THE STORYTELLER'S DEATH

A Novel

ANN DÁVILA CARDINAL

sourcebooks landmark

Published by Sourcebooks Landmark, an imprint Sourcebooks
P.O. Box 4410, Naperville, Illinois 60567-4410
(630) 961-3900
sourcebooks.com

Library of Congress Cataloging-in-Publication Data

Names: Cardinal, Ann Dávila, author.
Title: The storyteller's death : a novel / Ann Dávila Cardinal.
Description: Naperville, Illinois : Sourcebooks Landmark, [2022]
Identifiers: LCCN 2022011070 (print) | LCCN 2022011071
   (ebook) | (trade paperback) | (epub)
Subjects: LCGFT: Detective and mystery fiction.
Classification: LCC PS3603.A73526 S76 2022 (print) | LCC PS3603.A73526
   (ebook) | DDC 813/.6--dc23/eng/20220307
LC record available at https://lccn.loc.gov/2022011070
LC ebook record available at https://lccn.loc.gov/2022011071

Printed and bound in Canada.
MBP 10 9 8 7 6 5 4 3 2 1

For Carlos Victor Cardinal
I've been working on this story for most of your life...
It has always been for you.

CHAPTER ONE

death in a back room

There was always some old woman dying in the back room when I was a child. These women were just an expected part of the decor, like a lamp or a coffee table. I didn't know who most of them were, one ancient relative or another, and each summer I would usually find a new inhabitant. What I've come to understand, in the twilight of my own life, is that they were a nameless introduction to what would be my long and intimate relationship with death. They were also a doorway to true understanding of my Puerto Rican family and the gifts and curses that came with them.

I was eight years old in the summer of 1970 when I first encountered one of the inhabitants of the back room. That particular day, my cousins and I were running through Tío Ramón's one-story, concrete house at top speed, sliding over the slick, tiled floors, as adult reprimands in rapid-fire Spanish trailed behind us like a kite tail. We had to pass through the last room, a bedroom, before breaking free of the building and barreling into the back courtyard, scattering chickens and dust in every direction.

I remember I stopped short at the threshold, staring at the unexpected body on the shadowed bed. My cousins collided into me from behind and, seeing my apprehension, said in English, "Don't worry about her, Prima," as they pushed around me and pulled at my arms, coaxing me to follow them. "She can't hear you. Vamos!" I wanted to follow them, to be so unafraid as to walk through life as if there weren't something horrible waiting for me just out of sight.

The smell hit me first. Medicinal. Antiseptic. Stale. Like my father's hospital room back in New Jersey, that chemical odor that reached down into my stomach and squeezed. I pulled free of my cousins, my feet rooted to the doorsill, their voices fading as they scampered out into the daylight. I looked down at the scrubbed white Formica floor, the gray and blue dots forming moving patterns if I stared at them long enough, trying to pull me into their vortex, to get me to tip over and fall in headfirst.

The room was spotless: Tía Lourdes always made sure of that. She had been a nurse in the war, and so the care of the infirm family members always seemed to fall to her. These days, I can't help but wonder how she felt about that, or if she was even given a choice. This was one difference I found between the Larsen part of me and the Sanchez side. Even as a child, I couldn't imagine just blindly obeying someone simply because they were an adult, because they'd seen the sun rise and set more times than I had. Why did that alone impart the qualifications of authority? But that attitude was not understood nor appreciated by my mother's side of my family.

That summer afternoon, I stood in the doorway alone. The lights in the room were low; the bright afternoon glare permitted entry only through the wooden louvers that covered the windows, a narrow stream of sunshine spilling through the partially open back door, still swinging from my cousin Carlos's escape. Because of the near darkness, it was at least ten degrees cooler than anywhere else in the house. A large wooden crucifix was the only decoration on the white walls, the graphic dying figure of Jesus a ghastly contrast to the room's sterility. I imagined the blood from the wounds on his hands and feet snaking down and among the small white peaks of the stucco wall in a race to see which would make it to the floor first.

And there she was. An elderly female relative lying on the bed like an empty insect husk, her papery eyelids closed but quivering. A current of anxiety ran through my limbs. Or was it a thrill? The line between repulsion and fascination was blurred in that moment, but one thing was certain: I couldn't stay there forever. I decided to steal quietly but quickly through the room and not look over at the bed. If I didn't look, it would be all right; she couldn't get me. I had made it halfway across, escape mere feet away, when a crackly voice rose from the waxen figure under the chenille bedspread.

"¡Ay, Virgen! ¡Madre de Dios!" the old woman bellowed through her toothless mouth. I jumped, pictured her bony fingers reaching for me as I tore into the backyard, temporarily blinded by the summer sun but grateful to be free. I stopped and closed my eyes for a moment, imagining the sun was cleansing me, bleaching away the stain of dying that shivered across my skin.

I avoided going through the room for the rest of that summer. Not just because I was afraid but also because I felt a reverence for that shrunken woman teetering on the precipice leading from this world to the next. But occasionally, I would sneak away to peer at her through the slatted window from the safety of the concrete courtyard, sweat pouring down my neck, the sun on the back of my head reminding me that I was still outside the room and far enough away that she couldn't drag me with her when she went.

CHAPTER TWO
forgotten luggage

Nineteen seventy was also the first year my mother left me at Great-Aunt Alma's house for the entire summer like a piece of forgotten luggage. We had always gone as a family, the three of us, but that year, my father remained in his hospital bed, the bright-blue fluorescents an artificial and gloomy substitute for the Caribbean sun. I can still feel his cool hand on my face, still see him reaching up from his sheet cocoon. It was then, when I put my hand over his, that I realized his skin no longer fit. His body was shrinking inside its pale shell.

That night, back at home as we were preparing to leave, I watched my mother open the hall closet, watched her fingers hesitate over the handle of my father's large black suitcase and then pull her teal Samsonite bag from its side, leaving a shadowed hole like a missing tooth. As my mother stood silently beside me in the closet doorway, I ran my hand over his scratched black bag, smoothing out the wrinkled airline tag from his last trip that hung forlornly from its white rubber band.

"I guess we won't need this one this trip," I said, my voice sounding loud in the empty hallway. We'd had a routine, I remember. My mother always packed for him first and then helped me fill my pink duffel bag with shorts and tank tops. But that year, everything changed. At first my mother just stared at me, then anger flashed across her face. I thought she was going to yell. Instead, she slammed the closet door, shrouding the view of my father's bag behind the slab of wood. Then she just stood there, and I watched her face fall, her shoulders slump, her body fold into itself like a paper fortune-teller.

"Oh, Isla…" was all she said as she dropped to the floor, her suitcase falling between us with a thump. She sobbed then, hands covering her face, her legs awkwardly bent beneath her in the shadowed hallway. That was the first time I'd seen my mother cry, but it certainly wasn't the last. I knelt beside her and caught the faint citrusy smell of the gin and tonics she'd had with dinner.

"I can't believe Dad's not going with us," I said, my voice almost a whisper. I swallowed down a flicker of anger. Somehow it seemed her fault, though even then I knew that made no sense.

My mother choked out in between sobs, "I can't either."

The phone rang once, its metallic trill echoing through my parents' bedroom doorway, but neither of us moved. It was as though there were no air in that hallway and my father's absence was a tangible thing, like the ominous crawl-space door in the downstairs bathroom or the groaning boiler in the basement. Things I wanted to forget but always knew were there, lurking.

Later, as she drove to Newark airport with her fingers tight around the steering wheel, I begged her to let me stay with my father at the hospital. "I could sleep in the chair!" I offered, but I knew it was an empty suggestion. I knew the only people who slept in hospitals were sick. We parked, checked our bags, and boarded the plane in silence, the empty seat between us in the 747 an unfinished sentence.

A week later, I sat on the high, brass bed in Alma's guest room watching my mother repack, folding her cotton sundresses with shaking hands, then carefully placing them into her bag, her matching makeup case teetering beside her on the hideaway bed. The lipsticks rolled back and forth in the top tray, accompanying her movements in a rhythm section.

"Don't leave me here! Take me back with you. I can help take care of Daddy," I said for what felt like the fiftieth time. Truth was, I was panicked. She was leaving me on the island, alone, and the terror was immeasurable. The two most important people in my life would be an ocean away.

My mother's voice was tired, her repeated answer rote. "Oh, Isla. It's only for a few weeks, mi amor. You'll have more fun here with Tía than coming back to New Jersey. Daddy needs to rest so he can play with you when you come back." She attempted a smile, but I could tell from the tightness tugging across her lips and the way her glassy eyes stared off that she wasn't being truthful. I could always tell when she was lying.

I wanted to argue and plead some more—I was furious, disappointed, petrified—but the words wouldn't come. Then I had an overwhelming desire to climb off the bed, sit next to my mother, and hold her, but I couldn't make my body move. I wouldn't make my body move. This was her fault too.

Later, after my mother had disappeared through the gate door with only a quick glance over her shoulder, I stood next to Alma at the big plate-glass window that looked out on the tarmac of Isla Verde International Airport. We watched her walk in a line behind the other passengers toward the waiting jet, then slowly make her way up the stairway to the plane. She was wearing a straight green dress and thong sandals, her bobbed hair uncurling in the hot wind. She stopped halfway up the stairs, her left hand gripping the railing, and looked toward the window where we stood, her hand shading her eyes from the morning sun. She gave a quick wave, and for a moment, just a millisecond, I thought I saw hesitation, a shadow of regret. My heart leapt. I knew it! My mother couldn't leave me there alone.

I yelled into the wall of glass, "Mom!" a circle of steam from my breath forming, then retreating in front of me. I waved wildly at my mother, imagined her running back down the airplane's steps. But she said something to the woman a stair below and hurried onto the jet without looking back.

I stared at the plane as the rest of the passengers boarded and the crew stuffed suitcases and boxes wrapped with brown twine into the plane's belly. As they pulled the stairs away, then closed the door. I studied the teal globe skeleton on the side of the plane, repeating the name Pan-Am over and over to myself like a litany. Any moment, they would reopen the door, roll back the stairs, and my mother would hurry down them, carry-on bag flying behind her. As the plane taxied out, I stared into every small black rectangular window along its side, the midday sun glinting off them as if they were jewels. I stared until the plane was just a dot in the sky over San Juan.

Alma stood next to me, silent, but when the black dot finally winked out of existence, she put her hands on my shoulders and steered me away from the window. On the way to the parking lot, she bought me a soda, something usually reserved for special occasions, and held my free hand, occasionally squeezing it and clucking her tongue on her teeth as if disapproving of something.

We drove back to Alma's house in silence as I counted the corrugated tin-shack homes with oversized TV antennas that framed the highway from the airport.

Sixteen, seventeen, eighteen, nineteen.

She occasionally leaned over the Buick's red leather seat and patted my knee with her hand, murmuring, "Ay, bendito, pobrecita."

Twenty-two, twenty-three, twenty-four.

When we arrived at the house, Alma's guard dog, Guardián, barked and growled at us from the end of his chain, making me jump. Then, for the first time that day, I cried. The sobs came so fast and close together that I barely had time to gulp breaths. Alma led me into the house and sat me in the front parlor on the glider chair that was always my favorite. She rustled off to the kitchen, returning with a cold glass of water. I lifted the glass to my lips, the clean scent of chlorine wafting up as I drank. Alma sat next to me and carefully tucked her polyester skirt beneath her like the hospital corners on a bed. The lacy edge of her white slip appeared at her knees as she put her arm around my shoulders. She hummed quietly as we rocked back and forth, the only sounds the squeal of the chairs' rails and birds in the trees outside.

"Tell me a story, Tía." My voice was nasal from crying.

Alma stopped moving for a moment but then started again. "Ay, m'ija. You know I don't tell stories."

The thing is, until that moment, I didn't know that. Had I just never noticed? Back then, it had seemed to me that everyone on the island had a story at the ready, each one lined up behind the other like shark's teeth. I pulled back and looked at her, her visage fuzzy through my wet lashes. "But why?"

Alma just went on rocking and humming.

"Abuela tells stories," I said, knowing that bringing up Alma's sister, my grandmother, was sure to get a reaction. I knew Abuela was competitive with her sister, and I was banking that it went both ways. You see, Abuela was a true cuentista. My mother thought her evil, and given how the woman spoke to her, I tended to agree. Abuela was always yelling and judging and fighting; no one was safe from her wrath. Many times I'd watched her suck the life out of my mother with just words. But boy, could she tell a story.

When my abuela settled in a chair and the words "I remember the time…" escaped her lips, anyone nearby would stop and gather around her. She held court from her cane rocking chair, the smallest of her yappy dogs scattered over the expensive but severe dress that stretched across her breasts. I would sit at her feet, next to her support-hose-varnished leg, mesmerized by her ability to ensorcell with tales about the family, long-dead relatives and their lives on the island. What I loved best was that her stories always had a hint of magic woven through them, like a silver thread that glinted now and again. My abuela was never particularly kind to me, always criticizing and pointing out where I fell short compared to my cousins, but her tales were funny and nostalgic, and it was never clear if they were true. And, as I would come to learn, it didn't really matter.

Alma freed a strand of hair that was stuck in my drying tears. "Yes, well, I don't tell stories. As my father used to say, 'Stories are mere diversions for a lazy mind.'"

I sensed an undercurrent of judgment in the quote, so I crossed my arms and pouted.

"How about I play you a song on the piano instead? Hmm?"

I nodded and looked at her gratefully. When Alma played just for me, the notes hanging crisp and clear in the humid air of the parlor, it was a gift.

Alma walked over to the upright piano, the clean *thunk* of the cover being raised followed, and then she settled herself on the piano bench, back straight, eyes ahead. Soon the familiar notes of "Für Elise" were riding on the dust motes in the midday air, and I was able to forget for a time.

CHAPTER THREE
a boy like that

After Mom flew home that summer, Alma and I were insep-
arable. My mother's departure left a void, and my great-aunt
swooped in to fill it. She took me to visit friends and relatives
in the mornings, and I felt grown-up sitting in the rocking
chair my mother would have occupied, listening to the melody
of conversation in Spanish, sipping my syrupy Coca-Cola as
if at high tea. Our afternoons were spent walking through the
open-air market in Bayamón, sniffing papayas and playing with
hand-carved maracas, the words "Puerto Rico" crudely painted
on the gourds' sides. We walked arm in arm through the town
square, talking about nothing and everything. It took three
of my steps to equal a single stride of my tía's. Alma marched
around the town as if she owned it, and back then, I often
wondered if she did.

Alma was one of those women who seemed to have been born
sixty years old, as if she had always been matronly. Last year, I
ran across an old photograph of her, and I was surprised to see
she actually had a curvaceous figure in her youth. But her military bearing and, I would imagine, her entitlement made her
unapproachable and intimidating. She always walked with great

authority, her upper body leaned forward, her chin held high in the air, as someone striding up a hill with great purpose.

She kept her salon-styled salt-and-pepper hair short and beauty parlor curled and wore custom-made dresses in jewel-toned polyester fabrics. She wore stockings until her dying day, though they must have been impossibly warm and my mother tried her best to get her to switch to pantyhose. Her ensemble was never complete without the omnipresent patent leather handbag clutched over her left arm, its crisp satin-lined contents including an embroidered handkerchief, a Spanish fan, a rosary, and a mantilla. Oh, and a dusty mint to remedy church boredom.

Alma spent the rest of each day busy in her garden, which I found boring and insect-infested, so in the first two weeks of that summer, I used the time to explore the house. In the past, my mother was always with me, and each hour was carefully planned, so the freedom was exhilarating. I spent hours looking at the delicate robin's-egg-blue Lladro porcelain figures in the curio cabinet: Don Quixote, a young ballerina, and the Virgin Mary, all neighbors in their glass-walled nest. I wanted them, each and every one, though I can't imagine what I would have done with them. I think it was their inaccessibility that made them so appealing, their aloofness. I was fascinated by the marble-topped hall table in the parlor with the ancient rotary phone, and a piano-shaped music box. Even the collection of old sheet music in the womb of the piano bench was a treasure to uncover. That summer, I explored it all; I was an eight-year-old archaeologist.

But there was a room off the parlor in the front of the house that was unavailable to me, its door always locked. I asked my mother about it once. She shushed me, pulling me aside as if Alma were just around the corner, ears cocked for any transgression. In an angry whisper, Mom explained that the closed-off room had been Great-Grandfather's office, that he'd died in there, and afterward Alma had made the room off-limits to anyone but her.

Mom warned me that I was never to speak to Tía about it and never to go in there. But there was no need for such warnings: after she told me that, I couldn't even walk by the door without shuddering, especially since the wall behind the head of my bed was shared with that very same room. I pictured the door opening to a dark cave or a black chasm with flames licking from its bowels. It was the room that killed great-grandfathers. So, like the basement of our house in New Jersey, I would walk quickly by its door and try to forget it existed.

Once I had explored all there was to explore in the house, I became bold and ventured out into Alma's jungle. I understood it wasn't an actual jungle, but during those afternoons, as I ran among the trees, hopping over roots and stray coconuts, it certainly felt like one. Alma was comforted by plant life, and the vegetation was allowed to grow lush and wild around her low stone house. The plants reveled in her nurturing, enveloping the property in a rich, green sheath, shielding it from the neighboring maze of high-rise buildings that were multiplying as quickly as the foliage. To me it was heaven, a refuge from expectations. Under that canopy, I could forget that my mother had left me, that my father was sick. In that small wilderness, I was free.

Was it sad that I was left alone in a make-believe jungle? Perhaps. I had cousins my age, but they were still in school (the school year down there seemed preternaturally long to me), and honestly, it was a relief to be alone. I sometimes worried that my cousins only played with me because Tío Ramón insisted. They were always kind to me, but I often had the feeling there were other things they'd rather be doing. Real friends they wanted to play with, friends who spoke Spanish fluently, who understood their jokes. But me? Each summer, I had to pull my Spanish out from under the cedar blocks of winter storage in New Jersey, where the only Spanish I heard was one side of occasional phone calls from the island or at the local bodega where my mother bought her guava paste.

Among my cousins, I always knew I was different: larger, pastier, louder. I longed to be like them, switching so easily from elegant Spanish to an English that was more grammatical than my own. My play clothes that had seemed fine alongside the neighborhood kids in New Jersey felt shoddy and mismatched on the island, my hair ungroomed, too thin and dull. But the truth was, I didn't have any real friends at home either. Since my father had fallen sick, the other children acted as if I carried a contagion.

One glorious, solitary afternoon, I was playing detective, skulking from palm trunk to palm trunk and watching the workmen as if they were enemies on whom I was assigned to spy. I was scribbling on an imaginary notepad when I heard a crunch on the ground behind me. I leapt, my heart taking off in a run, and spun around. My shoulders relaxed when I glimpsed a boy standing a few feet away, his large eyes watching me. He looked to be about my age and was wearing nothing but a threadbare pair of navy shorts. He was tall but very thin, with a small round belly and deep-brown skin. I considered him and determined him no threat.

"¡Hola! Me llamo Isla. ¿Como te llamas?" I asked with a careful, friendly voice. But instead of telling me his name, he just ducked behind the hatched trunk of a nearby palm. I shrugged and resumed my surveillance duties: I was accustomed to not being understood.

"What are you doing?" he asked in accented English.

"I'm on a secret mission," I stage-whispered.

"Can I play?" he whispered back.

I assessed him again, looking closer into his dark-brown eyes. I had a gift, even back then. I could see meanness like a color in people's eyes, the sharpness at the edges, the extra glint off the surface. This boy was okay.

"Sure. I'm a secret agent and you can be my partner. What's your name?"

"José." He flashed a bashful smile.

"Okay, Detective José, we're on a stakeout." I pointed toward the workmen carrying materials from their truck to the shed. "These guys have stolen a secret invisibility machine, and we have to find out where they hid it. I'll watch the short guy with the mustache who looks kind of like a weasel. You watch the fat guy over there. Shoot him if he makes any wrong moves."

"That's my father," José replied.

"Oh. Well, you watch the other guy working with him, okay? Then we have to make a plan to capture them."

I remember we spent the afternoon running in and out of the trees, imagination painting stage sets of spy caves and international intrigue. José didn't try to control the game like my male cousins did, and he didn't make me feel a tomboy by worrying about getting dirty like my cousin Maria. By the time José's father called him to leave later that afternoon, we were friends.

"I'm going to see if my father will bring me with him tomorrow too," José said, his eyes bright. "See you tomorrow, Isla!" he called with an enthusiastic wave that started at his shoulder and ran all the way up his arm. I waved back as he and his father drove off in their dilapidated pickup truck.

Early the next morning, I ran outside as soon as I heard the truck pulling into the driveway. As my new friend shyly approached, his father and his coworkers watched and made approving comments to José about his already having a "girlfriend" and a "way with the ladies." We ignored them and ran off to plan the day's adventures behind the garden shed.

After a morning of pirates and buried treasure and running around the house like wild animals, Alma called me in for lunch. I reluctantly left our games and sat with my great-aunt at the small round table, looking through the iron bars to the backyard, trying to catch a glimpse of José. I used to look forward to lunches with my great-aunt, but that day, it was keeping me from my own plans.

"Isla, you're not eating! What's going on with you, m'ija?" She stared at me with her narrowed eyes like she was dissecting me.

"Nothing, Tía. I just want to go back out and play, that's all."

"Playing can wait until you finish your lunch," she chided, waving her finger in my face. In truth, Alma was a horrendous cook. The only spices allowed in her kitchen were salt and pepper, and she used those as if they were being rationed. While my tía shuffled into the kitchen to take the whistling teakettle off the burner, I poured the tasteless food through the patio bars and onto the waxy leaves below and rushed into the kitchen.

"I'm done, Tía. May I go now?" I asked.

Alma seemed exasperated but looked down at the empty plate. "I guess you were hungry after all, eh, niña?" she said with a hint of pride. "Bueno, go out and play. But don't get dirty! We're going over to Tío Ramón's for dinner tonight."

I ran out of the house and toward the back to hunt for José. I found him catching lagartijos behind the shed. He had one of the small electric-green lizards in his hand and was looking into its tiny black eyes. I walked quietly up behind him and watched as they regarded each other. I couldn't get within a foot of the creatures without them running away. After a few minutes, he put the lizard down on the ground, and it scurried away under the blanket of dried, fallen leaves.

I knew that José lived somewhere in the mountains, but I couldn't picture it. My worldview was narrow and privileged in those days. But I wanted to know what his life was like, to be able to picture where he was when he wasn't with me. "Is your house far away?"

He nodded.

"Do you have to walk far to get to your school every day?"

"Not every day. I wish I could, but sometimes I don't go."

This baffled me. Why would anyone want to go to school every day? So many mean children, such disappointed and harried teachers.

"Sometimes I have to stay home and help Mamá y Papá."

"Help with what?"

"I cut down plants around the house and work with my papá. And every day I get water from where it runs off the mountain. That's my job." He tapped on his chest when he said this, like it was something he owned, something of which he was proud.

"Why don't you just get water from the faucet in the sink?"

"We don't have one."

"But where do you wash your hands and face?"

"In the river."

We had four sinks, one in the kitchen, one each in two bathrooms, and one near the washer and dryer in the basement. Washing in the river. I pictured the water crystal clear and cool, bubbling over rocks as the sun glinted off its surface. It sounded as if he lived in a storybook, that his existence was in watercolor-washed illustrations from another time, while mine seemed as if it were shades of gray. "My house kind of scares me." I was surprised when the words came out of my mouth, words I'd never spoken before, to anyone.

José cocked his head to the side. "How can a house be scary?"

"I don't know, it just is. Especially the basement and attic."

"What are those?"

"The floor underneath the ground, and the attic is above the second floor where my room is."

José's eyes widened. "Your house has four floors?"

I shrugged. "Yeah. I try to forget about the first and the last, but I always know they're there. When I have to go down to the basement, I'm afraid there's something there, under the stairs, that's going to grab me. Like a monster."

José nodded as though he understood monsters. "But your father can protect you," he offered with the easy smile of someone whose father was strong and always there.

I swallowed hard. "My dad's sick. And my mom, sometimes it's like she forgets about me." The words sounded too loud, though I had almost whispered them.

José pulled his legs in and turned to face me. During that time of my life, when I told adults in New Jersey that my father was sick, they patted me awkwardly and changed the subject, avoiding my eyes. In Puerto Rico, the old ladies yanked me into a bone-crushing embrace and whispered in Spanish that I was a poor little thing. But José didn't say a word. He just held out a guineo niño in offering. Between us, we ate a dozen of the tiny yellow bananas in silence, the taste so sweet and concentrated that I wondered if the long, pale, tasteless variety back home were actually bananas in their larval state, only becoming themselves when they shrank to these.

When the sun started its descent, shining lower through the leaves overhead, we grew quiet, knowing our day together was coming to an end. After all we'd talked about, it was as if we were connected, a cord running from my chest to his. I wanted something to mark our pact as friends.

I leaned over, closed my eyes, and pressed my lips to his as I'd seen my parents do hundreds of times. Before the tubes had grown from my father's nose and mouth, blocking words and kisses. José's lips were soft and tasted of salt and bananas. He stared at me as I pulled away, his eyes wide and more black than brown, a shocked smile creeping from the corners of his mouth.

Neither of us heard my aunt tramping through the yard in our direction.

"Isla!" Alma shrieked, pulling me up by the arm so forcefully, I swear I felt it loosening from its socket. The violence of it left me numb with shock; Alma had never yelled at me, let alone been physical. She dragged me through the yard toward the house, scolding me in ferocious Spanish. My eyes never broke from José's face, his eyebrows knitted together. Alma stormed into the house, dragging me behind her like a rag doll, shoved me into my room, and slammed the door. I dropped to the floor and rubbed my throbbing shoulder. Tears fell while anger built in my chest. I could hear Alma outside yelling at the workmen. At José's father. Through the bedroom window, I watched the truck pull away with just the top of my friend's head peeking through the rear window.

All that week, the workmen's truck came and went without José. Alma and I occupied the house together but rarely spoke. I had no idea what I had done, and I could barely use my arm for days afterward. A week later, I came back from getting ice cream with Tío Ramón and my cousins to find Alma waiting in my room, sitting on the bed with her arms tightly folded across her chest. The air felt different, and my throat tightened.

"Do you know that boy showed up here today looking for you?"

"José?" I couldn't keep the excitement out of my voice, ignoring the sharp edges of her words.

Alma stood, glaring down at me between half-closed lids, hands on her hips. "Yes, José." She repeated his name in a mocking tone I'd never heard from my aunt before, one the kids at school used when they were pointing out my uncombed hair or mismatched socks. There was even a glimmer of meanness in her hazel eyes.

"He walked all the way from his backward mountain town to see you, in bare feet, no less! Well, of course I called his father right away and had him picked up. Obviously, you've given this boy the wrong idea. If you are going to live under my roof, you must act like a proper young lady!" She turned and straightened the already straight bedspread with jerking movements, the skin under her arms swinging.

Alma was always on my side, was the one person I could trust to truly take care of me, especially that summer. Falling from Alma's good graces was terrifying, but in that moment, I was more upset that she had taken José from me. "He's my friend!" I sputtered, wanting to say more, to yell at my aunt for scaring him off, for taking away my first real friend.

"Isla, it is my job to protect you. Protect you from making wrong choices."

Wrong choices? About what? I clenched my hands and bit into my lower lip to keep from crying. We stood there, glaring at each other. Angry words piling up behind my closed lips.

"It is clear I will have to keep a closer eye on you, and by the time you go home to los Estados Unidos, you will have forgotten all about that boy!"

There was something behind her words, something she wasn't saying, that I didn't understand. I wanted to ask why she was angry, when it was my friend who was pushed away. Instead, I stood with my fists tight beside my legs, wishing I could yell something, anything, that would fix things. The flame in my chest silently flared.

Alma started to walk out of the room, her back stiff and authoritative, her chin held high. Just before she reached the doorway, she turned on her heels. "We do not socialize with people like that."

"What do you mean?" My voice came out small and weak, and I hated that.

Alma sighed and her voice softened, just a little. "You are too young, niña. You cannot understand. It is for the best. Basta. Enough. Now go to sleep. We will not talk of this again."

Long after Alma left the room, closing the door behind her like a reprimand, I stared at the spot where she had stood. I pictured José's round, kind face. I thought of all the things I wish I'd said to Alma. I picked a book off the night table and hurled it at the door.

That night, the phone rang late, its trill echoing through the quiet house with sharp edges. I heard my aunt's shuffling slippers make their way to the living room, and the ringing stopped. I stumbled out of bed, cracked open the door, and strained to listen. It was my mother; I heard Alma call her by name, but I couldn't make out enough of my aunt's muffled Spanish to figure out what was going on. I wondered if I should go out there and ask. It was my mother calling after all. But I remembered the way Alma talked to me earlier that day, and I thought that talking to her would be losing somehow. Like it would make what she did to me okay.

Instead, I stayed and caught a handful of words, many I didn't understand. Was she telling my mother about what happened? About José? I heard murmured goodbyes, then the handset returned to the receiver with a clean *thunk*. I lurched a bit, ready to close the door quietly so she wouldn't know I had been listening, but she didn't come. Then I heard the wooden rocking chair creak as she sat, and the rocking began. And something else… Was that crying?

I was suddenly uncomfortable about eavesdropping and eased the door closed. I crawled back between the cool, cotton sheets. Though I felt bad Alma was crying, I hoped it was from guilt for how she'd treated me.

CHAPTER FOUR

a mound of earth

At the end of that summer, I had to fly home by myself for the first time. Alma tried to distract me with cheerful banter and a stop to buy candy, but I was petrified. And worse, I felt as though she was, too, like she knew it was wrong to let an eight-year-old fly by herself. She saw me to the gate, blowing sad kisses as she handed me over to a stewardess who filled the air with false chatter and pinned a plastic set of wings to my shirt, telling me they were just like the ones the pilots wore. I looked down at the pin, the gold paint already chipping off a wing, and wondered, did she think I could be bought that cheaply? Unlike my mother's flight, this plane had a tunnel leading right to it, the walls billowing like a vacuum-cleaner hose. As the stewardess and I walked, I felt as though the tunnel were shrinking around us, that by the time we got to the plane, I would have to crawl on my hands and knees until it finally crushed me.

When we arrived onboard, I caught a glimpse of Alma through the tiny circular windows. My great-aunt was standing behind the same glass window as we had when my mother left, purse clutched over her arm, watching the plane with wrinkles between her brows.

"Your seat's over here, honey."

I looked up at the stewardess who was pointing to an empty seat in the front row on the other side of the plane. I absently pointed toward Alma. "My tía…" But I knew it was no use. I would have to lose sight of Alma sometime. In the back of the plane, a child was screeching, accompanied by a thumping sound that I imagined was them banging their feet against the seat in front of them. The kid probably wasn't much younger than I was, but I felt as though I'd aged ten years that summer. I sat primly in my seat, feet dangling above the floor, eyes ahead. But inside, I wished I could make such a scene, could scream and kick until they had no choice but to take me off the plane and give me back to Alma.

Another stewardess adjusted my buckle for me, her shiny brown hair pulled up in a neat bun. The woman's scent of violets and soap was so nice, so gentle, that I thought I might cry. She pulled away with a smile, then went to help an old woman with her bag. A man in a suit in the next seat smiled at me as if he were being forced, then opened his newspaper, lit a stinky cigarette, and edged me off the armrest.

As the plane lifted off and the pilot's patronizing southern drawl murmured over the speakers, I looked over the laps of the people next to me and out the window. The sight of the expanse of blue and nothing else brought a wave of tightness to my chest. I was alone. Truly alone for the first time, and something inside me knew this was just the beginning.

When we finally landed in Newark, the attendant made me wait until everyone was off the plane to walk me off and through another tunnel. When I spotted my mother alone by the counter, I dropped the stewardess's hand, ran, and threw myself at Mom, hugging her middle as if she were the only thing tethering me to the earth. I knew it was a babyish thing to do, but I didn't care, my tears soaking her blouse.

As we drove home, the familiar Newark smokestacks marching by, I asked, "Can we go straight to the hospital and see Daddy?"

My mother gasped a little. She was quiet, then said, "Daddy isn't at the hospital anymore, Isla."

My heart lifted. "He's home?"

Silence again. Then, "No, honey. There's something I need to show you."

The tightening in my chest was back. My mother's tone was off, and she wouldn't look at me. Something was wrong. Really wrong. My mind flicked back to that late-night call at Alma's. My mother said that calls in the middle of the night were never good.

We drove to an unfamiliar place, with green hills and stones arranged in rows. My mother took me by the hand, and we walked, the birds singing in the trees around them as if it were any other day. The place was pretty, but in a false way that covered up something bad, flowery scent sprayed on rotting summer garbage. She stopped in front of a pile of soil, freshly patted down like the sandcastles my father and I used to build.

"This is where Daddy is."

I stared at the dirt and then gaped up at my mother. I didn't understand. And I did. All at once. And I hated her for that. I hated her for everything.

"I–I just thought it would be easier on you this way."

What would be easier? I looked down, and furious tears built up on the edges of my eyes. This pile of dirt had nothing to do with my father. Not a thing. My mother had abandoned me for an entire summer and then taken my father from me?

As we walked back to the car, I dropped her hand and didn't ask anything else about Dad since clearly my mother couldn't be trusted.

Later that week, my mother came looking for me. I was curled up, rereading *Charlotte's Web* in my father's butterfly chair. The smell of his cherry pipe tobacco smoke hung about me like a memory, and the worn leather was still molded to the shape of his body.

"What do you say we do some back-to-school clothes shopping? Wouldn't that be fun?" my mother asked in the forced cheery voice that I was hearing more and more from her.

I shrugged, irritated that she'd interrupted my reading. "Why? My uniforms from last year still fit."

But she pulled me up and snaked her arm around mine as if we were girlfriends going on an adventure. "Well, honey, I had to take you out of St. John's, but you'll be going to Anna C. Scott in a few weeks, and you'll want to look your best!"

I yanked my arm back and gaped at her. "What?" Anna C. Scott was the public elementary school where I didn't know anyone. "Why?" It felt like the house was shifting and tilting around me, and I put a hand on Dad's chair to steady myself.

She let out a long breath and threw her arms down, the cheery facade crashing to the floor in shards. "Because we can't afford St. John's anymore with just my salary, Isla. Your father's treatments ate up all our savings." Her hazel eyes looked paler, as if the life had been drained from them. "We're both going to have to make sacrifices." Her voice was drained too.

I stared at her, heat building in my chest. I knew it wasn't her fault, but I was still angry. It felt as though she was taking everything from me. I wanted to go back to Alma's. "Why don't we ask Tía Alma for help? She thinks school is so important, I'm sure she'd pay for—"

"No!" my mother barked, and I jumped, almost falling back into the chair behind me. "I will not ask my family for help when you are perfectly fine going to the public school for free." She put her hands on my shoulders, but hard, like she was trying to push me down and root me into the floor instead of comforting me. "I…we will be fine on our own, Isla."

She was scaring me, so I swallowed and nodded, my eyes brimming with tears. But even then, I knew that wasn't true. We would not be fine.

The first day of school came, and by the time I'd gotten dressed in my new clothes and come downstairs, Mom had already left for work, Pop-Tarts and a bagged lunch sitting on the kitchen counter with a note that read, "Have a great first day!" with a series of bulbous hearts drawn around it. I crumpled the paper up and threw it in the trash can.

My mother was right about one thing: I had to make a good first impression. Maybe at my new school, I could start again. After all, no one would know me, and I could build my own identity, make friends. I looked down at my crisp flowered dress, the tags cut off only the night before. I saw my lank, dirty-blond hair lying lifeless against my shoulders. Mom hadn't bugged me to take a shower last night, though I had expected her to, and I couldn't remember the last time I'd washed it. But there wasn't time to do it then, and I needed everything to be perfect.

I ran upstairs and went into Mom's room. The spicy floral sent of Maja perfume hung in the air, and underneath something sharper, more medicinal. I looked over at her dresser and saw the row of blank-eyed Styrofoam heads that sat sentry. I started to walk toward them but tripped on an empty bottle on the floor, kicking it across the worn wooden surface. I picked it up and sniffed. That was where the sharp smell was coming from. The label had a bat on it, which was kind of cool, but I had important things to do. I put it back down on the floor and went to the dresser.

The year before, when Dad was sickest, Mom had begun wearing wigs that looked just like her hair, only fluffier. "I just don't have the time to dye and style it these days," she would say as she lifted a wig and settled it over her increasingly silver-rooted hair. "This way, when I need to look put together, I can just wear these." When the wig was in place, the stray hairs tucked under the webbed cap, she would look in the mirror and smile at herself with a satisfied look. And she did look better, like she'd spent a lot of time getting ready.

It was just the extra something I needed.

I reached up and yanked the closest wig off, the white pitted head wobbling from the theft. I turned the wig around and pulled it over my hair, tucking my greasy locks under as I'd seen her do a thousand times. When it was in place, I looked up into the dresser mirror and smiled. It was a little big for my head, but I looked better, more grown-up.

When I stepped out of the house, new school bag on my shoulder, I stood taller. As I walked up our street, I noticed Mrs. Wagner staring at me, pruning shears forgotten in her hands. I waved and smiled. She never noticed me; she talked to children as if they were stray dogs she needed to shoo off her property, so it must have been my new look. It was a much longer walk to Anna C. Scott, but it felt good to be outside, and I liked the slight crispness in the air. I started thinking about autumn, my favorite season, with its pumpkins and apple cider and Halloween. I was smiling to myself as I walked. I could almost believe that year would be different, that I would be okay.

My heart was thrumming with nervousness as I made my way up the stone steps. As I went, kids started to notice me, moving to either side to let me pass. It was working! But as I started to walk down the unfamiliar hall, the linoleum polished to a high first-day-of-school shine, I began to hear the whispers and muffled laughter that seemed to trail behind me.

"Can I help you, dear?"

I looked over and saw a gray-haired woman with a kind face holding a clipboard.

"It's my first day," I said in a small voice, suddenly not so confident.

"What's your name?" she asked. She looked at me, but then her eyes darted down to her list.

"Isla Larsen." I left the Sanchez off because I knew that outside Puerto Rico, they cut off your mother's name as if it were an unnecessary appendage.

"Yes, I see you right here." Her voice was a little warbly, like a cassette tape that was wearing thin. "You're in Miss Long's class. I'll walk you there, dear." She smiled at me, but I could tell something was wrong. I wanted to run back down the long hall, out of the building, and all the way home to hide until Mom got home. Instead, I held my head up straight like Alma always told me to and followed behind the woman, her rubber-soled shoes squeaking on the floor as she walked.

I tried not to look at the kids as I passed by, the girls hiding their mouths with their hands like they were holding secrets back, the boys pointing. We arrived at the door to a classroom, a map of the flattened-out world hung on the board at the front, rolled down like a window shade. Miss Long was standing behind her desk, and when she looked up at us, her eyes rested on me and stayed there. She came rushing over as the bell rang and the kids settled into desks with a cacophony of scraping chair legs and excited voices.

She put her hand on my shoulder and smiled down at me. "Welcome, honey. You must be Isla." Before I could answer, the blue-haired lady and Miss Long started whispering to each other over my head, but I was busy looking at a boy in the front row. He had short, spiky hair like orange shorn grass and a spray of freckles across his nose. He was smiling at me, and I started to smile back just as he whispered one word, spitting it silently so the teachers couldn't hear.

"Freak."

My throat tightened and I fought the urge to cry with everything I had, the rest of the noise of the classroom becoming an indiscernible hum.

Miss Long bent down to talk to me, her silky hair falling on either side of her face like brown velvet curtains. "Isla, let's take a little walk, okay?" She turned to the blue-haired lady. "Mrs. Benson? Can you stay with the class for a bit?"

The woman nodded, and my teacher stood up straight and called out to the class in a voice that wasn't loud but everyone listened to. "Class. I'll be right back. Mrs. Benson is going to stay with you for a bit, and I expect you to obey her." Silence fell over the class, and all the students snapped into place like rows of chess pieces. Miss Long put her arm around me and walked me out of the room. I looked up at her with awe, a grown-up who made things happen, took care of things.

As we walked the now empty halls, she talked to me in a gentle voice. "Isla, does your mother know you're wearing that wig?"

I shook my head and felt tears building again.

"Do you know why I took you out of the class?"

I sniffled. "Because the kids were laughing at me."

"Partly." She stopped and bent down to my height, putting her face right in front of mine. "But I'm more concerned about why you wore it today."

I looked at her through my blurry eyes and felt in my roiling belly that she really wanted to know. That she cared. And so it came. The tale of how my father was sick for so long, about how my mother left me in Puerto Rico. About how he died while I was gone and my mother didn't tell me. About changing schools and needing to feel "put together." When I was done, I noticed tears in Miss Long's eyes too. She dropped to her knees, wrapped her arms around me, and as I began to sob, I could hear her whisper through the fibers of the wig, "Poor girl. Poor baby. It's going to be okay."

And I almost believed her.

That was the first of many trips to the guidance counselor's office while they called my mother. That morning, I sat in the corner drinking the ginger ale they proffered—a treat first thing in the morning—kicking my feet back and forth beneath the orange chair, wig in my lap like a deceased pet, while they talked about me in hushed voices. I was about to ask why I couldn't just stay there in that office for the school year, that I'd be quiet and study hard, when my mother arrived.

She entered in her out-of-breath, "Oh I'm just so busy" fashion, and I noticed she had touched up her makeup, primped the wig on her own head, and was using her "church" voice. She didn't even look at me, just turned to the guidance counselor when they were introduced, shaking her hand.

"And, Miss Long, how lovely to see you again," she said to my teacher with a strained smile.

I didn't like the sweet way she was treating my teacher, like the Frescas she drank with dinner, falsely sweet with a sharp bite. But I'd already decided that Miss Long was mine, not hers. She couldn't have her too.

"Mrs. Larsen, you understand why we called you in?"

I was glad they were talking to Mom as if she were a child too.

"Yes, I was so shocked to hear that Isla stole one of my wigs."

Stole?

Finally, she turned to me. "What on earth were you thinking, Isla?" Her eyes glanced back and forth between the other two women, as if making sure they were paying attention. "After all the new clothes and the haircut I got you?"

"You never took me to get a haircut." Now the edges in my voice were sharp too.

"Oh, I was sure we'd done that. But you should have showered last night when I told you to."

"You didn't tell me to shower. You haven't since I got back from Puerto Rico."

Anger passed across her eyes, but so quick I was certain I was the only one who saw it before she adjusted her affect again. "I'm certain I did, Isla." She turned to the other women, stage-whispering in a conspiratorial way. "We've been through so much this past year, losing her father. It's been especially hard on Isla this past summer."

I saw the women look at her with softness in their eyes, and I felt the rage stoke in my belly. "How would you know? You left me in Puerto Rico for the whole summer."

She grabbed me by the arm then, pulling me to my feet with shaking hands, the wig falling from my lap to the gray tiled squares beneath us. "I think you've taken up enough of these kind ladies' time, Isla." She looked at me with anger that stayed for a beat longer, until she turned to Miss Long and the guidance counselor. "Thank you so much for calling me. Nothing like this will happen again, we promise." Her fingers tightened, just a bit. "Don't we, Isla?"

I narrowed my eyes at her and said, "Yes," in a low steady voice. She hustled me out of the room, but as we got to the door, Miss Long called out.

"Oh, Mrs. Larsen?"

Mom turned around as if her body were one stiff piece, pulling me along with her. "Yes?" She pasted a big ole fake smile on her lips.

Miss Long stepped toward us, holding out the wig to my mother. "You forgot your wig."

Mom frowned, took the wig, and hustled me down the hall and out of the building. When we got to the parking lot and out of sight of the front door, she dragged me harder toward our car, muttering under her breath.

"I've never been so humiliated in my entire life, Isla! How could you do this to me? Now they think you're crazy and I'm neglectful!"

She opened the passenger door and basically threw me in, tossing the wig into the back seat in irritation.

I could hear her mumbling as she walked around the car, and the words came into focus as she climbed behind the wheel. She went to turn the key with jerky movements but stopped, her shoulders and head sagging. When she finally turned to me, there were tears pouring down her cheeks.

"What were you thinking, Isla?"

For the first time in a week, I felt as if she was actually seeing me, and I was suddenly ashamed. I answered after a silence, my voice cracking like a radio losing its signal. "I just wanted to look 'put together' like you do."

And then it was as if the air had been let out of her. Her eyes softened, and she began to sob as she pulled me toward her. We sat there, in the hot front seat of our Datsun station wagon, the car rocking with our sobs.

The wig stayed in the back seat of the car for weeks, like roadkill, until one day it just disappeared, along with the bald Styrofoam heads and other wigs from her dresser. I had to go back the next day, and though the class snickered and Michael Murphy whispered "freak" at me whenever I passed, Miss Long was always kind, and somehow, I got through that school year.

And the next.

But that first day set the tone, and things would only get worse from there.

CHAPTER FIVE
skin of my teeth

By the beginning of my eleventh summer, it was a relief to see New Jersey disappear beneath the clouds as the plane lifted. Mom had stopped going with me all together, and I had begun to have frequent nightmares about our house, some unseen menace hiding beneath the stairs, ready to grab my ankles as I went down to do laundry. Creaks in the attic were the scuffling of a demon's claws as it made its way down to get me, to pull me apart before devouring me.

I think Alma could sense my increased anxiety, because later that week, she arranged for my aunt Ileana to take me and my cousin Maria to a carnival. I'd seen the sleeping Ferris wheel peeking out over the high-rises as we made our way from the airport and squealed. But I had never expected to get to go. Alma considered such things frivolities, unbecoming of a young lady.

I was thrilled when Ileana—who insisted I call her Titi, the affectionate version of tía—arrived in her stylish minidress and stack of clicking bracelets on her arm. Alma didn't approve of how she dressed, "As if she were still a teenager," but I loved it. I wanted to be her when I grew up. She gave me a big smile and pulled me to her slim frame in a hug. I breathed in her spicy, vanilla scent of Chanel No. 5.

My cousin Maria was fifteen back then and was also in a short dress, her legs long and lean, shiny mahogany hair neatly held back beneath a wide headband. She already had breasts and had worn a bra for two years. I looked down at my mismatched Garanimals short set and grass-stained tennis shoes and felt ashamed. But even though she seemed so much older than me, so much more grown-up, Maria hugged me tightly, as if really glad to see me. When she pulled away, she clapped and said, "Oh, Isla, we're going to have so much fun!"

She put her arm through mine and pulled me toward her mother's waiting Lincoln Continental, and I knew we would.

It was a small carnival, nothing like Palisades Amusement Park used to be back home. I cried when they closed it a few years before, but the carnival had the sweet smells and bright lights that brought unbridled joy to my heart. After buying tickets, Maria and I took off toward the roller coaster, hand in hand, as Titi followed behind with a patient smile on her lips. As the car rattled its way up the tracks, then plummeted down with a *whoosh*, we screamed and laughed at each other screaming, then screamed and laughed some more. I had never felt so free.

We went on three rides in a row, then Maria suggested we get bags of rainbow candied popcorn, and I happily agreed. After her mother paid for them and snapped closed her wicker purse, we walked toward the games. I had begun to notice the boys—and men for that matter—staring at Maria as we walked by, creepy smiles on their faces until they caught a scowling look from Titi. I looked over at my cousin and realized just how much she had changed from the summer before. Her walk was slower, more swaying and deliberate, and she had more curves. She seemed aware of the attention but uninterested in it. "Do they do that all the time?" I asked.

She looked over at me with a scrunched nose. "Who? Do what?"

I gestured over toward a row of teen boys, hungry eyes staring our way. "Them."

She gave a dismissive wave with her delicate hand. "Boys? Who cares? I'm taken."

I stopped and gaped at her. "You have a boyfriend?"

"Shh!" She gestured toward her mother, who had run into a woman from their neighborhood and was busy chatting away. "Don't let Mamá hear you."

It was so exciting to be in on a secret, but a boyfriend? Such monumental news. "What's his name?" I whispered.

We locked arms again, and as she started to talk, I tossed a handful of candied popcorn into my mouth. As I bit down, it was as if lightning had struck through the top of my skull. The pain radiated down into my shoulders until I thought my head was going to explode. I stopped, my hand rushing to my cheeks.

"Isla? Isla, are you okay?" Maria looked into my face.

Tears welled as I shook my head.

She called her mother, and I couldn't stop crying as they walked me to the car, my hands cradling my face as if it were porcelain. Beneath the constant layer of pain was a strong current of embarrassment. I had ruined the trip for everyone and had been having the most fun I'd had in forever. These feelings only made me cry harder.

I sat in the front seat of the Lincoln, and as she drove, Titi put her hand on my knee, clucking, "Bendito, pobrecita. Tooth pain is the absolute worst."

I'd never felt anything like that before, but in some dark part of my heart, it felt expected, as if there were a voice saying *How dare you have fun!*

When we pulled through the stone gates, I saw Alma in the doorway, her face wrinkled with worry as she ushered me into the house. I cried as she brushed my teeth with baking soda, then settled me between the crisp sheets. She left the room and came back with a bottle of what I now knew was rum and poured some into a small glass. "Here, Isla, drink this, but swish it through your mouth before you swallow."

I shook my head, crying harder. "No! I can't."

"¿Porque no? Why not, m'ija? It's only a thimbleful."

"I don't want to be like Mom!" My sobs grew even louder, and I collapsed into her, pain bleeding exhaustion throughout my body.

I don't know how long she held me like that, cooing soothing words into my hair, but I woke up the next morning tucked back into my bed, my face swollen and throbbing.

We went to an office above a store in the main square of Bayamón, and Alma introduced me to the dentist, who she said was a cousin of ours. In those days, it seemed as if everyone on the island were some kind of relative or another. I don't remember much about the visit, only that once he examined my teeth, the cousin dentist was so alarmed, he brought in the other doctors from the practice. They stared into my mouth and conferred over me in hushed Spanish as if I was a broken pipe or car that wouldn't start. Eventually they put a mask over my face, and the next thing I remember, I was in the car next to Alma, drooling through numb lips.

She gave me one of the white pills the doctor had prescribed for the pain, and I slept for the rest of the day and most of the next. By breakfast of the third day, my mouth still ached too much to eat anything but creamed wheat, and I winced after each spoonful of that. As she went to clear the plates away, Alma stopped, turned toward me, and asked, "Isla, when is the last time your mother took you to the dentist?"

I thought, though my head throbbed with the effort. "When I was seven, I think."

She stared at me as her eyes grew glassy. Then she swallowed, patted my hand in her aggressive but affectionate way, and hustled into the kitchen.

That night, after I finished my weekly call with Mom, Alma asked to speak with her and sent me off to bed.

That was one of the few times I'd ever heard Alma raise her voice.

I was proud it was on my behalf.

CHAPTER SIX
shed skin

"Why don't we go over to Isla's house?"

My head shot up from the doodle I was drawing around the edges of my math notebook. Due to alphabetic seating, I was smack in the middle of a group of three popular girls and usually ignored them as they chattered over and around me as if I were invisible. "What?" I gaped at them. Patricia answered, though I was surprised she remembered my name. I had gone to her house for an after-school playdate in second grade, but she hadn't acknowledged me since.

She flipped her long, straight hair back and turned her body toward me. "You never invite anyone over to your house. Actually, it's kind of weird." Patricia said *actually* a lot, as if it were a new pair of shoes she was trying to break in.

All three girls were staring at me, waiting for an answer. My throat constricted around my vocal cords, and I could feel my heartbeat behind my face.

"I mean, it's not like you have to wait for a holiday or anything," Charlotte said from my other side.

I whipped around to look at her as if I were under attack. They were all still staring at me. When would the damn bell ring? I coughed, then said in a quiet voice, "My birthday is this Friday."

The minute the words fell from my lips, I wished I could gather them up and push them back down my throat.

"That's it!" Patricia squealed and clapped her hands. "It's settled. We'll come to your house Friday after school for a fourteenth-birthday sleepover."

"But…" I wanted to say I had plans, a weekend trip with my mother, anything, but the truth was, I doubted she even remembered it was my birthday.

"I can't wait to see where you live," Judy said with a one-sided smile and an up-and-down tone that reeked of cruelty.

The metallic ring of the bell sounded above our heads, and I almost jumped out of my skin. As the teacher began to talk about probability and polynomials, I sat with my elbows on my desk and held my head in my hands. How could I go on as usual when my entire life was careening down a hill like a bike with no brakes? I had to transfer schools or call in with a brain aneurysm, anything to keep them from coming to my house. And Friday night? That was my mother's worst night, as she was always anxious to slough off the workweek and dive into a bottle of Bacardi.

That night at dinner, I was silent, pushing the vague chicken shapes around in their tin Swanson tray, the sickly sweet smell of the apple-turnover-like substance mocking me from its corner compartment.

"So. How was school today?" Mom's voice seemed overly loud in the silent kitchen nook. We'd stopped eating in the dining room after Dad died. I hated the breakfast nook with its anemic yellow flowers that trellised up and down the wallpaper, but at least we didn't have to face the betrayal of the empty seat at the larger table.

"Fine." I was concentrating on spearing a pea on each tine of my fork.

"I was thinking… How about we get all dressed up and I'll take you out for a nice dinner on Friday?"

I looked up at her.

"For your birthday? You didn't think I'd forget, did you?"

I felt a small smile tug at the edges of my lips.

"We could go to that fancy Italian place in Englewood that just opened. I've been dying to try their wine list—"

I stopped listening after that because I could see the evening unfold as if it were playing out right in front of me. Mom flirting with the waiter, her wineglass refilling and refilling until the bottle was empty, her voice louder, sloppier, people staring. And the grand finale: the terrifying drive home.

She wouldn't stop talking, and I had to put an end to the charade. "Actually, I was going to have a sleepover with some girls from my class on Friday night."

Mom fell silent, staring at me with large eyes. I'd never had a sleepover. At the age when those normally began, my father was dying. And later? Well…

A huge grin spread across her face, and she clapped her hands like Patricia had. "Oh, honey! But that's fabulous! How many?"

"Three."

"Ooh! Well, we'll order some pizzas and get some bottles of soda." She stood and was swaying around the kitchen, waving her hands as if conjuring the party out of thin air. "You can set up your sleeping bags in the living room. And games! We should get some games!"

I put my hand out in the universal stop gesture. "Mom, I'd like to keep this…simple."

"Sure, honey. Of course." She started walking out of the kitchen, talking to herself. "Oh, there's so much to do! I'll have to get Lily to come a day earlier to clean, of course…"

I sat alone in the sad yellow light of the breakfast nook, wondering if I had just made a tremendous mistake.

———————————

When Friday arrived, I thought about ditching school, something I'd never done, and just hiding behind the couch if the girls showed up. But I went anyway. Mom hadn't mentioned the party as she was scurrying out that morning, and I was grateful. Maybe everyone would forget. But as I slid into my desk while the bell rang, Patricia leaned over to me.

"We can't wait for tonight, Izzie!"

Who?

Judy must have noticed the confused look on my face. "We decided that's your nickname. If you're going to hang out with us, you need a nickname." The other girls nodded, almost in unison.

Hang out with them.

As the teacher began the class, I allowed a small flicker of hope to bloom in my chest. Maybe it would be okay. Maybe this would be my turning point, the one I'd be waiting for, the one where I could have a real life and real friends.

I ran home after school and was pleased to see that Lily had indeed cleaned the house. It smelled of lemon and pine and looked almost normal. I changed my clothes a dozen times, deciding to go with my floral corduroy hip-huggers and a simple sweater. I wanted to look good but not as if I was trying too hard.

At five forty-five, Mom still wasn't home, but that was okay. I had heard her call and order the pizzas earlier that week, so there would be food. At six on the nose, the doorbell chimed—truthfully, I had forgotten we had one since no one ever visited—and I ran to answer it. The girls poured in through the half-opened door like Viking invaders, their voices high and all talking at once. Charlotte looked around the living room, Judy glanced into the side porch where I watched television, and Patricia appraised the dining room.

"Your house is actually nice, Izzie," Patricia said, sounding surprised.

What had she expected?

Judy arrived at her side and leaned on Patricia's shoulder. "My mom says her parents are architects, makes sense."

They knew what my parents did? How?

"Were," Charlotte stage-whispered.

Judy looked irritated. "What?"

Charlotte raised her eyebrows. "Her father…" she prompted.

Judy stood up straight. "Oh, right. Well, your mother still is, right?"

I just nodded. It was way too much to take in. I felt as though I were in the ocean, my head sinking below the surface of water as I stretched up and gasped, trying to take a breath.

The doorbell rang again—that certainly was a record—and Charlotte answered it. A pimple-faced teenager stood on the stoop, a stack of three pizza boxes in front of him and a bag of soda bottles and cups hanging from the other hand.

"Ooh! Pizza!" Judy squealed.

We set up on the dining room table, and the girls settled into the midcentury-modern chairs that surrounded it. I almost stopped Patricia from sitting at the head of the table in my father's spot, but I bit the comment back. It was just a chair, after all.

We dug into the pizza and started talking about last week's episode of *Saturday Night Live*. Patricia and I were the only ones whose parents allowed us to stay up late enough to watch it, so I felt special. We were just talking about how cute Chevy Chase was, and I was telling them about the "Wild and Crazy Guys" sketch when we heard the creak of the front door opening.

Everyone turned to look toward the door as Mom dropped her briefcase to the floor and shut the door with a shove. Then she turned our way and her eyes lit up.

"Oh my goodness! You're all here!" She walked over with her hands together, and I noticed the slight wobble in her step as she entered the dining room. "Isla! You didn't tell me your friends were all so pretty! What are your names?"

Then the girls were smiling and introducing themselves, and Mom was asking questions about their parents and the music they liked, laughing and being her effusively charming self. For a moment, I saw her as they must see her. She wore a silk embroidered dress with a Nehru collar that she had sewn herself from fabric my father had brought back from Japan during a business trip. Her leather-toe sandals were hippie enough to be cool but professional enough for the office, and her hoop earrings sparkled beneath the natural curls of her hair.

Mom put her hand on my shoulder. "So glad to see such a festive celebration for my sweet Isla." She beamed at me.

And in that moment, I was proud to be her daughter.

"Wait!" She clapped her hands. "I know! Let's go to Carvel! Ice cream's on me!"

The girls squealed and the chairs scraped, and I felt like the whole party was sliding off a cliff. My head snapped over to look at Mom, who was wobbling on her feet, the car keys already dangling off her thin fingers.

No. This was not a good idea.

"Wait! I can walk to the store and get us some ice cream! We can have it here!"

The girls were incredulous, and Mom put her arm around me. "Don't be silly, Isla. Mommy wants to treat her girls to some ice cream."

Mommy? And was I the only one who saw it? Who heard the blurred edges of each word? I felt a cold sweat break out on my upper lip as I followed behind the group, my mother holding the door open and them scurrying by. I swallowed and looked up at Mom. "Do you think you're okay to drive?"

"Of course. Don't be ridiculous." Her tone was suddenly sharp and angry, and she gave me a small shove as I stumbled onto the front step. The girls had piled into the back of the station wagon, and I climbed into the front passenger seat. Mom started the car and turned around to look behind, and I caught the sharp scent of rum on her breath.

Carvel wasn't far, but the drive felt like an eternity. A few years earlier, I had perfected my stamping-on-the-imaginary-brake technique in the hopes that I could control the car when she couldn't, like some kind of driver's ed teacher. The entire way there, I was silent, watching the car swerve near Mr. Carson's mailbox as Mom chatted over her shoulder with the popular girls from school. I don't think I took a breath during the trip there, and I felt a massive sense of relief when we finally pulled into the Carvel parking lot, the brightly lit building a beacon of safety. As I watched the girls pour through the glass door, I thanked God they hadn't seemed to notice anything on the drive.

"Hello, ladies, can I help you?"

The group grew silent as we looked up and saw Josh Hansen smiling at us from behind the counter. Josh was a senior, the handsomest guy at Leonia High, and everyone had a crush on him. Patricia started giggling behind her hand to Judy, and my mother stepped up to the counter.

"Well, aren't you a handsome thing?" she said, and I saw Josh's face redden all the way to his muttonchop sideburns.

I felt my stomach bottom out into my pelvis, and while Mom relayed the girls' orders to Josh—as if he couldn't hear them himself—I fantasized about running. Onto the highway. Out of New Jersey. Off the planet.

"And what does my sweet birthday girl want?"

I looked up and saw that Mom and Josh were looking at me, and I felt my eyes start to fill. "Nothing," I whispered.

"Oh no, we can't have that! Josh, honey, can you make her up a mint chocolate chip cone? That's always been her favorite."

She chatted and flirted with him, a boy half her age, and the girls stepped up one by one, dissolving into giggles as they took their cones from Josh. I had so many feelings at once, it felt like emotional white noise. It was as if I had left my body and was watching the scene play out below me, my head brushing against the pockmarked white ceiling tiles. But there was no part for me in this performance, even though the gathering was supposed to be in my honor. I stood frozen, saying nothing, and no one seemed to notice.

The girls filtered out, cones in hand, chattering and giggling about Josh. Mom threw some money on the counter and stepped out with her single rum-raisin cup, leaving me standing there alone.

"Isla."

I looked up, and Josh was holding out a cone with two towering scoops, one green, one white. I went to take it from him, my throat tight.

He smiled. "I gave you an extra scoop, for your birthday. It's my favorite too, but I like one of each kind."

It was so small an act of kindness, but it felt so big. Instead of smiling or thanking him, I felt the tears spilling freely down my hot cheeks.

Josh handed me napkins and touched my hand as I took them. I glanced up to find him looking at me with a serious face. "Is your mom okay to drive you girls home?"

I stared at him, feeling as if my skin had been peeled back, as if he could see all my internal organs, my exhausted and battered heart beating in my chest.

He shrugged. "My dad, he gets mean when he drinks, and he always insists on driving." Then he smiled, took off his white Carvel cap, placed it on my head, and tapped it down. "Keep that, for luck." He gave me one more big smile and said, "It's going to be okay, Isla."

I felt a wave of gratitude rush through me like fire and managed to whisper, "Thank you," before a couple came in with four small kids, and Josh was pulled away.

As I walked out the door, I licked at my ice cream, and when I got to the car, I noticed all the girls staring out the back window of the car at me, mouths agape.

I lost interest in my ice cream again, until I slipped into the seat and closed the door.

"Did Josh Hansen actually give you his cap?" Patricia asked, her voice tapped down with awe.

I lifted my hand up and felt the stiff white hat perched on my head and smiled. "Yes."

The car broke into screams as Mom drove out of the parking lot. Before she pulled out onto Grand Avenue, she looked over at me, pinched my cheek, and said, "My girl, a chip off the old block."

I didn't even notice the drive home, and by some birthday miracle, we made it back to the house safely even without my imaginary brake.

We moved the living room furniture to leave a big open space in the middle of the Persian rug and set our sleeping bags in a circle with the heads together so we could talk. Just after we settled, Mom appeared, wine bottle dangling from her hand, an exhausted look on her face.

"I'm heading up to bed, girls. Have fun."

After a chorus of "Night, Mrs. Larsen," I watched her walk up the carpeted stairs, her fingers wrapped tightly around the banister as if it was helping to propel her up. I heard her door close, and I let out a long breath.

The next couple of hours were a whirlwind of laughter, music (Charlotte had brought her Panasonic Toot-a-Loop AM radio), and conversation about movies, boys, and school. As Judy talked about her crush on Bobby Fitch, I looked around at their faces and couldn't believe they were there in my living room, and though I didn't talk much, I was part of a group of kids my age. I wouldn't use the word *friends* yet, not even in my head. It was too soon, too scary, but I was happy. By midnight, Charlotte had fallen asleep, her breaths whistling through her retainer, and Patricia and Judy were talking about what high school would be like the following year when I started to nod off. I cradled my head on my arms and drifted off with a smile on my face.

I woke to shaking.

"Izzie! Izzie, wake up!" Patricia pleaded, her voice urgent.

I looked around, trying to get my bearings. All three girls were wide-eyed and staring at me.

"What's wrong?" I was fully awake then.

"I think there's something wrong with your mother."

"What?"

And then I heard it.

A howling. Even through the closed door all the way upstairs, it echoed off the ceiling, reaching down the stairs until it hung over our heads like a storm.

I was up, jumping over sleeping bags and to the stairs in an instant. I took them two at a time, desperate to get to my mother, certain she was dying, someone was killing her. I shoved open her bedroom door and struggled to see in the closed-air darkness of the room. It started again, low at first, then grew like a fire siren, until the absolute grief of the sound weighed down on everything in the room. I ran over to my mother's form on the bed and shook her.

"Mom! Mom! Wake up! Are you having a bad dream?"

Her head bobbled on her shoulders like her neck was broken, her eyes open but unseeing.

"Mom, it's Isla. What's wrong?"

Her eyes jittered, and she looked around like she was trying to figure out where she was. Her unsteady gaze landed on me, and then her face fell as if it were melting. "Oh, Isla! He left me. He left me all alone." Then she was sobbing.

"Mom, you're not all alone. I'm here."

"But, Isla, he left me alone with all their stories. I can't do this alone. I just can't." The sobs were coming from the very core of her being, dredging up darkness even I didn't know was there. But whatever temporary awareness there was had fled. The howling started again.

I knew she was drunk and wasn't making sense, but despite this, the pain I tried to muffle in my own chest shed its carefully laid wrappings and uncoiled, and my quiet sobs mixed with hers.

I don't know how long we sat like that, me holding her head and shoulders in my lap like a reverse of the *Pietà* sculpture Alma had in her cabinet, Mary cradling her grown son, the crucified Jesus. Eventually Mom passed out, and I gently set her down on the bed and tucked the covers beneath her. After I quietly shut the door, I started for my bedroom, exhaustion weighing down my limbs, when I remembered.

I tore through the hall and flew down the stairs, but when I got to the bottom, I saw the living room was empty, my sleeping bag alone in the middle like a shed skin.

CHAPTER SEVEN
too many hospitals

I survived that last year of middle school, but the summer couldn't come fast enough. It had started to feel like the flight to Puerto Rico at the beginning was the flight home, that my life in New Jersey was marking time till I could head south again each year. As Alma drove out of the airport parking lot, I braced myself for the inevitable "How are things at home?" I couldn't lie to my great-aunt, never could. But how would I describe what our lives had become? I worried that if she knew what it was really like, she would try to spirit me away, but then who would take care of my mother?

Alma continued onto the expressway instead of taking the exit to get on Route 22 toward Bayamón, and I was about to ask her where we were going when she cleared her throat.

"Isla, m'ija. I am going to bring you to your cousin Maria's house in Old San Juan where you will stay for a few days."

Wait. Our routine had never changed before. Ever. She shared me with no one while I was there, not overnight. Normally this development would have thrilled me: Maria was eighteen, drove a convertible, and lived with a roommate in an apartment, but there was nothing normal about this conversation. I turned my body to face her. "Why?"

I watched her gnarled fingers grasp the Buick's steering wheel so tightly, her knuckles grew pale and blue as ice. "Tomorrow I must go to the hospital—"

I sat straight up, my heart picking up speed. "Hospital? What's goin—"

She held her hand up and did that tutting thing with her tongue, the one that had long ago quieted a full classroom of students, a small sound that demanded attention in the way only she could. It did its job and silenced me. "It is nothing to be concerned about, Isla. A routine procedure, that is all. I will be back home the next day, and after a few days of rest, you can come to the house, and we will have our summer together."

"But I can come right after and take care of you when you get out. I'm good at that, I—"

"Yes, I know you are. But you are here to rest, to be young. Not to care for an old woman. Your tía Lourdes will be helping me." She could see I wasn't comfortable and added, "Besides, your cousin is excited to be hosting you at her house."

Despite my anxiety about Alma, as we drove across the lagoon and then by the Caribe Hilton, I began to get excited. I'd only come to the old city on quick day trips or to buy Mallorca pastries before going to visit my grandmother. I'd certainly never *stayed* there. Alma was quiet during the trip, and I wondered if there were more to this "procedure" than she was telling me. But if she didn't want to talk about something, I knew from experience there was no use in pressing.

She wove the boatlike car through the narrow side streets, the blue cobblestones glazed from the noontime rain, eventually pulling up in front of a building with three large arched windows wrapped in ornate iron bars. When I was little and we took those short trips to Old San Juan, I would look up at the balconies with their flower-draped wrought-iron railings and wonder who lived there, what the buildings were like inside. I guessed I was going to find out.

There was no space to park, so Alma stayed in the car as I hustled my bags to the front door. It was huge and imposing, made of dark wood with iron fittings like something from King Arthur. "¡Ya voy!" I heard coming from behind the door. "I'm coming!" The door swung open and my cousin leapt forward, wrapping me in a warm hug.

"Oh, Prima! I'm so glad you're here!" she squealed in my ear, then held me at arm's length and brushed my overlong bangs out of my eyes. "And you've gotten so pretty and so grown-up!" Her smile was big, honest, and blinding. Then she noticed the car idling at the curb. She crossed the sidewalk in a flurry of linen, leaned in, and air-kissed Alma across the long bench seat. As a car pulled up behind and honked, Maria promised to take good care of me and stepped back. She put her arm around me as we stood and watched Alma pull away, turn the corner, and disappear. It was the first time I would be going somewhere on the island for any length of time without her. I felt both abandoned and on the edge of something very exciting.

"Well, now that the grown-ups are gone, let's get you settled in!"

Maria led me inside, and I looked around as she closed the door and threw the massive lock. The ceilings towered above our heads, with fans lazily spinning in each room. The floors were black and white marble and the walls painted a riot of tropical fruit colors.

"This is all yours?" I asked.

"Well, not mine. My parents are renting it for me for the summer since my internship is in town." She picked up my worn suitcase and carried it through the apartment.

Maria lived on her own in a city, like a grown-up. Awe spread through my veins like a drug.

She was still talking, but her voice was coming from farther in the house. I rushed to follow, entering a courtyard with bars instead of a ceiling, the late-afternoon sun reaching in and painting the floor in patterns of gold.

"This will be your room," Maria said as she lifted my bag onto a huge bed.

I stepped through the doorway and gawked at the orchid-purple walls, the ornate antique wooden bed and dresser.

"I can't take your room."

"Oh, this isn't mine. It's my roommate's. She's staying at her mom's this week. There's a bathroom right here." She flipped on a light, and I saw a claw-footed tub and a riot of art covering the walls from floor to ceiling. "I'll let you get settled, and then I'll take you out for an early dinner, okay?"

After I unpacked my things, tucking them in the dresser drawers that smelled like roses, I lay on the bed and looked up at the ceiling as salsa music wafted in from the courtyard. I found myself wishing I could come here each summer instead of Alma's and immediately felt bad, particularly with her going into the hospital the next day. But at my great-aunt's, I felt smaller, diminished. Here, though the ceilings were twice as high, the corners not filled with the detritus of old age, I felt bigger...seen.

Dinner was amazing. Maria ordered every appetizer on the menu, and I ate greedily. As we were walking home, the clean click of her kitten heels echoing on the narrow street, I asked the question that had been on my mind since the drive from the airport.

"What's wrong with Alma?"

Maria laughed. "Do you want a list?" She looked over at me, saw my face, and put her arm around me. "I'm just joking, Prima. I love her too. Truth is, I'm not sure. Something to do with her heart." She stopped, tucked her fingers under my chin, and turned my face to her. "Don't worry too much about her, Isla. She's one of the strongest people I know." Then she smiled.

It was enough for me.

The next day, we stopped by the hospital in Santurce to see Alma. Lourdes had called that morning and said the procedure had gone well, but I needed to get eyes on Alma myself. Just stepping into the antiseptic white hallways, the smell of ammonia and sickness reaching for me with spindly invisible fingers, I felt my skin tighten like it had become too small for my body. I hadn't been in a hospital since the last time I'd visited my father, the last time I saw him. But I swallowed my fear and fell in step next to Maria. Before we went into the room, she seemed to sense my anxiety and whispered in my ear, "We won't stay long, okay?"

I took a deep breath and walked in with her. Alma lay on the bed, her face slack in sleep, her skin drained of its olive color. Her gray hair was pushed back and wild, something she never would have been caught dead with. Her long pianist fingers were spread wide over the bedsheet, as if reaching for the keys on either side.

Maria stepped up to the side of the bed. "Tía. Tía Alma," she whispered, taking our great-aunt's hand.

Alma's papery eyelids fluttered up, and when her hazel eyes saw us, a smile spread across her face. "Mis primitas bonitas."

Maria bent down and planted a gentle kiss on Alma's cheek and stepped back. They were both looking at me. As I took slow steps toward the bed, the smell of disinfectant and urine, with something sweet and overripe underneath I couldn't identify, invaded my nostrils. I leaned over and brushed my lips to Alma's cheek for a second, then jumped back. My breath was coming in faster and faster, but no one seemed to notice.

"You have some visitors, Alma, how wonderful." I hadn't heard the nurse come in, and I stepped aside so she could get closer to the bed. She changed out the IV bag while talking to Alma in a calm, gentle voice. "How are you feeling, amor?" she asked as she took my great-aunt's pulse.

"I'd be better if you'd tell those dogs to pipe down."

The nurse smiled at her and patted her hand. "I will, Doña," she said, and as she turned to go, she told us quietly, "She's still under sedation and it will make her a bit confused for a few more hours." She smoothed Alma's sheet, then silently padded out the door.

"Well, Tía, we'll let you get some rest. I think—"

But then Alma was gesturing to me to come closer, her finger hooked and her eyes insistent. I glanced over at Maria for guidance, and she nodded. I moved forward in tiny, slow steps, swallowing hard. When I was next to the bed, Alma grabbed my hand.

"Elena. Elena, you must do something for me," she urged in Spanish.

"Tía, I'm not Elena. I'm Isla, her daughter," I answered in English, trying to emphasize the error.

But she didn't seem to hear me. "Elena, m'ija," She pointed over to the far corner of the room where a wheelchair sat patiently waiting. "See your mother over there?"

I squinted. "You mean Abuela? No, Tía, she came to see you this morning, but—"

She shouted right into my face, making me jump. "I know what I see! She's right there! Are you blind, child?"

I looked over at Maria with pleading eyes.

She shrugged.

Alma yanked on my hand, pulling my attention back to her. "Tell her that I know." She pointed to her chest with her finger, eyebrows narrowed. "That story she always tells is wrong. She knew what really happened that day." She nodded slowly.

I wanted to pull my arm free and leave. Tears clouded my vision. Alma said something under her breath. I leaned closer. "I'm not sure I understand, Tía."

Then her eyes went wild. With one hand, she grabbed the front of my shirt with her bony fingers; with the other, she pointed off in the distance. "The shot! The shot in the trees!" Her voice was strung tight and thin, spittle gathering at the sides of her mouth.

A scream cowered in my throat as I stared into Alma's cloudy eyes, feeling as though I were falling into their confusion.

Maria yanked me backward, settling me on my feet, pulling me from their spell. "Okay then. Let's give Tía besitos and let her sleep, yes?" Then we were brushing lips again as Alma's eyes shut, heavy with sedatives and age. The speed with which Maria left the hospital made me realize I was not the only one who had been frightened.

───────────────

The next four days were a blur of day trips to forts, shopping, and trips to the beach. When we were driving back from the Condado, the fancy tourist area between Old San Juan and the airport, I was enjoying the feeling of salt tightening on my skin, the warmth of the sun still held in the strands of my hair. "I love the beach." I sighed. "Alma never takes me to the beach."

Maria scoffed. "Yeah, her generation thinks it's only for poor people."

My head snapped toward her. "What? Why?"

Then Maria broke into a perfect imitation of Alma's wavering voice, each word precise and enunciated. "Why would you want to darken your skin, m'ija? You are descended from the Spaniards who founded this island, not the slaves who built it."

I didn't want to admit I didn't understand, so I stayed quiet.

Maria sensed my discomfort and patted my arm. "Don't worry about it, Prima. It just means the older generation of Sanchezes are still living in medieval times." She gave me a wide grin. "I'm thinking it's ice-cream time, no?"

I smiled and nodded, but my mind was still worrying the threads of what she'd said, pulling at each word to find understanding.

CHAPTER EIGHT
abuela's story

The next night was my last at Maria's, and I was already mourning the return to the house in Bayamón that felt like stepping back in time. We were invited to Abuela's for dinner and therefore had to dress accordingly. Our grandmother believed one should dress for dinner and that young ladies had to appear a certain way. Maria loaned me a white cotton dress with a flouncy skirt that I had to admit made me feel like a princess. But as we got closer to the gated community in Guaynabo where our grandmother lived, I felt my skin tighten and felt like the dress was a costume that Abuela would mock me for, sensing the skinned knees and clumsiness within the pretty wrapping.

Mom never went to visit her mother; they despised each other. Abuela didn't approve of anything my mother did, or what I did, for that matter. The rare times I did see her, she was quick to point out that my shorts were dirty, that I didn't speak English clearly, and why couldn't I behave like my cousin Maria? Being in her presence made me feel inadequate in every way possible. I can only imagine what a lifetime in her presence had done to my mother.

The house was elegant and spare, the opposite of Alma's. The furniture was stately and "imported from Spain, of course," and servants skirted around in the background, trying to avoid stepping into the matriarch's radar. I understood that impulse all too well. I stayed silent while Maria worked her magic, fawning over new artwork, feigning interest in society gossip.

We sat down at the dinner table, and as I spread the cloth napkin on my lap, I breathed a sigh of relief that I had avoided interaction thus far. I started a bit when her cook, Genara, placed a steaming plate of filet encebollado in front of me. The strips of steak marinated in traditional spices, rings of fresh white onion, their juice reaching over to the starchy slices of plantain, olive oil and garlic scents reached for me like old friends. I looked up at Genara gratefully, and she gave me her warm smile.

She had always been nice to me when Alma left me at the house for a few hours a couple of times each summer, bringing me frosty Cokes after my grandmother yelled at me for playing in the dirt or blending up virgin piña coladas when I sat alone, crying for my mother. It always seemed so weird to me that Abuela had servants at all—only the superrich in the States had servants—but as Genara walked away and I glanced into the kitchen after her, for the first time, it struck me that all of them were dark-skinned.

"Isla!"

My shouted name jerked me back into the moment. Startled, I looked over at Abuela.

"That girl's head is always in the clouds, just like her mother," she said to Maria as if I wasn't in the room, cutting at her steak as if it had wronged her in some way.

I put down my own fork and knife and swallowed, the food suddenly less appetizing.

Maria put her hand on mine. "That's why she's going to be an artist, or a writer, verdad, Prima?" She gave me a secret wink, and I could almost feel a small transfer of her power.

Abuela scoffed. "Exactly, something useless like an architect."

I swallowed a flush of anger. "I'm sorry, Abuela. Were you asking me something?"

She took her time, chewing her steak her requisite thirty-two times. *You must always properly masticate your food.* Then she asked without turning toward me, as if she couldn't stand to look at me, "I asked what you are taking in high school this year." She looked over at me, fork in hand. "That is, if you *are* going to high school this year."

I narrowed my eyes, silently letting her know I heard the dig, and answered, "I will be taking algebra, biology, history, English, and typing."

She nodded begrudgingly, as if disappointed there was nothing she could pick apart in that list.

I continued, divulging something my mother had been hiding from her. I knew I was poking the bull, but I wanted to. Needed to. "I'm going to the public high school in town."

Her head shot up. "What? You're not going to a private Catholic high school?"

"No, Abuela," I replied primly, suddenly interested in my food again.

I knew this would probably only backfire on my mother, but my grandmother had made people so miserable for so long, it felt victorious to me.

After dinner, we retired to the back patio, relaxing to the music of the rocking chairs, the beginnings of coquí song, and the quiet landing of bright-red flamboyán blossoms in the azure water of the swimming pool. This time of evening was the only part I liked about visits to Abuela, because it meant we would be getting a story.

It would have to be quiet for her to start, a lull in the conversation, the breath of a sigh for the cooling of the evening air. Then she would begin the telling, slowly weaving a tale from the air like fabric, until the colors, sounds, and smells came to life in front of us. Though I had heard her tell this particular story before—she would rotate them, bringing them back every few years to keep them fresh—it was my favorite, and each time she told it, she added some detail that made it new.

"It was that hour in Bayamón when the noontime rain had passed... You know how everything gets shiny as if it's covered in a sugary glaze like Lourdes's pastries? The heat rose again, and with the wet ground, the air became heavy and moist. The dampness that day was particularly heavy around our house.

"That afternoon, the monkeys escaped from the local zoo. No, it's true. I remember it well. It was all over the radio news, and everyone was talking about it while sipping their afternoon cafecitos. The policemen scoured the streets while the zoo workers frantically drove around, looking up at the trees for the runaways.

"Sitting on the back patio, I was oblivious to all the commotion, enjoying a well-deserved break from my afternoon chores. Papá worked us all so hard! You kids today don't know how easy you have it. Anyway, as I lifted my coffee cup to my lips, I heard something running over the roof of the house. I set my cup down quietly and grabbed a broom—the closest thing to a weapon a good Catholic lady has—and carefully walked to the end of the patio, looking up through the black gates at the roof of palm leaves. I saw a movement, quick and brown, and squinted, trying to make out what it was. Suddenly, a second figure ran across the gated roof, gripping the bars with long russet fingers. It was as the tail skirted by that I finally realized what I was seeing. I began to wonder if I was losing the good sense that God gave me, but then I heard men's voices, shouting excitedly.

"'They're over here! Bring the nets!' Three men in dark-green uniforms appeared in our backyard. The large one was carrying two portable cages by their metal handles. The second man was tall and slim and held a net that seemed to mirror his big head and sticklike body. The third and smallest had a bushy mustache and a loud voice that blared like my father's old-fashioned car horn. He was obviously the boss, or at least thought himself one, and he barked orders at the two other men. I watched with great amusement as they stumbled about our foliage, and I slinked over to the side behind a potted plant so I could observe without being seen. It was like those old films... What do they call it? Slapstick, yes.

"The men were peering up at the canopy. I followed their gaze just as the monkeys began screeching and swinging with abandon from tree to tree, occasionally taking breaks to eat freely of our bananas. For almost an hour, I watched the bumbling zookeepers as they attempted to corral the playful monkeys and return them to their cages. It was more entertaining than the afternoon telenovela! The tall man was particularly aggressive and began to lose his temper, jabbing at the animals with the long pole of the net. One of the monkeys, a chocolate-brown one with an intelligent face, grew angry at this. I could see the planning of ideas in his large, cunning eyes. When the man got rough with him, the monkey stood on his branch and began to pee on his tormentor. I stifled a giggle, and the other men began to laugh and point. I watched the tall, skinny man get angrier and angrier, humiliation clouding around him in the afternoon heat.

"After a while, one by one the monkeys scurried down the trees to the ground: the fun of their afternoon jaunt had passed. The tall man scooped them up and put them in the cages while the boss called out apologies to me through the foliage, his head bobbing up and down as if he were bowing. As the men walked around the edge of the house, I peered around the corner and into the cages and found that the chocolate-brown monkey was looking at me. I smiled at him and waved goodbye, chuckling to myself at my silliness. How could he understand? But just as they were going out of sight, my little brown friend put his finger to his mouth as if the afternoon adventure was our little secret."

When the last words faded away and the spell broke, Maria and I said our goodbyes, gave our obligatory kisses on the cheek, and headed back to Old San Juan for one more night.

If I had known then that that was the last time I would hear Abuela tell that story, I would have paid better attention.

Maybe I would have been better prepared.

CHAPTER NINE
death of a cuentista

I looked out the plane's window at the carpet of white and realized that after eighteen years of being shuttled back and forth, I was most comfortable right there, among the clouds high above the Atlantic Ocean, halfway between New Jersey and Puerto Rico. Beside me, my mother lined up the little empty airplane bottles of rum on the tray table in front of her like a tiny Bacardi army, oblivious to the rock and sway of the plane and the second glances of the flight attendants. I wasn't surprised when my mother ordered the rum and Coke before the plane had even begun to taxi.

The fact that my mother hated my grandmother didn't make the news of her death any easier. In fact, it was worse. Eventually my mother passed out, mouth open, head tilted back against the blue nubby fabric of the seat. At that point, I much preferred to fly alone, and I was grateful that I wouldn't have to fly back with her in a few days after the funeral. I put on my Walkman headphones and thought about how I would be heading off to college in a few months and would never look back. Well, not entirely since I had to live at home. We didn't have the money for me to live in the dorms. If it weren't for my scholarship, I'd have no way to afford any part of college.

I had to shake my mother from her drunken stupor when we landed. As we lined up to exit the plane, I noticed a smartly dressed woman whispering to her husband and looking over at Mom. At that point, I was no longer embarrassed by her drinking. Well, that wasn't entirely true, but I had grown protective calluses over the years. I looked right back at the couple, staring until they got uncomfortable and turned away.

As we passed through the baggage-claim area, I could see our relatives waiting for us on the other side of the wall of glass. For a moment, I imagined it was a family portrait that only the two of us could observe. This was the first time so many people had come to the airport: only in death could my abusive grandmother actually bring people together. As we walked, my mother grabbed my hand and held it tightly like she hadn't since I was little. I could feel the tremor that radiated up her arm as she prepared to step from one of her worlds into another. I wondered if for her, it was a step forward or backward.

The minute we pressed through the sliding doors, the family was upon us. All dressed in black, they were a flock of crows descending to pick at something on the road, and I felt my mother's hand slipping from mine. I stood there as the wave of relations enveloped us, words of Spanish swelling and cawing over my head. There was the obligatory cooed discussion about how grown-up I was, what a beautiful lady I had become. I smiled and said gracias as was expected.

We drove straight to where all Sanchez religious events occurred, la Iglesia de Santa Cruz in Bayamón's Parque Central. I knew the old church well, as Alma and my abuela dragged me there for mass every Sunday morning during my summer visits. As Mom and I walked in, I swung back the flat, black rubber strips that hung down in a drape over the huge open doorway. Abuela told me they were there so the doors could stay open, allowing the air to circulate but preventing birds from flying into the church. Much to my abuela's dismay, I would run back and forth through them, pretending I was a bird breaching the church's defenses, flying among the high stone buttresses. Exasperated, my grandmother would snap at me about how Maria wouldn't behave that way. That would only make me run faster.

I followed my mother into the church and down the aisle toward the front, the smell of incense hanging heavy in the church's stagnant late-morning air. We were stopped every few feet by mourners dressed in black who popped out of the aisles to impede our progress and hug my mother like some kind of Catholic pinball game. When they noticed me, they too talked about what a lady I'd become but then pinched my cheek as if I were forever five. When we finally made it to the front pew, I sat down hard as people continued to flock to my mother and express their condolences. If they knew what my mother really thought about the woman, they wouldn't have bothered.

My eyes swept over the white-fabric-draped altar, the bright Caribbean sunlight blasting its way through the stained-glass window above, the image of the Virgin Mary lit like a movie marquee. I breathed in my mother's Maja perfume as the last people filed into the church. The spicy sandalwood scent reminded me of her linen drawer at home, where I used to spend hours pulling out hand-embroidered handkerchiefs, painted fans from Spain, olive-wood rosaries from Bethlehem. Music swelled from the organ behind the altar, and the priest slowly made his way up the aisle, a vivid red flame embroidered on his white robe like a splash of blood. He was followed by a group of men carrying Abuela's coffin on their suit-clad shoulders. I recognized a few of them; Tío Ramón was in the front. There were so many people holding up the coffin that some were only touching it with the tips of their fingers.

"Jeez, Abuela wasn't *that* big. The whole town's carrying her!" I whispered to Mom. She chuckled, just as the woman in the row behind shushed us.

"You can say that again, m'ija," she said in a conspiratorial whisper, glancing back at the shushing woman behind. "Your abuela certainly weighed heavy on me." Her eyes were weary, but her mouth was set in an angry line that I'd only seen a few times before, and always with my grandmother. Over the years, I had seen Abuela berate my mother about everything. For marrying an Americano with a weak constitution. For being too lenient with me. For drinking too much. Sometimes when my mother was drunk, she used to rant about Abuela, about how she was cruel like Great-Grandfather. But for me, the most painful part was that my mother, the woman who took shit from no one, never stood up for herself with Abuela. She just stayed away.

As the men balanced the glossy wooden box on the stand in the front of the church and the priest began the mass, I noticed my mother staring at the coffin. Staring at it as if she were watching a pacing tiger in the zoo and worrying about whether the bars could contain it.

CHAPTER TEN
and the monkeys came

That night, my belly filled with lechón and the sweet guava cakes that Tía Lourdes had brought from next door, I sat on the front porch and listened to my mother and our relatives converse in Spanish. Between the music of the leisurely conversation and the excess of comfort-food calories, I could feel my eyelids getting heavier. I was biding my time until I could escape to the air-conditioned bedroom, but truthfully, I felt too lethargic to move.

I watched my mother as she talked, her hands dancing with her words as they always did when she was on her home island, the ice in her lowball glass of rum providing a clinking backbeat. As usual, the edges of her speech were slurring. I doubted anyone else noticed, or at least no one had any interest in talking about it. I often fantasized about having all the inappropriate and badly timed conversations, making all the controversial statements, and shouting all the obscenities I'd held back over the years in one fell swoop. I would air all the dirty laundry on the front lawn where everyone could see it, then I would take the deepest and freest breath imaginable.

"Oh! It looks like I need a refill!" my mother chirped, stumbling to her feet.

Need was not the first word that came to my mind.

She stopped in front of me and pushed my hair out of my eyes. "Do you want a cocktail, querida? My girl is so grown-up now!"

My only response was an ice-cold glare.

"I know! Let's all name the thing we admired most about Marisol," Tía Lourdes offered enthusiastically.

My mother sighed, walked back to her chair, and dropped into it, her glass of rattling ice forgotten in her hand. I could see her work to manage her feelings beneath her carefully made-up face.

Ramón spoke first. "Her piousness. My sister was such a good Christian." He raised his index finger as if giving a lecture, which he usually was. "She never missed a day of church in her eighty years. Not one!"

Alma was next. "Her gardens. She could make anything grow. I always wish I had her touch with flowers."

Each family member went on to pull something out to honor my cantankerous grandmother, until Mom was the only adult who hadn't said anything. The silence hung heavy on the humid evening air as everyone turned to look at her. She brought the glass to her lips for another sip, even though all that remained was ice.

Ramón cleared his throat, but my mother's voice cut him off from whatever social saving maneuver he had in mind.

"Her stories."

I breathed a sigh of relief. When my mother drank like this, there was no predicting what she was going to say. But when we were in Puerto Rico, she was always better behaved, as if she were playing a part.

"Tío, will you tell one of Mami's stories?"

Ramón harrumphed. "Ay no, Elena, this is not the right time—"

"Oh, Tío, por favor? What better way to honor her? Besides, you know her stories by heart. Won't you tell one? For me?"

Mom had that cloying "I'm manipulating men with my femininity" voice going on, two octaves too high. My jaw tightened. I saw her request for what it was: deflection, pure and simple. Or perhaps my mother actually wanted to hear her mother's stories. She couldn't stand the woman, but she loved to be told stories, someone else's stories...anything to escape real life.

I leaned forward and wondered if this was the distraction needed to make my escape, but when my great-uncle began to tell the story, it was as if he were conjuring Abuela, as if I could hear the high cadence of her voice, not his, echoing off the concrete walls, and I got pulled in as I always did, as I had in my fourteenth summer, the last time I heard her tell the story of the monkeys getting loose from the zoo...

After, it was Ramón's voice that came into focus as the tale came to an end, and I shook the memory of my grandmother's lyrical tone from my head.

I used the pause to execute my escape. I had no interest in hearing more about my grandmother or seeing my mother dive deeper into the almost empty bottle of Don Q. I stood, stretched, faked a yawn, and excused myself.

I curled up beneath the mosquito netting in Alma's guest bedroom with a thick novel. I was just falling asleep when I heard a strange skittering sound coming from the roof. I pulled the sheet up over my head and tried to ignore the sound. The adults were still awake and talking on the front patio. *They'll take care of it*, I assured myself. My eyelids had begun their slow fall when I heard it again, something running on the roof toward the back of the house. I threw back the sheet, pulled up the netting, and ran barefooted to the front porch. My relatives were still scattered about in the rocking chairs, drinking out of elegant crystal and prattling in Spanish.

My mother noticed me first. "Trouble sleeping, honey?" she asked in slurred English.

"I heard a sound on the roof," I said, panting for breath. They just stared at me, and my impatience loosened my tongue. "Didn't you guys hear it? Something's running across the roof!" After a pause and a look from one to the other, they all started to laugh. It infuriated me when adults did that. God, Mom was just talking about how grown-up I was, so why couldn't they treat me as one?

Alma piped in with, "Oh, m'ija, it was probably just a mango hitting the roof. You know how much noise they can make. Go back to sleep."

At that moment, I heard the sound, right above our heads. I looked over at the adults, who had resumed their conversations. "Hear that?" I yelled, pointing to the ceiling. "That! That noise!" They just stared at me. "You really can't hear it?"

It was Alma who finally spoke, a slight edge in her voice. "Enough silliness, Isla. Basta. Now go to bed."

They really didn't hear it. I stood there for a few moments but finally decided to investigate on my own since the adults were useless, as they so often seemed to me in those days, particularly when they hung around in packs.

I ran to the open-air kitchen in the back of the house, slipping on the tiles in the dining room, going in the direction of the scuttling sound, my heart beating faster than my feet. The side of the kitchen that faced the backyard was open, a web of black iron bars replacing the wall, and I could see the full moon reflecting off the shiny leaves of the thick canopy of palms. My senses were heightened as I caught the sweet scent of night-blooming jasmine in the light wind that rustled the plants outside. I looked up and saw movement on the branches closest to the roof. I blinked, and when I opened my eyes, daylight was filtering through the trees.

I glanced over at the clock on the wall: it was still nine. I could hear the adults' low murmur and the clinking of glasses in the front of the house, and I could still smell the jasmine. It was still nighttime. So where was that light coming from? I looked back to the trees and saw the shadow of a small brown figure swinging from frond to frond, followed by a second, and a third. I stood, my heart racing but my feet rooted to the floor. Faint voices came from around the side of the house, and when they rounded the corner, I saw men in starched dark-green uniforms and brimmed caps carrying cages.

I realized what I was seeing: it was Abuela's cuento. But how was that possible? My legs began to shake, and I could feel my lungs constrict, but I still couldn't move.

I jumped at a voice behind me. Tío Ramón entered the kitchen and walked toward the refrigerator for his late-night glass of parcha juice. "What are you doing, Sobrina? Do you see something out there in the dark, or are you listening to the coquis?"

He had to see the play being acted out, didn't he? But it didn't appear that he could. For a moment, I considered yelling at my tío, wildly gesturing toward the men, the monkeys, but as he calmly poured his drink, I remembered the indifference of everyone on the porch earlier, of how little I could depend on adults in my daily life. I had to try something, however.

"Um, Tío?"

"Yes, m'ija?" he asked kindly.

I pointed out the back of the patio. "Do you…see something out there?"

He looked, his eyes crinkling beneath his thick white eyebrows.

"Like what, Isla? Do you see someone in the trees? I don't see anything. Do you want me to go check?" He put his hand on the holster that was ever present tucked under his arm, beneath his suit jacket.

"Oh. No, Tío, thank you. It must have been a trick of the light," I said, hoping he would be satisfied and return to the gathering, leaving me to puzzle it out. He smiled at me, mussed my hair with his thick fingers, and walked out of the kitchen, sipping as he went. I was on my own.

I spun back toward the action, and in the moment I had turned away, a woman had appeared to my left, hiding behind the large potted plants, enjoying the exploits of the men and monkeys. I gaped at her. Looking closely, I saw that the woman was about my age, with dark curls tight to her head and an old-fashioned dress grazing her ankles. She grasped a straw broom in one hand and had a wide smile on her face. I stepped closer and confirmed: it was my grandmother.

Her face was smooth and pristine, like the framed photographs that Alma kept on her lace-covered dresser. Was she a ghost? She didn't look like one. Though my mind was full of caution, I wasn't frightened by the apparition. I called softly, "¿Abuela? ¿Eres tu?" But my grandmother seemed unaware of my presence and continued to watch the events unfold. I took a cautious step closer and caught the faint spicy scent of Santa Ana Alcoholado, the bay-leaf-scented alcohol that my abuela had splashed on every morning.

The zookeepers—looking foolish and impotent on the ground—yelled up at the monkeys. Abuela appeared delighted by the simians' antics. It was clear she was rooting for them, not the zookeepers, and I couldn't help getting caught up in her joy. Then the small monkey began urinating on an already-humiliated zookeeper, and

Abuela's hand rushed to her mouth as she tried to stifle a giggle. I became distracted by a monkey on the bars overhead, and then I heard the scream.

"NO!" Abuela yelled next to me. I jumped straight up in the air as a gunshot echoed among the trees. Shaking, I huddled closer to my grandmother. I looked back toward the door that led to the front of the house. Was it Tío Ramón? Was he shooting at something outside? But no, the room was empty except for me, and, well…them. Everyone in the apparition stood in silence as my heart continued to hammer in my chest, my breath coming in short and shallow. I had heard that story of Abuela's half a dozen times, and I was certain there was no gun in it.

The earlier model of my grandmother and I stood side by side as the monkeys came down from their perches and the men brusquely shoved them into their cages. I stood behind Abuela as she watched them round the corner of the house. The brown monkey looked back at us, his long finger to his lips. But with the addition of the gun to the story, this gesture did not seem playful or mischievous, rather one of shared silence. Of secret keeping.

Then they were all gone. Just like that, Abuela disappeared, and the curtain of night returned to the kitchen, the coquis resuming their song. I stood there for some time, tears threatening as I struggled to understand what had happened in the darkened room. I continued looking at the corner where my grandmother had stood, half expecting her to return.

I put my head in my hands and tried to think. I considered going to talk to my mother—but then I remembered the empty glass and the likelihood of subsequent refills. No.

Alma. I had to get Alma alone and tell her what had happened. She would help me puzzle it out. I ran to the front porch, interrupted the conversation, and pulled at my great-aunt's arm, gradually coaxing her inside to the darkened parlor.

"Okay, niña, what is it that's so important?" Alma asked, her hands on her hips in the shadows.

My breath was coming in big gulps. "Titi! I saw Abuela!"

"What? What are you babbling about, Isla? This is not a good day for your jokes—"

"No! Alma, I saw her! It was her story about the monkeys, but there was a shot and—"

"What? She never told that version to the children. There is no way you heard—"

"But that's what I'm trying to tell you! I didn't hear it, I saw it! And there was a gunshot... I—" And then I remembered when Maria and I visited Alma in the hospital a few years earlier. "Wait, was that the shot in the trees you mentioned after your surgery?"

"Isla!"

Her shout hit me as if it were a blow. The talking on the porch stopped. Alma noticed and pulled me farther into the house, her fingers digging into my arm like fork tines, reminding me of when she yanked me through the yard away from José when we were just kids. When we reached the dining room, Alma leaned closer, so her eyes were glaring straight into mine.

"Isla, stop talking about this!" she hissed. Then she looked up at the ceiling. "I should have known something like this would happen. How old are you, eighteen? Why is it always eighteen?"

I would have thought she was talking to herself if it weren't for the grip on my upper arms. But then she locked her eyes on mine again.

"First, I never talked about any such thing, in the hospital or anywhere. And second, you are never, ever to mention any of this nonsense about your abuela and her ridiculous monkeys to anyone, comprendes?"

I just stared at her, open-mouthed. Her face was red, her mouth twisted and tight.

She shook me by my upper arms, the forks digging deeper. "Do you understand?" she translated, as if after all these years, I couldn't understand a simple Spanish word.

Though I was already taller than Alma and certainly stronger, she frightened me. This version of Alma anyway. This was not the woman I'd known my whole life, who cared for me when my mother hadn't. No, this was the Alma who took José away. I hadn't seen her for ten years, and I was surprised to find she still struck terror in my heart, still made me feel powerless. I nodded. I was not confident my mouth would work.

Finally, she released me, and I rubbed my arms, still staring at Alma while her face slowly changed back to the one I knew.

"Good. Bueno. Good girl," she said in a shaky voice as her hands went to smooth her hair, then her dress. She held her head high and returned to the porch, jumping back into the conversation as if nothing had happened.

I stood there for a while in the dark, dazed. A familiar pain burned in my stomach, one I thought I'd banished years earlier. But here it was again, like an uninvited guest. After a time, I padded off to bed. I lay awake, wondering what Alma meant about being eighteen and why she had gotten so angry. Images of my grandmother and Alma's angry face blew across my mind, questions trailing behind in their wake, but sleep eventually took me.

I woke in the middle of the night, my mouth parched. I stumbled into the kitchen and poured myself a tall glass of cold water straight from the tap. I stood looking out the window over the sink and drank it down, feeling the liquid replenish all the air-conditioning had taken from my body. As I was refilling it, I heard footsteps below the window coming toward the house on the garden path. I turned off the water and ducked down. Then, the gate to the back patio rattled. I looked around and grabbed a large heavy pot that was drying on a towel and tiptoed toward the door. Just as I was sneaking around the corner, I ran headfirst into Alma and screamed.

Alma's hand rushed to her chest. "Madre de Dios, Isla. You are going to give an old woman a heart attack!"

As I was catching my breath, I noticed the soil on my aunt's fingers.

"Tía, are you gardening in the middle of the night?"

She sighed. "As I told you many times, Isla, it is my prerogative and my business." She looked down at my hands. "And what are you doing with my good pot?"

The following night, Alma and my mother went next door to Tío Ramón's house, and I pretended I wasn't feeling well. I had trouble even looking at the two of them after the previous night. Between Mom's booze and Alma's erratic rage, I felt unable to predict which versions of themselves they would be from one hour to the next. Now and then, their laughter carried through the louvered windows next door, taunting me. I tried to keep myself busy by putting together a puzzle in the dining room, the chandelier spilling a pool of light onto the shiny walnut table, the faded image of Big Ben filling out piece by piece.

I was thinking about getting a soda when the whole room brightened. I looked up at the skylight and saw the sun beaming overhead…at almost nine o'clock. Then I saw it: a small brown figure scrabbling across the thick glass toward the back.

"Oh, hell no!" I yelled into the empty house.

I jumped up, knocking the wooden chair to the floor, and ran to the kitchen. There was Abuela crouching in the corner with her broom, the monkeys and their keepers scurrying around among the sunlit trees.

I stood there open-mouthed as the story played out again. But when the gunshot came, I crouched down and squeezed my eyes shut until the sounds ended and night returned to Alma's kitchen patio.

It happened again the next night, and the next.

Beyond worrying about my own sanity, I was petrified by the addition of the gun. It lent a layer of darkness to the previously innocent story, and it made me so nervous, I jumped at every loud noise. I stopped going out to the kitchen at night, trying to hide from the vision in my room. Each night, as the hour drew near, I pulled the sheets over my head, gritted my teeth, and prayed that the scuttling would not return, that I wouldn't hear the sound of the gunshot. But it always came. I couldn't tell anyone about it, not after the experience with Alma. Besides, they would just dismiss it as my colorful imagination and grief over the loss of my grandmother.

After four nights of this haunting, as I had begun to think of it, I'd had little to no sleep and was walking around the house in a daze. When the sun began to set, my heart raced and sweat beaded on my forehead. After the performance that night, I swore to find a way to stop them.

Or I really would go crazy.

CHAPTER ELEVEN
a detective's return

The next morning when I awoke, my mother was still dead to the world, her snores loud over the air conditioner, the smell of last night's rum hanging around her like bad cologne. Alma had already left to do some errands in town, so I took advantage of the quiet morning to sit, think, and try to find a solution to my problem. I grabbed my journal and pen and settled on the patio with a café con leche and a guava pastry.

Gazing out at the sun filtering through the trees, I was contemplating my ridiculous yet terrifying situation when I noticed several men working around the shed, the triangular tips of shovels occasionally rising like seesaws in the bright morning light. Alma had said something about a new shed being built, but I had been too tired to pay much attention. I watched them for a few minutes, hypnotized by their rhythmic movements, when one of them stood and stretched, his face rising to the sun as he held his lower back with his hands.

This was not the usual pudgy, middle-aged man Alma tended to hire but rather a young guy with warm brown skin, a crown of glistening black curls, and strong, sculpted arms. I couldn't help but stare at him. Then his eyes turned my way. His face was as chiseled as his arms, strong and angular, but complemented by the most beautiful lips I'd ever seen. I locked on his dark eyes fringed by long black lashes. There was something so familiar in those eyes, something from long ago. I saw a look of recognition in him as well, and I stood abruptly, almost knocking the china plate to the floor as he walked closer to the house.

"Isla? Is that you?"

I watched the handsome face smiling through the black iron bars of the patio. He knew my name. Boys who looked like that didn't know my name.

"Don't tell me you've forgotten your favorite partner, Detective Isla?" His smile broadened.

"José?"

He nodded and brushed back a dark curl, leaving a stripe of soil on the smooth skin of his forehead. I tried to reconcile this gorgeous man with the small, thin boy I had played with all those years before. I walked slowly as my legs regained their ability to move and opened the gated door.

We stood facing each other for a moment, unsure but not quite awkward, the sound of shovels hitting dirt like a heartbeat behind us. José moved first, stepping forward and pulling me toward him, his warm, bare skin wrapping me like a blanket. I froze and though my body was still, my mind and heart skittered. Then I wrapped my arms around him and felt the muscles across his back, so different from the boy I knew. He smelled like sun and earth, a scent that was familiar and oh so comforting.

He pulled away suddenly. "Wait, is your tía around?" He squinted as he peered into the house.

I watched his eyes dart around as he stepped away from me. It was a small step, but I wanted to pull him back, to feel his warmth again. "No, she's gone to town. Besides, nothing is wrong with two friends greeting each other, right?" His eyes locked with mine again, and warming coals smoldered beneath my cheeks. I knew he was looking at me and smiling, so I pretended to be very interested in the work being done behind him. "Hey, what are you doing here anyway? Are you working for Alma?"

"I'm working with my father through this summer, and by then, I should have saved enough to not work and start at the University of Puerto Rico in the fall." His smile was wide, and he stood taller.

"Wow. Congratulations! What are you studying, crime scene investigation, Detective José?" We laughed.

"¡José! ¡Ven aca!" an older man yelled from across the property.

"¡Voy!" José shouted, then turned back to me. "I have to get back to work..." He pointed over to where the men were pulling a dead tree trunk from the ground.

"Oh, yeah, of course..." I said as we both stood there awkwardly again, like actors without a script. "Well, I guess I'll...see you around?"

José smiled back, his white teeth dazzling. "I sure hope so, partner." He started to walk away.

"Wait! José!"

He turned around with a radiant smile. "Yes, Señorita Sanchez?"

I smiled, but I didn't like him addressing me so formally, as if we were talking to each other across a great distance. As if I were like Alma. But seeing him, I once again wanted to talk to him about things I couldn't with anyone else. Because even though ten years had passed, I just knew he was...safe. That he was not going to change into someone else. But how was I going to ask the question I needed to ask? "Um, do you..." I just rushed into it, like jumping into cold water to get it over with. "Do you believe in ghosts?"

At this, he tilted his head to one side but then said, "¡Claro! Of course. Why do you ask?"

"I mean, do you think people…some people can see ghosts?"

"Sure, don't you?"

I nodded and shook my head at the same time, making a noncommittal circle.

"In fact, Pablo over there?" He pointed to a heavyset man with salt-and-pepper hair and a thick mustache who was hauling bags of cement. "His mother is an espiritista. She gets paid to talk to the dead."

My heart lifted. "Really?" This could be my answer. I knew telling José was the right thing to do. "Is she near here?"

"Sure, two blocks that way." He pointed toward the back of the property. "She also sells food. The yard is surrounded by chain-link fence… You can't miss it." He added in a stage whisper, "But if you go there, don't drink anything she gives you." Then he blessed me with that smile.

I smiled back. "Thank you." I didn't think I'd need to go, but it was good to have a plan B. And it felt really good to talk to somebody about my…situation. Somebody who wouldn't judge.

"Sure thing, partner." José tipped an imaginary hat, swung his shovel over his shoulder, and walked away.

One of the men smiled at me, and I realized I'd been staring. I hurried back into the house, the warmth behind my face returning yet again as I closed the gate behind me.

Maybe the visions would stop, and I wouldn't have to go find Pablo's mother.

And maybe they wouldn't.

CHAPTER TWELVE
claridad means clarity

That night, I withstood the sixth occurrence of Abuela's escapade and slept little, so the next morning, the minute Alma left for her daily stop at church to light a candle for her sister and while Mom slept it off, I grabbed the house keys and headed out the back door. There was no gate in the back, but I easily hopped the short stone wall that surrounded my family's property. The morning was clear and hot, and I slowed to feel the sun on my face. As I walked, I noticed the sounds of construction coming from all directions. A hospital was being built north of the property, an office building to the south. But on the Sanchez land, it was still the 1940s. I wasn't sure if I loved or hated that.

A block behind the property, the houses became more and more run-down, the sidewalk broken like something had heaved through the concrete while trying to escape. A group of men who were clustered around a corner store called to me, making kissing sounds as I picked up my pace. I realized this was the first time I was out on my own on the island. I was always being brought places, escorted, dragged. But though I knew the town well, I stood out with my pale skin and shambling gait. I was just beginning to question the wisdom of this quest when I noticed a tiny building surrounded by chain-link fencing, a counter open to the street with stools along the front. It had to be Pablo's mother's store.

There was one customer, a man in a business suit and hat perched on the stool farthest on the left, a cup of coffee clutched in his hands, a newspaper on the counter in front of him. The glass cases were lit with warm yellow bulbs but empty of food. I walked up tentatively and saw a tiny brown woman behind the counter, her gray hair pulled back in a tight bun.

I pulled out my careful Spanish. "Good morning. Are you Pablo's mother?"

The woman crossed her arms, and her eyes turned to slits as she examined me.

My voice shaking a bit, I continued. "José sent me. He works with Pablo?"

Again, nothing. Just cold, hard staring. I looked over at the man at the counter for help, but he only shrugged.

The woman mumbled something to the man, and I caught the word *blanquita*, little white one. This wasn't going to be as easy as I'd imagined. I looked back at the woman and felt like we were in a standoff in an old western film.

The man leaned over and whispered conspiratorially, "I think you should try her mavi."

"What's mavi?"

"It's a drink, made from the bark of the mavi tree. Claridad is famous for it." He nodded toward the old woman. Seemed her name was Claridad.

I remembered José's warning about not drinking anything I was given, but it was clear that I wasn't going to get anywhere unless this woman accepted me. I took a folded-up five-dollar bill from my pocket, slapped it on the counter, and announced, "Un vaso de mavi, por favor."

The old woman continued to stare for a moment, then took the five and put it in her apron pocket and said, "Bueno." She shuffled out through the open back door in her slippers, chickens scattering as she walked through them, and disappeared.

I looked at the man in confusion. "Did she leave?"

He shrugged again and went back to reading his newspaper.

I was wondering whether I should just give up and head back when the chickens scattered and squawked, dust flying again in their wake, and Claridad reentered and placed a disposable plastic cup of amber-colored liquid on the counter in front of me. Nothing about it looked appetizing.

I stared at the cup. The customer and Claridad stared at me. Apparently not one of the three of us was convinced I would drink it. Then I remembered the chain-smoking professor with rings on her toes who taught the early college cultural anthropology class I had taken at Columbia my senior year of high school. She had spoken of being in a community where they offered her the delicacy of ants whose bellies were filled with honey. The anthropologist asked, "So what do you do when faced with that situation?" The room of teenagers stared at her, and we braced for the answer. "You bite the ant in half and savor that honey."

I looked at the other two, who were smiling now, clearly content with their assumption about my inability to drink the mavi. There was nothing for it: I knew I had to bite the ant in half. I took a deep breath, picked up the cup, and drank.

It was almost thick with sweetness, but with an underlying earthy flavor. The closest thing I could compare it to was ginger ale. It was odd and rooty, but I liked the taste. I drank the entire cup in one go, tried to slam the cup down on the counter in dramatic fashion, continuing with the western movie theme, but the plastic just crumpled.

When I looked at Claridad, the woman was beaming, and then she started laughing. A bent-over-holding-her-belly-type laugh. Then we were all laughing, guffawing, tears streaming from our eyes. In that moment, I felt more at home on the island than I ever had before.

Claridad cleared her throat and asked in Spanish, "What do you want, m'ija?"

I swallowed and came out with it. "My abuela died, and I... Well, I see one of her stories, and her, every night."

"Ah, she was a cuentista?"

"Yes, she told stories."

"You must be one too, then."

I shook my head hard and found it spinning, just a bit. "No, I don't... My aunt says—"

Claridad waved her hand in dismissal. "You are young. It will come."

"But how do I stop them? The visions, I mean."

The old woman thought for a moment, then asked, "Your abuela, she liked telling these stories?"

"Yes, very much." I didn't add that she didn't seem to like much else in life.

"I'm sure she doesn't want them to stop with her death. Perhaps she wants you to keep telling them for her."

I shook my head again. "No, she didn't like me. And I'm not good at that. I don't even like speaking to more than one person."

"Does anyone else see these visions?"

"Not as far as I can tell. Seems to be just me."

"Well, your abuela chose you for some reason."

"But my tía Alma says—"

Claridad jolted, then stood stock-still. "Alma? Alma Sanchez is your aunt?"

"Yes, my great-aunt, actually, but—"

And then the old woman was moving, clearing off the counter. She shoved my five-dollar bill at me, then pulled the shutters closed across the front. The man at the counter didn't seem surprised; he picked up his coffee and stepped back, tucking his newspaper under his arm.

"But…Señora, what did I say?" I yelled through the closing gap in the gates. I was finally getting some answers, and then this.

Just before Claridad pulled the dented corrugated-metal shutters completely closed, she said, "Doña Alma is a good Christian, but I know what she thinks of people like me." She pointed her bony, bent finger at me. "Do not tell her you were here. For both our sakes." And slammed the shutters closed.

I was stunned. I turned to the man, "What did she mean 'like her'?"

The man shrugged again. "I try to stay out of such things, young lady. I am Switzerland. Perhaps you should be too."

I stood there for a moment, then tried to take a step back. The earth spun and the man steadied me with a hand on my shoulder. When I looked over at him, he was slightly blurry.

He sighed. "People say Claridad's mavi packs quite a punch. You'd never catch me drinking it."

I wobbled a bit. "Wait, you mean it has alcohol in it?"

"It's fermented. Downing it quickly like that probably wasn't wise." Then he was walking away, whistling.

I somehow made my way back to the house, let myself in after several attempts to get the key in the lock, and promptly passed out, a mirror image of my hungover mother in the next bed.

I woke up in the late afternoon, alone, with a cottony feeling in my mouth and a pounding in my head like my brains wanted out. I saw Alma working in the garden, heard my mother's overly chipper chatter from the porch at Ramón's, so I swallowed some aspirin with a glass of cold water and retreated back to the bedroom. I decided to look for the magazines I'd purchased in the airport and started rooting around in my carry-on. I was wondering if I could even read, given how I felt, when my journal fell to the floor.

As I stared at the book, Claridad's words came back to me. About how perhaps my abuela wanted her stories to continue, that she wanted me to tell them. I looked over at the stack of paperback novels on the night table next to my bed. Storytelling wasn't only done out loud.

I jumped to my feet, opened the rolltop desk in the corner of the room, and sat down on the worn upholstered chair. Shoving aside Alma's faded stationery, I found a pen and opened the journal. Beneath the air conditioner's hum, I wrote out my abuela's story, the blue words filling the prescriptive lined paper as I tried to capture the heart of the tale. The monkeys. The secret shared between my grandmother and her little comrade. I left out the gunshot, since that was not the story I had heard her tell. I filled three pages, transcribed the last line of the cuento, and stopped. I didn't feel any different, but time would tell. I slept for a few more hours and missed dinner all together.

Just before nine that night, I woke up starving. I shuffled into the kitchen and was rustling through some leftovers when I heard shouting. I stood up, eased the refrigerator door closed, and listened. I glanced out the kitchen doorway and saw Abuela crouching behind the potted plant.

"Fuck."

I half expected Abuela to chastise me, but she was too busy acting out her story over and over. As she screamed, "No!" into the woods, it hit me. "The shot in the trees." I had only heard one version of this story, and here she was telling me another. I ran back to the bedroom and wrote out the version from the vision, not the G-rated version I had heard. When I set the pen down, the air in the room felt different somehow. I looked around, but everything appeared the same. I shrugged, closed the book, and headed back to the kitchen to resume my foraging.

The next night, I lay in bed after dinner, looking at the clock every few minutes. By 8:45, my body had already begun to tense in anticipation of the sounds of the monkeys' scurrying.

8:50.

8:55.

9:00.

Nothing.

9:05.

Silence.

About this time, I should have been hearing the shot. I jumped out of bed and darted to the kitchen and looked through the iron bars. I saw and heard nothing, just Alma humming to herself as she did dishes at the sink.

No Abuela crouching in the corner of the kitchen.

No playful monkeys festooning the greenery.

And no shot in the trees.

Nothing but black night and coqui song.

I thought of Claridad and of the two versions of the written story in my journal. "Did it stop because I wrote it down? The version *she* wanted?"

Alma turned off the water. "What was that, m'ija?"

"Nothing, Tía. Just talking to myself."

The water began running again.

I took a long, deep breath, exhausted. Shuffling back to bed, I couldn't help wondering *Why me?* Abuela had talked of nothing but my shortcomings my whole life. I was surprised to find I would miss seeing Abuela, but I was grateful the nightly performances were over. I could sleep, and my evenings could go on as they had before Abuela's passing.

Or so I thought.

CHAPTER THIRTEEN
the last word

The morning Mom was due to fly back to the mainland, Tío Ramón came calling, hat in hand. He seemed oddly formal, but I assumed he was there to say goodbye to my mother, so I left them to their visit in the sitting room. After the first summer my mother had left me down there, I looked forward to her departure. I looked forward to not having the tension tighten in my shoulders when I heard the telltale crackle of rum pouring over ice. And since my grandmother's funeral, it had been coming earlier and earlier in the day.

I was rustling up some corn flakes for breakfast when I heard raised voices coming from the front of the house. Despite the stereotype of Latinos being overly emotional people, the Sanchezes were downright stoic, so the yelling was unexpected. I tiptoed from the kitchen to the dining room where I could hear what was being said without being seen.

"Elena, you can contest it. You *should* contest it."

"No, Tío. I don't want anything from that woman, dead or alive."

"But that makes no sense, niña. She might have been misguided and angry, but she was still your mother."

"Bah! No, she wasn't. She was a shitty mother and you know it!"

Wow. Mom never cursed around her family. At home, she swore like a truck driver, but in PR, she behaved like a proper "lady."

"Elena! You will not speak badly of the dead!"

"And why not, Tío? The woman is dead, and she still manages to give me a solid 'fuck you' from beyond the grave!"

I could hear my great-uncle gasp. And all this with no alcohol (but probably a throbbing hangover).

"I will not stand here and listen to that kind of language!"

His steps made for the door, and I could imagine him putting on his hat. He always tipped it slightly downward in front when he was angry, as if to shield the fire coming from his eyes. But I didn't hear the gate open, and when I next heard his voice, the edge of anger was gone. "Just think about it. I will contact you when you're back in New Jersey. Adiós, Sobrina."

The gate creaked open, then snapped close with a clunk, and the crunching sound of his boots on paving stones receded.

I heard some sniffling, then Mom's angry steps, so I rushed back to the kitchen. The sound of my mother's suitcase banging against the doorframe followed. I don't know what they talked about, but I was certain of one thing: Abuela always got the last word.

I walked into the dining room and took the suitcase from her, setting it down by the front door. When I came back, I found her standing outside the door to the bedroom we'd shared, her arms tight across her chest, her face hard and lined.

I touched her shoulder, and she looked up at me with tired eyes. I held up the small box of corn flakes that I still held in my hand. "Want some cereal?"

She smiled and hunched a bit, the weight of my abuela still pushing her downward. She shook her head slowly. "Just coffee. I could use some coffee."

I put my arm around her and walked her to the kitchen table. "Sit. I'll make you some café con leche."

She put her hand on my arm. "No, black. A cafecito. But I can get it…" she said, starting to get to her feet. I patted her shoulder, and she settled back in.

"Nah, I got it, Mom. You sit." I went into the kitchen and got to work, filling the bottom portion of the battered stovetop espresso maker with water, spooning the Bustelo coffee into the filter in the top, screwing it back together, and lighting the flame beneath. While it heated, I got out the delicate cafecito cups that Alma had brought from Spain and the sugar that still held a pale-brown memory of the sugar cane.

When I placed the rich, dark coffee in front of my mother and the version with steamed milk at my spot, she took a sip and looked up at me with awe. "I had no idea you knew how to make cafecito."

I shrugged. "I've been making it for years. Alma taught me."

She looked at me with glassy eyes. "Thank God for Alma. She's more of a mother to me than my own ever was."

I took a slow sip of my sweet milky coffee to keep the two words that sounded in my head from coming out.

Me too.

CHAPTER FOURTEEN
everyone loves a parade

One overcast morning, two weeks after my mother left, I woke to red lights reflected on the ceiling. Peering through the lace curtain, I cursed the thick shield of foliage. I leapt out of bed, shoved my feet into flip-flops, and tore out of the room, careening toward the front door. I could hear Alma's voice in my head, *You are too old to be running like that, Isla. You're a woman now!* I smiled as I ran anyway.

The gate was unlocked, and my great-aunt was already next door offering coffee to the medical personnel while Tía Lourdes spoke to a policeman on her front porch. I stopped just out of their view and watched as two men in white jumpsuits navigated a gurney over the patio stones. I stared at the reclining figure topped with a starched white sheet that waved in the breeze, wondering what the body looked like underneath. I hadn't ever seen a dead body, but when I was about ten, I had gotten the *Merck Manual* from the reference section of the Leonia library and looked up what happened to a body after life had left it.

I learned decomposition starts almost immediately; the skin pales as the blood gathers at the bottom of the body. Postmortem lividity is what it's called. Morbid research for a young girl, I know, but it was something I felt a burning need to know at the time. I guessed from overhearing conversations that the body of this particular woman in the back room had belonged to my great-aunt Lourdes's mother, a reportedly cranky ancient woman named Teresa, who had lived way longer than anyone anticipated (or probably wanted). I wondered if she'd been dead long enough for rigor mortis to set in.

"¡Isla! ¡Ven aca!" Alma had spotted me.

I scuffled across the yard, kicking the dried seedpods from Ramón's tamarind tree. Hadn't we had enough death lately? I hadn't even known the woman. But I knew that such excuses would never fly with Alma and would result in lectures about "obligation" and the priority of family. I reluctantly made my way over to Ramón's house.

I helped in the kitchen most of the morning, assisting in the preparation of food for the influx of relatives that could now be expected later that day. Puerto Ricans still buried their dead quickly, a holdover from pre-refrigeration days. As Lourdes chopped green peppers and crushed spices with her mortar and pestle, she would cry on and off, Ramón coming in to offer his wife comfort as the morning wore away, Alma telling her it was God's will. I felt bad for Lourdes, but all the drama made me uncomfortable. At home, I was basically left to myself and did my best to avoid *all* drama. I bided my time until I could sneak away.

Just before noon, I walked out behind the house, breathed deeply, and took note of the rustling of the trees, the crowing of the rooster from the next block. It was so good to be back on Alma's land. It was the closest feeling to home I'd ever had. Or what I imagined home to feel like. I closed my eyes for a second, feeling the warmth of the sun on my face, taking in the rich, earthy smell of the dense foliage that surrounded me. Without warning, the sound

of horns, cars, and many voices came out of nowhere, and my eyes
flew open. Alma's private jungle was gone, and I was standing in the
middle of a crowded dirt road surrounding a town square.

My head whipped around as I attempted to get my bearings,
the ground spinning slightly with my disorientation. The road was
bordered by small wood-framed stores with hand-painted signs over
their doors. The square was tree-lined, its carpet of grass dotted with
people in formal, old-fashioned dress seeking the little shade that
the leafy ceibas offered. As my eyes reached the edge of the park, I
gasped to see the Iglesia de Santa Cruz. The stones of the church's
facade were cleaner, a mottled caramel color, and in place of the
rubber strips were massive wooden doors with dark iron hinges and
handles. I tried to imagine the fragile old priest pulling the heavy
panels open...but as I glanced around the rustic street that I knew
as a bustling urban center, I remembered how my grandmother had
looked in the other vision and wondered if the priest was a young
man here.

It had been only a few weeks since I had last seen Abuela's monkey
story, but in that time, I had convinced myself that it had all been
my imagination. That the heat had made me see things. Now, as I
looked around at this vintage version of Bayamón, I wondered how
I could have ever doubted it. But what family story was this?

A horn barked like a seal to my right, and I whipped around to
see a cavalcade of antique cars and trucks with rounded edges and
elaborate front grills like sets of teeth, decorated with hundreds of
American flags, heading straight for me. I leapt over to the side,
losing one of my flip-flops in the road. I examined the faces of the
people crowded around me, wearing what I guessed from seeing
family photographs as 1930s-style clothes, the women smiling
beneath the brims of their large hats. I scanned the throng clapping

and smiling at the oncoming parade, trying to find a familiar face. Would I even recognize anyone?

I followed the crowd's gaze to the head vehicle, where a handsome man waved from his stance on the flatbed of a red truck. His hair was dark and wavy; his thick and bushy mustache roofed his smiling lips. I looked around at the patriotic flags, heard the melancholy notes of the song that would become the island's anthem, "La Borinqueña," floating on the muggy air, and considered who the man on the truck could be. Politician. Had to be. But he was unlike any politician I had seen before.

He wore the sleeves of his neatly pressed white button-down shirt rolled up over his thick forearms and had the footwear of a farmer. He was clearly a man who worked outside as his skin was paler where his sleeves raised up, a deepening red across his nose and brow, and had fine lines that drew years into the skin by his eyes. His smile was warm and open, and as he grasped the men's hands that were held toward him, he looked directly into their eyes. Everyone smiled up at him as he passed, and he seemed to know them all. As the truck neared, a graceful but pinched older woman next to me yelled out, "¡Ramón! ¡Felicidades, Ramón!" She beamed at the woman next to her and said in Spanish, "My son-in-law, Mayor! Can you imagine?"

Ramón? Tío? I studied her as the woman beamed lovingly toward the road. Her lips formed a thin line that slashed across her face, her nose a sharp triangle that jutted out like a traffic cone, and her eyes were small and close together. Teresa, I presumed.

Just then, the politician's eyes lit up as he saw the woman, and he blew her a kiss with both hands as the truck carried him past us. I watched the vehicle move down the road, the cars behind it honking loudly as they went, belching exhaust behind them as a band on the back of another flatbed truck began to play "The Star-Spangled Banner." I stood there gaping as the last vehicle of the parade clattered down the street and the people flooded the road and closed in around the cavalcade like a wave refilling a hole in the sand as it comes back in to shore.

When I turned back to look at the woman again, she was gone. Or rather, everyone was. I spun around wildly, looking for any remnant of the spectacle that had just crossed my path. Nothing. The lizards skittered among the fallen palm fronds around me, and the rooster was unimpeded in his midday serenade.

My heart was beating fast, still keeping the rhythm of the patriotic drums that had marched past me. Or had they? Then I noticed my flip-flop on the ground a few feet ahead. I crouched and approached it slowly and carefully, as if it were a suspicious animal. When I got close, I picked it up and searched for the mark of tire treads.

CHAPTER FIFTEEN
a liar's truth

Later that evening, there was a get-together at Ramón and Lourdes's house. I ate my fill of Lourdes's arroz con pollo and tostones, the deep-fried, golden plantain fritters sinking in my stomach like a lead weight. After adding some dessert to my already-full belly, I ambled among the old and still older people, their conversations like a constant hum. My cousins had been and gone, and once again, I was left with the viejos. I stopped by a table of framed photographs of the deceased, picking up one portrait to examine it closer. Yep, there were the close-set eyes, the traffic-cone nose. It was indeed Lourdes's mother in the vision. But what was that parade? I knew it was not the time to grill my great-aunt for information. I retreated to Tío's darkened study, tired of smiling while ladies I didn't know pinched my cheeks.

I threw myself into his wooden desk chair and twirled it around once on its squeaky wheels, looking at my great-uncle's things. I'd always loved that room. The smell of leather and tobacco, the dark wooden furniture that was worn but polished to a high sheen, and the papers on the desk that appeared important and organized in their tidy piles. To me, back then, that room was the epitome of masculinity. I scanned the dust-covered bottles of alcohol that lined his desk, the windowsills, and dresser in an array of colors and degrees of fullness. Ramón had stopped drinking fifteen years earlier and liked to keep the reminders of his addiction and harder times around him untouched. He forbade Lourdes and their cleaning woman from even dusting them.

Ramón was my mother's favorite tío as well as mine. Most of the time, he was proper and elegant, like he had been when he'd come to see my mother before she left, but sometimes, he acted like one of the children, chasing us around the bushes with a water pistol, not like the gin-and-tonic-drinking, authoritarian men that passed for fathers back in New Jersey. No, to me, those men seemed like the dads on television shows, one-dimensional, cold, and unknowable.

"Tired of all the people too, niña?"

I jumped at the voice coming from the darkened corner of the room. Only then did I see the glowing orange light of his cigar tip.

"Sí, Tío, too much boring conversation. And too much pinching." I rubbed my sore cheeks. "They treat me like I'm a baby or something."

A warm laugh rose above the smoke, and I saw Ramón's kind, weathered face lean forward from the depths of his armchair. "We understand each other, cielito. I'm hiding as well. In truth, I didn't even like the woman. Or rather, she didn't like me."

I was intrigued to learn more about the recently departed Teresa and the possible context of the vision. However, I couldn't conceive of anyone not liking Ramón. He was warm and funny and always took the time to talk to me, to ask me about my life. Of course, I could never tell him what my life was *really* like. No, though that was the truth, it would have mobilized the family against my mother, and I just couldn't live with that. For better or worse, Mom and I were a team. "Why didn't she like you, Tío?"

"Ah, she never thought I was good enough for her daughter. A simple farmer? For her princesa?" At the last words, he put his hand to his chest in mock astonishment.

I giggled.

"What really didn't make sense is that Teresa was a Sanchez too, so she had no right to judge."

"Wait, what?"

He nodded. "Teresa's great-grandmother married a distant relative of mine."

"Wait, hold on... You and Tía Lourdes are...cousins?"

"Oh, m'ija, it was many generations ago, our blood has been so watered down by now. Besides, in my great-grandfather's day, that was done all the time. It kept the money in the family and the bloodline controlled."

I shuddered. "Still. It's kind of weird." I realized that was impertinent and hurried to add, "Sorry."

He chuckled. "No need to apologize, Isla. I like that you speak your mind, just like your mother used to." Then he sighed. "Well, Lourdes married me anyway, as you know. Much to Teresa's unhappiness. We were in love; it didn't matter if she liked me or not." He snorted. "Of course, that all changed with the election."

I sat up straight in the chair, leaning toward my uncle. "Election?"

"Yes, yes," he said with a dismissive wave. "It was many years ago, and the two candidates both dropped out due to some kind of pissing match—oh, excuse me, niña—some kind of disagreement. I was mayor of Bayamón for one month. Just one month. It went by so quickly, but to Teresa, well, she lived off that most of her life. All of a sudden, I'm acceptable to her? I don't think so. A Sanchez does not forget such treatment, verdad, niña?" he asked, sitting up straight and proud at the edge of his chair.

Things were starting to fall into focus. "Did you have a parade, Tío? I mean, when you were made mayor?"

"Parade? Ha! I was barely sworn in before one of the candidates decided to grow up and accept his responsibilities. It was a relief, m'ija. A huge relief. I just did it because I felt it was my civic duty. I am a humble man who prefers his farm to a stuffy office. But Teresa, she talked about it around San Juan as if I were president of los Estados Unidos." He sank back into his chair and took a long puff of his cigar. "The woman was loca."

"¿Ramón? ¿Ramón, dónde estás? ¡Te necesito!" Tía Lourdes called to him from the living room.

He extinguished his cigar in the ashtray on the arm of his chair, put his calloused hands on his knees, and pushed himself up to standing with a groan. "Ay, Isla," he said as he walked by me. "Duty calls, eh?" He chucked me under the chin, smiling into my eyes, and for just a moment, I could see the handsome young man on the flatbed truck. He then shuffled out of the room with his hands rubbing the center of his back while calling out, "Sí, sí, mi amor. ¡Ya voy! I'm coming!"

I sat there in the darkened room and thought about Teresa. About the stories from her and my abuela. It seemed that this story wasn't true, but I saw it anyway upon Teresa's death. It didn't make sense. My head and stomach began to ache, and I sank back in my uncle's chair. The squeaking of the seat, the murmur of conversation from the other room, even the coquis' song outside in the night were beginning to grate on me.

I didn't write Teresa's story out right away. From my previous experience, I was certain it would happen again, and I wanted another look. I wanted to see this exaggerated cuento Lourdes's mother had created, especially now that I understood the truth—Teresa's truth. I also enjoyed seeing a younger version of my great-uncle, so handsome and strong. For the next two days at noon, I stood by myself among the trees in the back, staring at the air. On the third day when Teresa's story came to a close under the thick roof of palms, I walked back to my room and took out my journal. But as I held my pen above the paper, I stopped.

Do I write Teresa's version from the vision or the truth? I thought about the issue of the gun in the second version of Abuela's story, the one she told when children weren't around, the one that was probably true for her. I put pen to paper and carefully wrote down Teresa's version of a day in my great-uncle's life.

The next day, the hour came and went without incident.

Barely a week had passed before a new occupant had been installed in the back room of Tío Ramón's house. What if she was a cuentista? Would it ever end? The thought exhausted me. I imagined an assembly line of dying old ladies each with their own cuentos to tell, their rolling beds arranged single file, head to foot, for miles. Leading out of Bayamón. Out of San Juan. Off the edge of la isla. Into the sea.

CHAPTER SIXTEEN
the party of the red head

For as long as I could remember, Alma was a night owl. Once, I even caught her cleaning the floors at two o'clock in the morning, happily sloshing an ammonia-soaked cloth mop around the dining room. When confronted about the ridiculousness of it, she had replied with a wry smile, "¿Y por qué no? There is no one around to track up the wet, newly clean floor, it's quiet, and since this is my house, Señorita, I can clean whenever I care to!" But that summer, I noticed my great-aunt was going to bed earlier and earlier, making me wonder again about that "treatment" she'd had a few years before.

One night in particular, Alma was looking pale around the eyes, and she retired to her room right after dinner; the sounds of snoring followed soon after. I settled on the gated front porch, reading and rocking in one of the cane chairs. This was how most of my summers on the island were spent, sitting and rocking. Rocking and sitting. The night was clear but hot, and I was just considering a retreat to the air-conditioned bedroom when a wave of noise rose from the street.

I stood and looked around the quickly darkening property, wondering what on earth was coming. Hesitating just a moment and looking toward the dark interior of the house, I decided to risk it. I grabbed the keys off the sitting room table, unlocked the front door gate, and ran down the stone pathway. There were bright lights and a flood of voices coming up Calle Santa Cruz in front of my family's property. Leaning over the front wall, I looked down the street and saw a cavalcade of trucks, people, and white flags featuring a straw-hatted man's head silhouetted in red.

As they drew closer, I felt my head spin. It was as if Teresa's parade vision had been brought into the modern world: the antique belching cars replaced by shiny trucks, the patriotic music updated to a salsa beat. I pinched myself and wondered if it were some other Sanchez story. Had someone died? Then I heard my name being stage-whispered from behind.

"Isla! *Pssst!* ¡Ven aca! Come here!"

I squinted back to see my aunt Lourdes creeping toward me in the shadows, her shawl wrapped tightly around her shoulders as if the night were actually cold. Lourdes was one of those women who was always cold, always cocooning herself in shawls or softly knit sweaters even in the midday sun.

"Hi, Titi!"

"Shhh!" Lourdes dramatically put her finger to her lips, then gestured impatiently. "Come away from there, niña!"

So she saw it too. It was no vision then. "What? Why? What's going on out there?" The crowd had reached the front of the neighbor's property, music blasting from large speakers mounted on the lead truck. "It looks like fun."

"Ay no! That is a rally for the PPD. Your tío Ramón would not approve of you being out here with all that going on."

"PPD?"

"Partido Popular Democrático."

I caught the words *popular* and *democratic*. Didn't sound bad. "What's that?"

My aunt hissed through her teeth, "Something a young girl shouldn't concern herself with. Come along." She grabbed my arm with her pincerlike fingers and pulled me back toward the house.

"What's with the red head with the hat on the flag?"

"It's a jíbaro, a country man, with a pava, the straw hats they wear."

I was stumbling to keep up with my aunt who pulled me as if I were on a leash. It reminded me of that time Alma pulled me from José in the backyard, and it was starting to piss me off. But I wanted more information. "Why doesn't Tío like them?"

"Your uncle supports statehood and the PPD does not. Ay, I don't know from politics, Isla. I let your tío handle that. Bueno, go back inside and lock the door. Rallies like this can get out of hand quickly."

I stood staring at my aunt for a moment, hoping she'd walk away so I could take a closer look, but Lourdes wasn't budging.

The woman waved her hands as if I were a pesky insect. "Well? Go! Shoo!"

It became clear that she would not leave until I went back inside Alma's house. I looked back at the empty porch, gangs of mosquitoes hovering around the flickering blue fluorescent lights. From the street, the rally was calling me as if it knew my name. I was determined to go, but I had to get rid of Lourdes first. "Okay, I'm going in." I smiled innocently at my aunt and made my way inside. It wasn't until she heard the locking clunk of the front door gate that Lourdes finally shuffled back to her house. I stood there until I heard my uncle's front door slam closed.

What was that all about? "Get out of hand" how? And why on

earth would Lourdes let her husband decide her political opinions? Some things in my family truly baffled me, but I had learned to keep my mouth shut.

I tiptoed toward the back of the house to avoid being seen by Lourdes, let myself out the gate that served as the back door off the kitchen patio, and listened for a moment for Alma. The woman had superhuman hearing, even while sleeping. I locked the kitchen door gate behind me and headed out the shadowed path to the back wall of the property. It was very dark among the thick greenery that filled the backyard. The dried palm fronds on the ground rustled loudly, but I was certain even Alma couldn't hear me back there. As I walked, I breathed deeply, the air scented with sweet night-blooming jasmine.

I got to the waist-high stone wall and clambered over, grateful for my "boyish" shorts as Alma called them. I ran beside the wall, following it around the corner to Santa Cruz. From the side street, it was clear the rally was in full swing, no end in sight to the parade of vehicles and people. What really surprised me was the light. The side street was dark, the palms on either side muting whatever streetlights there were, but it was as if the parade were lit from within. Music and an orchestra of voices rode the air, yelling, laughing, talking. When I got to the corner, I stopped dead at the sight.

The crowd in the street moved like one being, rising and falling and waving their arms. The parade was a creature all its own, a boisterous, showy animal with a loud heartbeat. The red-headed flags were on everything, attached to car antennas, carried by old women, painted on children's foreheads. The atmosphere was festive but directed, a party with a purpose. A young girl with flags in her pigtails and a huge smile on her face hooked her arm into mine, and just like that, I was caught up in the throng. My heart was pounding, I felt on the edge of losing control, but there was something so exhilarating about it. Like everything in Puerto Rico, it felt foreign yet so familiar, like it brought my island blood to the surface. The girl handed me a flag, and I waved it as we walked, grinning so hard my face hurt.

The vehicles slowed, and those who were walking buckled up a bit, laughing and jostling as they too stopped. The girl dropped my hand to get her mother's attention about something, and I looked back into the crowd behind me. My gaze skipped over a group of guys and came back as my brain caught up to who I was seeing at the center. José! His smile was huge and glorious, and he had his arm wrapped around the neck of a guy next to him in a joking choke hold. I watched him for a minute, the smile widening on my lips. I was glad he would see me there, being involved in something important on the island. I picked my way backward, throwing perdónames left and right, until I stood in front of him. "Hi, José!"

He was still smiling as he turned his head, but when he saw me there, his face froze. "Isla?" He looked around at his friends, who glanced at me curiously. "What are you doing here?"

My stomach dropped as if it were no longer supported by my pelvis. "I'm… It was going by the house…" I pointed back toward the house but found I no longer knew where I was exactly and did a small spin. The noise and colors and José's weird reaction made me more and more disoriented.

The crowd started to move forward again, and José took me by the upper arm and pulled me toward the sidewalk, nodding at his friends to buy him a minute. "You shouldn't be out here," he said in that same loud whisper my aunt had employed to say the same thing.

"Why?" I hated how little my voice sounded, but my throat was tight.

"Because this doesn't concern you."

I felt the heat rise to my face with his patronizing tone. "Yes, it does! My family—"

"Your family are probably PNP, Isla."

I looked at him blankly.

He rolled his eyes and looked like someone else entirely. "Pro-statehood, right?"

I hated even more that he was right. At least in terms of my uncle. Why hadn't I ever inquired about the island's politics before? What was the PNP, and why was there the assumption that I would blindly follow? I lifted my chin. "Well, that doesn't mean that I am."

He laughed, an ugly sound like a car bumper scraping concrete. "You didn't even know what the PNP was!" José looked at me, and he seemed to notice my now-glistening eyes. "Look, Isla, it's just not a good idea for you to be out here alone. Does your family even know?" He started walking me back along the sidewalk toward the tail of the parade.

I didn't answer, but my inability to look at him said everything. I wanted to yell at him, to tell him I was old enough to make my own decisions, to do what I wanted to do, but the words got stuck in my throat and tears threatened. God, I felt like a child in that moment.

He stopped and let my arm go, and I saw we were standing in front of my family's property. I pulled my arm in tight, hugging myself as if I too were now cold.

José held out his hands, palms up, as if proving he had no weapons, that he would not hurt me. Too late. "Isla, I'm glad to see you. It's just—"

I took off, running through the stone pillars that guarded the front, tears flying off the sides of my face. I fumbled with the keys, slipped in between the gate, only looking back at the road once the lock was thrown. I could see José's silhouette on the other side of the wall, the festive colors and sounds of the parade mocking me from behind him. He put his hands in his pockets and walked back toward his friends, and I ran into the bedroom, burrowing under the covers in hopes of drowning out all sound.

CHAPTER SEVENTEEN
a sleeping rose

Later that week, I decided to pay a visit to the newest inhabitant in Ramón's back room. If there were any possibility I would have to deal with a vision after their death, I wanted to know as much as I could about them, perhaps even hear some of their stories firsthand, if they were coherent. It was a diversion from the humiliation of my encounter with José at the rally earlier that week. I still didn't feel I had done anything wrong, but my mind kept rerunning the scene over and over as my own private vision, shame heating and reheating in my chest like coals. Besides, it felt good to have a plan, to have something to do.

I walked over to Ramón's house, the air heavy with the scent of sun-soaked trees and morning coffee. The day had started out warm but not yet oppressive. I knocked on the front door, and right away, the sound of shuffling came from within.

"¡Ya voy! I'm coming!" Lourdes opened the slatted wooden door, exclaimed when she saw me standing on the veranda, and immediately smothered me in her ample bosom. I felt the pearlized snaps of Lourdes's housedress pressing into my cheek, the slightly sweet scent of Persil detergent overwhelming all others.

"Isla! Now *this* is a lovely time for a young girl to venture out! I'm so glad you came to visit your old aunt."

Interactions with Lourdes were not complete without a dash of guilt.

Then Lourdes added the obligatory cheek pinch. "Ay, so beautiful! Just like your mother. Too skinny though, niña. Bueno, no matter. A big serving of your tía Lourdes's plátanos and we will fatten you up. Well? Come, come inside."

She put her arm around me and pulled me into the house. Back then, it seemed that I was always being pulled or pushed somewhere.

"So can I make you something to eat?"

"No, no, Tía, thank you. I'm not hungry."

"Ay, living all summer on Alma's cooking, I'm not surprised you have no appetite!" She chuckled. "Then what can I do for you, querida?" Lourdes let me go and began to walk to the kitchen, her domain.

As I followed, I was comforted by the signature scent of garlic and lavender soap that trailed behind her in a whisper.

"Titi, I was wondering… Who are you taking care of in the back room now?"

Lourdes was reaching into the fridge for a carafe of passion-fruit juice when she stopped to look at me. "¿Qué? Why?"

"I'm…I'm doing a project for the school paper on family stories, cuentos, and I thought since they are usually members of the family, I would see if they had any stories I could use." The white lie only stung a little. Especially since she must be used to lies, having had Teresa for a mother.

Lourdes finished retrieving the juice and closed the refrigerator. "Oh, well, yes…"

My aunt put down the pitcher and started wiping the counter with a rag, though it was already immaculate, her movements brisk and jerky.

I waited a moment, then asked, "Is there some reason I can't visit whoever's back there, Titi?"

"Ay, niña, I just don't think your aunt Alma would approve."

"What? Why?"

"Because Rosa is a cousin of mine from a…different side of the family."

I was baffled. "And? Why would Alma care if I talked with her?"

"Isla, she's not going to be able to say much anyway. Rosa's been in a coma for many weeks now. That's why they brought her here." She distractedly poured the golden juice into two glasses.

"So why would Alma care if I visited her?" I asked again. Now I really *was* curious, and to top it off, the overwhelming feeling of ignorance that had started with the political rally was rising in my chest again.

Lourdes threw the towel to the counter. "Bueno, I suppose there is no harm in you sitting with her for a moment. I think Rosa would like that."

I followed Lourdes. I hadn't been in the back room for many years, since my cousins and I had gotten older and stopped racing around the property as if trying to touch every square inch. My heart was beating rapidly with memory, but as I looked around, it was as if it were a different room. Smaller and less forbidding. The louvers were open, and the breeze darted through the room, carrying the heady scent of flowers from Alma's gardens next door. And it was so very clean. *A scary room is never so clean*, I thought.

I turned toward the bed and saw a large, still form: Rosa, tucked in neat and tight, the sunlight striping in from between the slats. As I stepped closer, I noticed the plump, deep-brown hands lying on top of the white bedspread. I looked into the sleeping woman's peaceful face accented by a gorgeous head of white curls. It was clear

Lourdes was taking special care of her; her nails were beautifully shaped and painted a bright coral. She even took the trouble to apply matching lipstick.

Lourdes lifted the sleeping woman's hand into her own. "Rosa, querida, my niece Isla is here all the way from Nueva Jersey."

Lourdes stood and stared at Rosa while she gently placed her hand back on her chest. "Pobrecita, her heart is big but not so strong." The sun shone on Rosa's face, giving it a warm glow. "She always liked the warmth of the sun." Lourdes's voice sounded far away, like she had forgotten I was there. "I'm glad Ramón let me bring her here. That shack she was in was so bad for her lungs."

"Shack?"

"Yes, Isla, not everyone is as fortunate as we are." There was an edge to her tone I hadn't heard before, a judgment in its timbre.

"But isn't *she* part of *we*? I mean…couldn't *we* have helped her out? The family, I mean, so she didn't have to live in a shack?"

"Ay, Isla…" Now there was impatience. "I do what I can, but my brothers and sisters won't even acknowledge that she is family, let alone give her money. They don't even call her by name. They just call her La Negra." Lourdes brushed a tendril of white hair off her cousin's face and tucked it neatly behind her ear. "Luckily your tío Ramón is a generous man and did this for me, despite his own misgivings. He knows how much she means to me. I'm not sure Alma understands, however."

Heat rose to my face at these last words. I just stood and stared at the beautiful woman on the bed.

"Bueno, I have to get cooking or your tío will have nothing to eat when he comes back from work."

"Wait, Tía, was Rosa a cuentista? Did she tell stories?"

Lourdes smiled for the first time since I brought up visiting the back room. "Oh yes. Her stories were always funny. Even with her difficult life, she never lost her sense of humor." She patted my shoulder. "Sit with her awhile, m'ija. She'll like that."

I sat on the edge of the metal chair next to the bed while Lourdes shuffled back to the kitchen. The sound of pots clanking and oil sizzling followed soon after.

Rosa slept on, her face glowing as if she had just stepped off the beach, the edges of her lips curled into a hint of a smile, as if she were thinking about something funny. When the sounds in the kitchen reached a certain level and I knew my aunt could not hear me, I began to talk to Rosa. I told her about Abuela and the monkeys, about the gunshot and the parade that never happened. I talked about my visions, or what I understood of them, that I thought I saw the stories the cuentistas wanted me to see, the ones they wanted to leave behind. I told her that while I was not sure why I was seeing them, I was looking forwarding to seeing hers. Would I even see her stories? Did we share enough blood? Lourdes's great-great-grandmother married a Sanchez, after all. Either way, it felt good to talk about it all. Though Rosa and I didn't exchange a word, I felt approval coming from her like warmth.

There was much living in Rosa's pleasant face, more than could be discovered from a photo album or biography. Or a cuento. I thought of Alma and felt the pulse in my head beat harder, faster, until it might burst. In that moment, it seemed as though Alma's house was miles and miles away instead of just next door.

I sat with Rosa for almost an hour, talking quietly about everything and nothing, watching the woman as she slept her dreamless sleep. I told her about José, of Alma's reaction to our friendship all those years ago. That no wonder he thought I didn't understand if this was how my family behaved, if this was what they believed. I was disappointed that so little had changed.

Finally, I patted Rosa's cool, powdery hand. "Sleep well, Cousin Rosa. If, when you go, you have a story to share with me, I would be honored. I could use a funny one right about now."

I headed back to the kitchen to nibble on whatever Lourdes was cooking. At that moment, I preferred to stay there rather than go back next door.

CHAPTER EIGHTEEN
the pit with the fruit

That weekend, there was a party at a family member's house in Vega Baja, on the coast just west of San Juan. The Sanchez clan was boundless, tendrils of the family tree reaching to all corners of the island, and every summer, I was dragged to some fiesta, christening, or wedding (not to mention numerous funerals). For me, much of each event was spent watching old ladies talk. There were often kids my age at these festivities, but the idea of speaking Spanish with them and feeling like a specimen under a microscope made my stomach lurch. And at eighteen, I wasn't adequately boring enough to enjoy hanging with the adults but was too old to play with the kids, so where would that leave me? Even worse, that night, Alma insisted on dictating the evening's wardrobe.

"You always dress like a boy, Isla, with those jeans and shorts." She said the word *jeans* as if just the utterance exposed her to some strain of disease. "Tonight, you will wear this," she proclaimed as she held up a flowery sundress. "And some makeup would bring out your pretty blue eyes, no?"

I knew there was no use arguing with the woman, and truthfully, I didn't care. I just wanted the evening to be over with. I grabbed the dress and hanger from my aunt and stormed off to the bathroom to

comply. I had been short-tempered with Alma since the visit with
Rosa. Well, my version of short-tempered. I'd never snap back or
yell like I'd seen the girls at my school do with their mothers. I just
gave one-word answers to Alma's questions and avoided her when I
could. It was possible that Alma didn't notice these small rebellions,
but even the sound of her slippers shuffling from the next room
grated on me.

As we drove off in the fading afternoon light, I made the mistake
of asking Alma how we were related to those having the party. After
a list of about thirty cousins and about as many turns on side roads,
I lost the thread of relations as well as a sense of where we were going
and decided to just stare out the window. Usually the summers at
Alma's were uneventful, much of the same, but with Abuela's death,
a different feeling had fallen over the days like a shroud.

Especially with the addition of the visions.

It was dark by the time we pulled into a driveway that was flanked
by high stone walls. The palm trees that lined the drive were strung
with white lights, the glow against the dark-green fronds giving
the property a magical ambiance. As with most arrivals at Sanchez
family gatherings, we were greeted by a pack of dogs, small to large,
all scraggly and probably rescued from a supermarket parking lot,
with patchy fur and missing ears as tokens of their previous lives. As
soon as I opened the car door, I heard the throbbing of music and
a chorus of laughing voices seeping from the open-air patio in the
back. Like so many houses on the island, this one was low and flat,
the gates pulled aside as if the very walls had opened up to invite
guests to enter. I walked behind Alma, trying to shield myself as we
made our way through the house.

I stopped short as I entered the main room, though one room
flowed into another with only a suggestion of walls. Unlike Alma's

close quarters stuffed with musty, worn antiques and every surface covered with knickknacks, this house was spare and modern, more like Abuela's but with style. The furniture was angular and funky with splashes of color sprinkled about among the yards of chrome and black and white marble-tiled floor.

As Alma hunted out the hostess, I looked around the gathering, people spilling out into the kitchen or onto the patio, the lights flickering off the backyard pool, the aqua-blue water illuminated from beneath. Women in short, sparkling dresses and sky-high heels flirted with men with slicked-back hair, crisp guayaberas, and polished shoes. Cocktails glittered in thin crystal glasses and platters of food covered every surface. The smells of roasting meat and expensive perfume mingled as if made for each other. Parties in Puerto Rico seemed like parties in the movies, not the rare and uncomfortable gatherings I was dragged to that passed for fetes in New Jersey.

"Isla! Isla, ven aca. Come here, Sobrina."

Alma impatiently beckoned from the middle of a sea of coiffed gray-haired ladies.

I moaned beneath my breath and shuffled over as if attending my own court-martial. I always felt as if it were the Spanish Inquisition when they drilled me with questions about school, whether or not I had a boyfriend, why didn't I try a little makeup, their dentured smiles belying the fierce cross-examination.

"I want you to meet your second cousin twice removed." Alma put her arm around my neck and yanked me close with her classic hug/wrestling hold. "Marta, this is my grandniece Isla." I pasted on a smile as we moved from one relative to the next, my lips sliding over clenched teeth. I shook their hands and made polite small talk while planning to make a quick escape. And as usual, they rapidly switched to Spanish, talking about me as if I weren't there while I shifted my weight from one foot to the other. I could indeed understand them if I made the effort to pay attention, but I'd long ago realized that adults could talk for hours about nothing.

Just when I thought I would never escape, I felt a hand on my shoulder.

"Hey, Prima! I'm glad you came."

I whipped around and my heart lifted with the sight of my cousin Maria.

"Titi Alma, is it okay if I steal Isla for a while? I have some friends I'd like her to meet." Maria's voice was pure sugar-cane syrup as she tugged Alma's arm from mine and held it for a moment as if they were two girlfriends whispering secrets.

I could see Alma melt. Our aunt chuckled. "Certainly, querida, but you girls behave, yes?" She pinched Maria's cheek, and my cousin smiled sweetly, then Maria took my arm and turned us both around.

"Quick! Run for your life!" Maria whispered as she quickened her pace despite her towering heels.

"Oh, I owe you big time for that one!" I giggled as we navigated among the guests balancing china plates in their hands and made our way to the patio.

Maria led me over to a large bamboo table next to the pool where the younger guests congregated. There were about a dozen of them, some sitting at the table, others on it, all attractive and chatting away in Spanish. The girls were wearing stylish short dresses and high heels that made their legs seem six feet long. The boys were dressed in crisp, elegant but cool garb, their eyes catching glints from the tiki torches that surrounded the patio.

The woody scent of bay rum reached me like a wink, and

I realized that I had always fantasized that my summer trip to Puerto Rico would look just like this. I imagined that I'd look sleek and confident and would kiss a dark-eyed boy with soft lips and tumbling hair. But I looked down at my out-of-date sundress and scuffed sandals and realized I was the same old misfit destined for the edges of parties, never the center. I slowed down and let Maria pull ahead of me, intending to quietly disappear before she realized I was gone.

But just as I was about to sneak away, Maria doubled back and grabbed me. "Oh no you don't! Get over here. I want you to meet my friends."

Maria dragged me over to a girl on the end with thin, long legs, wavy auburn hair, and olive-green eyes. She had a large, angular nose that only added to the unique beauty of her face.

"Valentina, this is Isla. Isla, this is my roommate, Valentina."

I smiled. "It's nice to meet you."

Valentina smiled at me, took my hand warmly, and kissed my left, then right cheek. "I've heard so much about you. It's nice to finally meet you."

Maria talked about me? I was surprised at the wave of emotion that rose from my chest.

"Where are you staying? Can you stay with us instead?"

Maria laughed. "I wish! Alma would never give her up! But I'm going to come and steal you away for a shopping trip one of these days. Isla, I bought that building where you stayed with me a few years ago. Valentina and I have been there ever since."

She bought a building. I was beginning to understand that Mom and I were in a different economic category than most of the other Sanchezes.

"How long are you here for, Isla?" Valentina asked. Though a moment ago, I had heard her talking with a handsome guy in full-tilt Spanish, her English was accentless. People who were completely fluent in two languages were miraculous to me. On paper, I could understand nearly everything in Spanish, but speaking was another thing all together. I just couldn't imagine the humiliation of all the mistakes I would undoubtedly make.

"Until August twenty-third," I answered.

"Oh! Then, Maria, you must bring her out with us this Friday! Isla, there's a new disco in Santurce…"

The conversation continued with all parties doing their best to include me while I looked around at the group of impossibly attractive people and told myself I should enjoy every minute, that this was what I'd wished for all those nights stuck on Alma's porch listening to the coquis and the squeak of Alma's rocking chairs. I tried, really I did, and they were so kind and continued to talk in English for my benefit, but as I listened to my voice cracking like a frog among songbirds, the little I said sounded stupid and my movements felt clumsy. It was as if I had woken up in someone else's body and couldn't quite figure out how to operate it.

There was a loud commotion near the small concrete bathhouse, and everyone turned as the door opened and a guy stepped out. He was wearing a tiny Speedo bathing suit and had the lean, muscular body to go with it. As he walked out, the crowd went wild, wolf whistles coming from all directions. He stopped for a moment, seeming surprised by the reception, but quickly recovered and began to strike bodybuilder poses, sucking in his already washboard stomach as the catcalls got even louder, and he finally dove into the pool in a clean slice.

Maria gave a belly laugh. "Seems the swimming has begun, thanks to your brother."

Valentina scoffed. "What else is new? Show-off."

My cousin took my arm. "No one ever wants to be the first one to swim at these parties. You can see why after that entrance."

In that moment, the boy leapt from the water and grabbed Maria's ankle with a dripping-wet hand.

My cousin looked down calmly. "Victorio, if you pull me into that water, I will personally make sure you'll be singing falsetto for the rest of your life."

Victorio let go, held his hands up in surrender with a Cheshire cat grin, then silently disappeared under the water.

She turned to her friend without missing a beat. "Hey, Valentina, did you bring your suit?"

"¡Claro! Of course! You guys ready to swim?"

"Isla, I have an extra one so you can join us," Maria offered.

She had to be joking. After that spectacle, she could *not* expect me to put on a bathing suit and walk around with an audience. But it seemed Maria was serious as she extricated two tiny bikinis from her colorful straw bag.

I could feel beads of sweat gathering on my upper lip. "Um, no, I… Chlorine makes my skin itch."

"What are you talking about? Your mother used to have to drag you out of the pool in the dark, your fingers and toes all puckered. You love to swim!"

"I know, but I…changed. Besides, I just ate and should wait awhile."

Maria regarded me for a moment. "Okay, Isla, but don't go far. You don't have to suffer with the old ladies, chica. You can hang with us, okay?"

Warmth rushed through my chest, and the misfit feeling receded a bit. "Okay, Maria, thanks."

The group of girls made their way to the pool house, their hands darting about as they chatted, every set of eyes following them. I let out a long breath, feeling as if I had dodged a bullet.

Walking down the other side of the pool, I followed the stone path around the corner of the house. It was darker on that side, the lights of the party barely reaching more than a few feet from the windows, and I was grateful for the shelter of the shadows. I wrapped my arms around myself and watched the ground as I walked.

I reached the patio at the side of the house and turned out into the yard, walking down the shadowed grassy field between the two rows of trees that framed the yard like spectator stands. My sandal kicked something, and I heard it spin away over the short, dry grass. Scattered around my feet were small green balls. I looked up at the tree's branches and waxy green leaves and determined that the fruits must have come from there. I liked the clean *thonk* sound they made when they hit the ground. I began to kick them, soon laughing maniacally as I stomped about like a four-year-old in a sandbox.

"They're actually quite delicious, you know."

I froze, my foot in midkick. My eyes searched around in the dark for the source of the voice. I saw a figure silhouetted, leaning against the tree's thin forked trunk. The voice was sonorous and familiar.

"They're called quenepas," the voice said, its shadowed hand indicating the green orbs scattered around us. He stepped forward, and by the ambient light of the house and stars, José's smiling face appeared.

"Oh! José...um, hi." I became very interested in the ground again as my heart took off at a full gallop.

José bent down and picked up one of the green balls. "It's interesting. They are actually a pit with fruit instead of the other way around."

Part of me had hoped I'd never seen him again after the parade. Another part looked for him every day in Alma's backyard. And here he was, at some distant cousin's party, in the dark. "What are you doing here?"

He looked at me for a moment. My rude tone had not been lost on him since it was the same thing he said to me the last time we saw each other. He turned and pointed at the far end of the yard where I could see a group of figures darting among the trees, passing a bottle from one to another in the dark. "Andrés is my best friend."

I just looked at him.

"This is his house. Well, his parents' house."

"Oh."

"Oye, Isla, about the other night at the rally. I was…surprised to see you there. You just…"

"Don't belong?" It came out before a second thought could silence it.

"No, it's not that. It's just…not your fight."

"Why does it have to be a fight?"

José sighed. "Good question. It's just…the PNP party has been in power for four years, and this election… It's so important we win. They just want to complete the colonization of our island by becoming a state, so we can lose any identity we have."

I didn't understand, and that embarrassed me. This was half of who I was, and my ignorance was inexcusable. I needed to educate myself about these important issues. I was trying to think of something meaningful to say, something to contribute to the conversation, when José absently picked up one of the small fruits scattered around us.

"Would you like to try one?" He held out one of the hard, green fruits and then brought it to his mouth. I saw a flash of teeth, heard a brisk snap. Then his long fingers worked the crack and slowly peeled the thin, tough skin off the fruit, exposing a light peach-colored flesh beneath. When it was completely peeled, its pale fruit open to the night air, he held it toward me, and for the first time that night, I looked up into his eyes and felt any remnant of discomfort seep away.

My fingers reached for the fruit, but he pulled it back.

"Don't let the color fool you. The juice dries a dark brown. I wouldn't want you to stain your pretty dress."

I looked down at the dress that had so recently seemed infantile.

"Let me hold it for you." He held it out, and it was as if the glistening fruit hovered in the darkness in front of me.

I took a small step forward and tentatively held my mouth near the quenepa, looking up at José, seeing hints of his face in the dark, his smile warm and inviting. The smell hit me first, citrusy and tropical in the evening air. I opened my mouth and slowly leaned into his hand, into the fruit. The taste hit my tongue as I took half in my mouth, a hint of lime puckering my lips until the melon-like taste took over, the moisture of the fruit filling my mouth. I scraped my teeth along the hard pit, gathering what little fruit there was. It was unlike anything I'd ever tasted. Sweet, but sharp at the edges.

I smiled at José and then quickly looked away as I swallowed, feeling as exposed as the small, peeled quenepa.

He dropped the pit to the ground and sucked the juice from his fingers.

"Aren't you going to have any?" I asked.

"No. I've eaten too many of those in my life."

I ran my tongue over my teeth, the sharp, sweet taste renewed in my mouth. "I can't imagine eating too many of those. It would be too much work to peel so many for so little fruit." I laughed but saw that his face was serious.

"When I was a boy, there were days when I was hungry and those were all I had to eat." He looked up at the stars for a moment. "I can't taste them now without feeling that familiar gnawing in my belly from childhood." His eyes came back down to earth, landing on me. "I promised myself I'd never have that feeling again."

I looked down at the quenepas, scattered about randomly like billiard balls, imagining them as a source of sustenance, as the only food for the day. "Oh." I hadn't understood when we were children just how poor he was. Even though that was ten years earlier, the ignorant feeling rose again.

There was silence between us for a moment.

"Isla, would you like to meet my friends?" He pointed in the direction of the group of guys, and then as if on cue, a chorus of laughter and curses in Spanish rose, two boys shoving each other on the grass.

"No. I mean—" My mouth stumbled, and I worried I sounded abrupt again. "Thank you, but I'd rather stay here."

He smiled. "Me too."

I couldn't look at him, but it was all I wanted to do. Even worse, I couldn't think of anything to say. Luckily, he spoke first.

"Why aren't you inside at the party?"

"I don't really feel...comfortable in there. Besides, I didn't bring my bikini." I snorted at that and then realized what I'd said and to whom. I could feel the heat rise to my face, grateful for the dark. "Um, what about you?"

"Me? No, I didn't bring my bikini either."

His grin was wide and glorious. I was comforted by the thought that my face couldn't get any redder. "No, I mean, why aren't you inside at the party? Or over with your friends?"

He leaned back against the tree trunk again. "Sometimes I prefer to be alone."

I nodded. That I understood. So often it seemed like one long family gathering down there.

"And I will be spending the entire semester with most of them once the summer is over."

"You mean that group over there?"

"Yes. Well, some of them, anyway. Others are going to the States for school."

"Oh." College. Yet another world about which I knew nothing.

"Isla?" Alma's tired voice crackled in the dark from the direction of the house.

For a moment, I considered not answering, ducking behind the quenepa tree. I wanted to spend just a few more minutes with José. But why prolong the inevitable? I was sure he was anxious to get back to his college friends anyway.

"Isla! Ven aca! It's getting late and we must go!"

The one time in my life I wanted to stay at a party, and Alma was all ready to go after an hour. "Okay, Titi! I'm coming!" I looked up at José and smiled, though I was certain the sadness was seeping out through the lifted ends of my lips. "Thank you for the quenepa. It was delicious."

"My pleasure. I'm glad you liked it."

"Okay… I'll see you soon."

"I hope so."

I waved awkwardly, then took off running toward Alma. I was out of breath when I reached my aunt, my face warm in the cool evening air.

Alma craned her neck to look behind. "What were you doing? Who were you talking to?" She looked exhausted, but she still managed to be nosy.

"Nobody." I walked toward the car that waited patiently in the full lot, savoring the taste of the fruit that lingered in my mouth like a secret.

CHAPTER NINETEEN
shadow and storm

Late one afternoon the following week, I was helping in the garden, hoping to see José, when an ambulance pulled up to Tío Ramón's house next door and I knew that Rosa had died. My eyes filled as the red lights danced over the walls of green palm fronds. I had been so preoccupied with thoughts of José that I hadn't made it back to sit with Rosa again.

I watched them wheel the stretcher out, a thin white sheet stretched across Rosa's girth. This time, I knew who was beneath the shroud, so the sight held more meaning, fewer secrets. I smiled. Rosa wasn't gone, not yet. Except for Lourdes, Rosa's own family didn't appreciate her, but I would be honored to see one of her stories come to life if she chose me. I put down the gardening trowel, brushed off my clothes, made excuses to Alma, and headed inside with purposeful steps. I had work to do. I got the book of cuentos out from my suitcase and cleared a place for it on the little desk. This time, I would be ready. I stayed in the room reading until Alma called me for dinner.

Things had felt so strained between Alma and me over the last few weeks, though I'm not sure she noticed as she'd been going to bed early and sleeping late, but Rosa's death had only renewed my

conflicted feelings about my great-aunt. We ate in silence and afterward I helped clean and dry the dishes. Then I excused myself and
padded off to bed early with the explanation that I wanted to read.
I lay on the bed with a novel open on my chest. I stared through
the mosquito netting at the tiny stalactites on the white stucco ceiling and waited, the image of José holding the quenepa out to my
mouth filling and refilling my mind. No matter how much I told
myself to forget, that we were both going off to college and would
forget all about each other, thoughts of him kept creeping back in
like the surf. Eventually my eyelids grew heavy with the rhythm of
my thoughts, and the book slipped to my side unread.

I woke to the sound of screaming.

I jolted upright in bed, the book thudding to the floor. I searched
for the source of the screams and found I was no longer in my
aunt's guest room. The walls were wood, the floor worn, the furniture spare and utilitarian. Three people huddled in the corner, a
woman and two small children, a boy and a girl. But the screaming
was not coming from them. The walls themselves were shrieking.
Howling. Groaning. The wooden shutter over the window to my
right suddenly splintered and blew open, wind squalling in, rain
pelting me like bullets. I jumped up and ran to close the shutter but
found I couldn't move it. I could feel the cracked frame, the peeling
paint—that was new—but still I couldn't budge it.

I stepped back when the woman got up and pulled the shutter closed against the driving wind and rain, latching it shut.
She seemed unaware of my presence, so I looked closely into the
woman's brown, careworn face, searching for a resemblance to Rosa,
but she turned quickly to get back to her children. Wait, was Rosa
the girl? Or the mother? My heart jackhammered in my chest, and
I followed the woman back to the corner where the family cowered

and threw myself on the floor next to them, hugging my knees to my chest, no longer caring who was who.

At that moment, there was the sound of metal rasping, tearing, and all eyes went up to the ceiling in the same instant. The ridged, rusted tin roof squealed and stretched, and suddenly it was gone, the ceiling replaced by furious, swirling gray and black sky, rain crashing in at an angry angle. The furniture began to move across the room as if possessed, menacingly scraping over the uneven wooden floors. The small dining room table propelled itself toward the corner where we huddled, narrowly missing us and banging into the wall on the other side.

I was finding it harder and harder to breathe, as if the wind and my terror were stealing the air out of my body. The chairs followed, circling around each other in a macabre dance. One of the wooden straight-backed chairs started to move in my direction, its velocity increasing as it went over each floorboard, willing itself toward me like metal to a magnet. I threw my arms up just as the chair hit me, the sound of wood splintering all around, blood pouring off my arm and onto my forehead. I closed my eyes and let out a scream.

The next thing I heard was Alma's voice, high and thin with concern, breaking over the sound of my cries. "Isla! Isla! ¿Que pasó? What happened to you? Are you okay?" I fought her at first, swiping her hands away with my arms, my eyes still clamped shut. Slowly I calmed down, my aunt's familiar voice dragging me back from shadow and storm. I opened my eyes, and Alma's face was right in front of me, alarm carved into the folds of skin around her mouth. I looked around the room frantically and saw the bed, the ornate carved dresser topped with Tía's perfumes and doilies, the book sprawled on the floor near the night table, the solid ceiling above. Through the window, the evening was clear, the stars visible in the black velvet sky. Then I noticed a wetness on my arm. I lifted it in front of my face and saw the gash, my freckled skin streaked with blood. Alma carefully brought me to my feet, and I could hear her voice as if from very far away, clucking about the cut and the bleeding.

"How did you do this, niña? What a bad dream you must have had! We must disinfect this right away." As she led me to her room, she gave the lecture I had heard a thousand times before about how cuts can go septic in the tropics—"This is not Nueva Jersey, you know!"—then sat me down on her bed. The texture of the chenille pattern pressed against my bare legs; water ran in the bathroom as she scurried about, gathering bandages, cotton, alcoholado. Alma spent ten minutes fussing over me, bandaging my wound, asking questions to which she didn't seem to expect an answer. I just sat there watching, removed from the scene, a silent spectator.

By the time I was able to ask, my aunt seemed so glad to hear me speak that she didn't find the question odd. "Was there a really bad hurricane here?"

Alma paused for a moment, then answered. "Yes, many over the years. ¿Por qué?"

"Was there one that could take a house's roof off?" My voice sounded robotic, emotionless.

She paused again, probably concerned, but then she continued. "Sí, it was in September of 1928. San Felipe Segundo, it was called. I was twenty-four. It was very scary. Every Puerto Rican learned about preparing for the worst after that storm." She looked at me again and put her hand over mine. "Do not worry, mi amor. You are safe. That is why our roof is concrete."

I didn't explain that I was not afraid of real hurricanes. I didn't have the energy to talk. Or to care. Alma walked me to my bed, covered me up with the cool cotton sheets, tucking me in as she had when I was small, and sat at my side holding my hand until sleep took me.

All night, I had terrible dreams of crashing storms and bending trees, and I bolted awake in bed in the wee hours of the morning, breathing hard. As I was falling back to sleep, I heard the back gate squeal and Alma walk through the house. I had a fleeting thought that I should go and check on her but instead fell into a blessedly dreamless sleep.

I spent the next day in bed, only getting up twice: once to eat and once to record the terror of the previous night's events in the book of stories before the sun set. Knowing that the hurricane was in 1928 helped determine that Rosa had been the young mother in the corner hiding with me and that the roof blowing off was one of her cuentos. Lourdes had said she told funny stories, but clearly, she'd also been carrying around this dark one. But why show me this particular story? Was it a warning? And why could I now feel surfaces in the visions? Did that mean they were getting stronger?

And the most pressing question of all: Why could it hurt me?

I wouldn't get all the answers right then, if ever, and that was not an experience I cared to go through again. Monkeys and parades were one thing; hurricanes were another.

Until that night, I had thought the visions were a gift from the dead. An odd one, but still a gift. As I looked at the dried blood darkening my bandaged arm, I wished it were a gift I could return.

CHAPTER TWENTY
great-grandfather's office

One rainy evening as I sat curled up in the parlor reading a science-fiction novel and Alma played the piano to soothe her arthritic fingers, a neighbor appeared at the front door gate.

"Doña Alma, may I borrow that math book you told me about in the supermercado? Cecilia is not doing so well in her classes, so I want to spend some time helping her this summer."

I watched a wide grin spread across my great-aunt's face. When Alma's mother died, she had become a math teacher, and nothing elated her more than seeing a child suffer through algebra while the sun shone. I teased her that she must have taught half of Bayamón at one time or another.

"¡Seguro! Of course, of course, Carmen. Just wait here and I will get it for you."

Carmen stood next to the gated front door as Alma retreated to her secret front room that had been her father's before her. As always, she opened the office door only a crack and slipped through, closing it swiftly behind her.

When Alma emerged in the same guarded way and went onto the porch to give the book to Carmen, I stared at the closed door as if my gaze could bore a hole through the thick wood. What was in there? Alma was a very practical and not superstitious woman; there was no explanation for her protectiveness of an empty room.

"Gracias, Doña Alma!" Carmen called from the front walk as Alma locked the gate.

"My pleasure, m'ija, and God bless."

Alma shuffled back into the parlor and looked at me with tired eyes. "Ay, Isla, I'm going to bed. Old ladies like me need our sleep, yes?" She smiled and kissed my forehead, the same way she had for eighteen years, her scent of talcum and roses settling on my skin like a security blanket.

"Good night, Tía."

I tried to concentrate on my book but found my mind still focused on the office door. What was in that room? As I sat there, the dark cave images from my childhood morphed, taking on new details. Shadowed shelves with jars of body parts in cloudy fluid, leather-bound books that, if opened, released an ancient demon into the modern world. The bodies of every dog Alma had had over the years—they'd all been named Guardián so their jobs were always clear—stuffed and snarling from every corner, their glass eyes shining in the dark.

For a moment, I considered that perhaps I'd been reading too much Stephen King of late, but after all I had been through that summer, after Alma's reaction to my…situation with Abuela's story, I was tired of Sanchez family secrets. And with the dangerous acceleration of the visions with Rosa's, I wanted some answers. I padded to the middle of the house and saw that Alma's bedroom door was closed, her light off. I made my way back to the phone in the hallway. I wasn't naive enough to investigate the room by myself at night—I actually paid attention to the plots of horror movies—but at the very least, I could do some research.

I looked at my watch: 9:35. My mother might not have passed out yet.

The phone rang and rang, and just when I was about to hang up, my mother's breathless voice reached through the crackling phone line.

"Oh, Isla, I just got in, didn't think I'd make it to the phone on time."

"Just got in? From where?"

"I was working late."

"On a Saturday?"

I could hear the it's-none-of-your-business tone creep into my mother's voice. "Did you call for a reason, honey?" The last word seemed tacked on as an afterthought. I felt an angry heat rise behind my face and really was not up to a long-distance argument, so I cut to the chase.

"Mom, what's the full story about your grandfather and Alma's front room?"

Silence.

Shuffling of the phone.

More silence.

"Isla, what a thing to ask over the phone." She whispered as if there were scores of people listening in on our conversation, dying to overhear any Sanchez family scandals.

"It's not a big deal, Mom. I just want to know."

"Where is your great-aunt right now?"

"In bed. Jeez, Mom, you don't think I'd be that insensitive, do you?"

"Ay, Isla. Look, it was no big secret. He found out he was sick and didn't want to burden the family, so he took his life."

"What?" I looked at the receiver as if I'd heard wrong. "He killed himself?"

"Yes."

"In that room?"

"Yes."

I looked at the closed door with newfound or, more accurately, confirmed fear. "How?"

My mother sighed, getting impatient. "He shot himself."

"What?" This was getting dark even for me, too dark for being the only one awake in the house…at night. I spun around a bit, looking for moving shadows in the corners. "What was he sick from?"

"Tuberculosis. There were other rumors among the family, but I never paid them much mind. But listen, Isla, you are never to speak to Tía Alma about this, comprendes?" I could almost see my mother's finger pointing at me over the phone.

"I know, I know." I couldn't get a full image of the man, and I wanted one now that I knew his fate. "But I'm just wondering, what was he like?"

I imagined my mother leaning back into one of the dining room chairs, the only illumination from the streetlights out front. "I was very young when he died, so I don't have many memories of him. All I remember is a feeling, really."

My mother's voice had that faraway timbre that threatened a lost thread of conversation, particularly if the evening had included a cocktail or three. "What feeling?" I prompted carefully.

A long sigh. Then, "Fear. He frightened me. He would bellow at the servants, hurling insults at them and occasionally even a fist. Even my mother, the strongest woman I knew, acted differently around her father: 'Sí, Papá, no, Papá, lo siento, Papá,' apologizing when she hadn't done anything wrong, so eager to please him. Bah! She was a bitch to everyone but him!" Her anger sputtered in my ear like a backfiring car.

"Everyone knew that Alma was his favorite, especially Mami. He would scream and yell at her, and she would cower from him. Can you imagine your grandmother cowering to anyone? Well, she did. I wondered what he had done to earn that fear from her and how I could bottle some for myself."

I stood there in the darkened foyer, trying to integrate this information with the dapper man in the white suit who stared out from the frames across Alma's dresser.

"Isla…how are things down there? Are you having fun?"

I imagined my mother told herself and anyone who would listen that her daughter was on the island having fun for the last ten summers so she could feel better about abandoning her only child in order to drink. Another secret protected. I could hear a hint of desperation in my mother's voice, like she needed me to assure her it was all right. That made me even angrier.

"Sure, Mom, tons."

She let out a breath. "Bueno, I'm glad."

Once again, I wondered if my mother was really that oblivious that she couldn't detect the sarcasm. A muffled sound from the background on my mother's end.

A man's voice.

"Who was that?" The edges of the three words were sharp as razors.

"No one." The answer came too quickly. "It was the TV. Isla, I have to go. Sleep well, mi amor." And she hung up.

I stood there in the darkened parlor, rage building in my belly, my fingers so tight on the phone's receiver, I wondered if it would shatter. My father had been dead for ten years. Why shouldn't my mother date someone? But in our home? While I wasn't there? Were they drunk?

I set the receiver down slowly, feeling my dinner rise and push against the back of my throat.

CHAPTER TWENTY-ONE
not one drop of blood

Early the next day, I made my way next door to talk to Tío Ramón. The conversation with Mom had not been helpful on any level, and I decided to focus on finding out more about my great-grandfather. I was intent on this pursuit, particularly because no one seemed to want me to know more. Which meant they were hiding something. Besides, it kept my mind off the man's voice on the other end of last night's conversation. I couldn't even think about it without feeling as if I were going to be sick. So since Alma was off-limits, Ramón seemed to be the next logical person. As was his daily habit, I found him sitting on the wooden glider on the front porch, café con leche in hand, staring off into the trees.

I leaned over and gave him a kiss on his scratchy cheek. I thought it odd as he used to always be clean-shaven, his clothes pressed, and his boots shiny. That summer, he seemed to live in a V-necked white undershirt, baggy pants, and his mud-covered rubber boots. But as I sat down, I realized that he'd gotten old when I wasn't looking. I'd always thought of my family as eternal, that there would always be Ramón and Lourdes next door, that my summers would be spent with Alma forever and ever. But just the momentary consideration that this might not be true caused my chest to tighten, so I practically yelled an innocuous question at my great-uncle.

"What do you think about when you sit out here, Tío?"

He took a deep breath, and when he let it out, it looked as if he had deflated. I wondered if that was what old age did to you. "Ay, niña. Many things…and nothing."

I smiled. It was a classic Sanchez response, evasive but poetic.

He turned around and faced me with a grin. "And what about you? What do you think about, Sobrina? Boys, I would imagine, yes?"

I laughed but then thought of José, and the heat started to rise to my face. Not for the first time, I damned the pale skin I'd inherited from my father.

My great-uncle slapped his knee. "See? I knew it." His chuckle was clean and clear as the sound of water tumbling over rocks.

"Actually, I'm trying to figure out what being a Sanchez means." I was surprised by the words even as I said them.

A pause. A glance at me. Then, "I am not the person to answer that question, m'ija."

"But that's the thing. No one here wants to answer questions like that."

"What kind of person feels they can speak for an entire blood-line, huh? An arrogant one, that is for certain."

"True." I thought for a minute as we sat in companionable silence, the only sound the squeak of the glider's tracks. "Okay, tell me one thing that a Sanchez is. Just one thing."

"Hmm." He squinted in thought, breathed deeply, then said, "This kind of inquiry requires ice cream."

"For breakfast?" I laughed.

"¡Seguro! Why leave the best thing for after dinner, verdad?" He downed the last dregs of his coffee, picked up his hat from the chair next to him and placed it on his head just so, then stood. "Come, niña. Let's us go get ice cream and discuss your question."

I never turned down ice cream, and Bayamón had the best ice cream parlor around. Dozens and dozens of flavors, tropical, traditional, even chili con carne. But despite the array of options, I always got the same thing: a cone with a scoop of chocolate chip and one of mint chocolate chip. Well, since I was fourteen, at least.

We loaded into Ramón's jeep and pulled out of the property in a belch of smoke and dust. As we drove along Calle Santa Cruz, I considered how the neighborhood had changed. The small linen shop was gone, replaced with a quick mart, the windows crisscrossed with thick black bars, a big check-cashing sign above. And next door, where the bakery used to be, was now Esteban's Gun Shop.

"Gun shop? When did that open up?"

"When the neighborhood began to change. It is hard to believe now, but when your mother was your age, this was all farmland. Can you imagine?"

I looked at the gray, trash-strewn street and shook my head.

"Now, I am afraid there are tiroteros every weekend, and good people must defend themselves, tu sabes?"

Tirotero. Shootout. I remembered the day I learned the word. The entire family was gathered on Alma's porch. I was sitting on the floor near my parents, playing with Barbies, humming a little song. The adults' conversation was lively, and the scent of roasted pork hung in the air. Then a series of cracks sounded in the not-so-far distance, like a string of firecrackers, and I jumped. Then my family was up, rushing inside and dragging me with them, bodies kept low to the ground, Barbies left splayed between the cane rocking chairs.

I shook the memory from my head and focused on what Tío was

saying about the new stores that had seemed to sprout along the road like mushrooms.

We got our ice cream, the cones frosty in the humid morning air, and sat on a brightly painted wooden bench out front. Cars would honk as they went by, my great-uncle raising a hand in greeting as if he were royalty. I suppose he was, in a way. We were quiet in our concentration, carefully licking the ribbons of ice cream that snaked their way down the sides of the cones.

I watched the traffic buzz by, realizing that the strip used to be half the width, the traffic half as much. A lot of things were changing.

Ramón popped the bottom point of the cone in his mouth and sighed deeply as he chewed. "Now I can think." He smiled. "If I remember correctly, and I always do, you had asked me to describe one thing that embodies what a Sanchez is. I would have to say: hard-working. A Sanchez always works hard, Isla. It doesn't matter if you sweep the floor or own the building, you must do it—"

I finished with him, "'To the best of your ability.'"

"Ah, so you've heard that one before."

I rolled my eyes. "Only thousands of times from my mother and Alma."

He laughed. "Thousands, ay? Well, there's a second thing then. We're predictable."

"And weird."

"That too."

"Tío, can you tell me about Bisabuelo?"

He looked at me sideways. "Hasn't your mother told you about her grandfather?"

"No, she says she was too young when he died and doesn't remember him, and Alma…won't talk about him. Was he nice?"

Ramón sighed and combed his thick gray mustache with his fingers. "It was not his role to be nice. It was…a different time. Men like my father had to be strong. Comprendes?"

I shook my head, not because I didn't understand but because I wanted more.

"Those were difficult times here on the island. Your great-grandfather wanted to protect the life that his great-grandfather had built after arriving from España, and in his youth, it was a time of great unrest. But he stayed strong and was proud of his pure blood, just two generations from Europe. And you should be too, Isla. Not one drop of blood, ni una gota de sangre, that is not European. Yes, you should be proud." My great-uncle sat silently now, staring at the ground ahead of him.

I felt the familiar heat growing behind my face. All this talk about European blood seemed like just another way of feeling superior. I was disappointed that my great-uncle, who was usually the most forthcoming, also seemed to be keeping secrets.

He stood, his huge ring of keys jangling at his waist. "I know. Let's drive back a different way. There is something I want to show you."

Ramón turned down a road I'd never noticed before, and as we drove, the buildings gave way to more and more trees, the cars became fewer and fewer, until we were surrounded by an unending carpet of green. Brown cows spotted the hills on either side of the road. It was the opposite of the buzzing route we had taken out, and I smiled.

"I've never been this way before. It's beautiful!"

"Isn't it? It belongs to the family, you know."

I turned around in my seat and stared at him. "What? You mean"—I gestured around us—"all this is Sanchez land?"

He smiled. "¡Seguro! Of course. The property is called 'El

Tesoro,' the treasure. You asked about your great-grandfather. He built the family by buying land like this bit by bit. He built the Sanchezes into what we are today."

I watched the green roll by the windows and breathed in the lush scent. Was my family rich? I'd really never considered this before. They lived simply, nothing ostentatious, no bragging.

"Part of it should be your mother's...but your abuela...she—"

"Cut my mother out."

His head snapped as he looked at me, but he didn't say anything. "Yes, well, I'm hoping your mother will reconsider and fight for what is hers."

I looked around and tried to imagine what it would be like to own a piece of this land. Would it look different to me if it were ours? I supposed I'd never know, and that was okay. At eighteen, I didn't own much of anything anyway.

After he dropped me off in front of Alma's, I kissed his stubbly cheek and said, "Thank you, Tío." I always enjoyed my time with my uncle, but as I walked up the path, it struck me that though we had talked a lot, I didn't know much more than when I'd left the house an hour before. And to me, that, more than anything, captured what being a Sanchez meant.

CHAPTER TWENTY-TWO
the many meanings of bueno

The summer was nearly over, the Caribbean sun setting earlier and earlier, more of the orange-red blooms of the flamboyán trees falling to the ground as small fiery phoenixes. After I'd spent several weeks being sequestered in Alma's house, I was thrilled when my cousin Maria invited me to spend an afternoon shopping in Old San Juan. Shopping was not a sport that I was drawn to, but I admired Maria, and the idea of yet another day under Alma's watchful warden gaze was not at all appealing. However, a trip with Maria necessitated a morning of primping.

Maria was one of those women with effortless style. To my mind, there was a proliferation of such women on the island. The previous summer, I had visited Old San Juan with Maria and I'd dressed as I always did in New Jersey: ripped jeans shorts, a pair of comfortable, worn sneakers with a frayed backpack slung over my shoulder, all prepared for a day of trekking up and down the cobblestone streets of the old city. But Maria had pulled up in her Datsun 280Z convertible wearing a bold 1950s sundress covered with large orange flowers that set off her dark hair and carrying a vintage straw handbag. I spent the afternoon feeling wholly inadequate and frumpy and considered crawling underneath the table of the sidewalk café when Maria introduced me to some handsome classmates from college.

I swore that would never happen again, and thus I spent an inordinate amount of time getting ready, pulling out a never-worn dress and replacing my omnipresent flip-flops with stylish thong sandals my mother had forced on me. And though I would never admit it to Mom, I even applied a bit of makeup.

A car honked and I called goodbye to Alma, then bounded down the front steps, inhaling deeply the moist smell of Alma's jungle after the noontime rain. When I looked toward the car, I saw a guy leaning in the window and talking to Maria, a pair of pruning shears slung over his shoulder. I stopped short and my hand went automatically to my hair, smoothing a stray strand before they saw me. For several weeks, I had been looking while pretending not to look for him, and there he was. I smiled at José as I ducked under his arm and slipped into the white leather passenger seat. He smelled of earth and soap and earned sweat, and he made my head swim.

"Oh, hi, José!" I tossed over, grateful that I was sitting down so my shaking legs were not apparent.

Maria's grin threatened to split her face. "You know each other? Fabulous! José and I go way back, Isla. He's best friends with our cousin Andrés. They went to grammar school together."

Maria looked from José's sweating and extraordinarily handsome face to my increasingly crimson one. She never missed a thing.

"I have an idea! José, why don't you join us in Old San Juan?"

I grabbed my cousin's arm and wasn't sure if I wanted to scream NO! or YES! But I kept my lips in a tight, straight line as we waited for his answer.

He chuckled. "I wish I could, Maria. I have to work. But thank you for the invitation. I would much rather spend the day with two lovely ladies than work in the hot sun."

Two lovely ladies, two... And he was looking only at me now. I could feel the warmth of his gaze as I stared at my feet on the black rubber car mat.

Finally, Maria put the car into reverse. "Bueno, shall we go, Prima?"

José tapped the car twice. "Have fun, señoritas." Again, he spoke to both of us but looked only at me.

I didn't breathe until we pulled out onto Calle Santa Cruz, the stone wall buzzing by my window as I put my face in my hands. Despite my cousin's oversized and expensive sunglasses, I could tell she was still watching me out of the corner of her eye as she drove down the street. The concrete houses and storefronts breezed by, and I tried to concentrate on the Ronrico rum banner or the old-fashioned ladies' beauty parlor that still teased women's hair like it was the 1950s. Finally, I couldn't take it anymore. The silence was excruciating.

"What?" I griped at Maria. "Why are you smiling at me?"

Unruffled, Maria just looked ahead. "So, José's cute, huh?"

I crossed my arms and grunted. I knew I looked like a petulant child, but I didn't care. "I hadn't noticed." But I couldn't maintain my grumpiness in the face of Maria's unwavering cheer, and by the time we parked the car on a narrow side street in Old San Juan, I was feeling downright festive. We spent the day wandering up and down the blue cobblestone streets, zigzagging in and out of shops, arm in arm. I actually let Maria talk me into getting a fitted and low-cut blue dress that brought out the color of my eyes and hugged my body like a whisper. Of course, having seen José right before our expedition might have something to do with why I capitulated. The sun was setting over Alma's jungle by the time Maria dropped me off, and despite the late hour, my eyes darted around the grounds of their own accord as I slowly walked up the path, the light from the inside of the house beaming between the black metal bars of the front porch gate.

The night before my flight home, I stood by the high, metal bed in Alma's guest room, folding clothes into my suitcase. I was distracted with thoughts of what I was leaving behind and what I was to face in New Jersey. All day, I noticed things I hadn't before: the innumerable variations of the color green in the flora that surrounded the house. How the heady, sweet scent of ripe bananas always hung in the kitchen air from the ever-filled fruit bowl. That when the truck with loudspeakers mounted to the hood did its daily pass in front of the house, I realized I understood the muffled Spanish list of fruits and vegetables for sale.

As usual, I didn't want to go home. That house in New Jersey that I shared with my mother hadn't felt like home since Dad died, certainly not with the way things had been. I would be starting college not long after I returned, so everything was going to change. It was as if the ground beneath me was shifting.

I realized with a start that Alma was standing in the doorway watching me.

"Tía! You almost gave me a heart attack!"

She said nothing in response and continued to watch me as I carefully placed my sandals in the corner of the bag, my great-aunt's eyes never leaving my hands as if I were conducting a symphony.

Alma's voice finally cut through the silence. "That boy José, the one you used to play with when you were younger, stopped by today."

My head shot up. I knew I shouldn't show any emotion, but I was starting to care less and less what Alma or anyone else thought. "What? When?"

"When you and your uncle were out souvenir shopping at Plaza las Américas."

I feigned interest in my packing job. "Did José say anything?"

"Yes, he asked me to say goodbye to you for him." Her voice was flat and even, beach glass worn down by the ocean.

I attempted to hide my disappointment. "Oh, that was nice of him."

Alma stood there for some time, looking at me as if she was waiting for something to happen, her arms held across her chest like a shield. I had finished packing but continued to arrange and rearrange, pretending to be very busy. I was afraid Alma could hear the beating of my heart. I felt my muscles stiffen with memory, bracing for my aunt's expected judgment of my friendship with José, for the verbal blow. But I would not just take it like I had when I was a kid. I was older, stronger. I was starting to understand who I was.

Finally, Alma broke the silence. "I didn't realize you knew him. I mean, except for when you two were children."

I looked up at her. Though I heard disapproval and unspoken questions in the timbre of my aunt's voice, the words were carefully chosen. They treaded much lighter than I had expected. I noticed the creases that framed Alma's eyes and pursed lips, the papery skin of her hand.

She was waiting for me to say something.

"He is my friend." I was surprised by the formality of it, the lack of contraction.

A pause.

A sigh.

And then, "*Bueno.*"

Alma unfolded her arms and was gone.

Bueno. Good. But not in the affirmative sense of the word. Like so many Spanish words, this one had shades of meaning. From Alma, on this day, it was meant more as an acceptance: very well then. One word could have so much weight and substance in my mother's language.

I closed the suitcase and sat next to it, the edges of the old mattress lifting with my weight. I looked around at what had been my summer bedroom for as long as I could remember. The wooden furniture, dark and severe but intricately carved, the upholstered fabrics paled by sun and time, a light layer of dust covering all. Nothing had changed, but it was as if I were looking at it through a camera with a new filter. I saw scratches and gouges I'd never noticed before, saw how the speckled pattern of the linoleum floor was faded from years of ammonia and scrubbing.

I wondered how things would look to me when I returned next.

CHAPTER TWENTY-THREE
home at last?

I scanned the waiting, glass-masked faces beyond Newark airport security, the row of eyes searching for their deplaning family, friends, colleagues. But no eyes were searching for me. I chided myself for being surprised, felt my shoulders fall a little under the weight of familiar disappointment. I hadn't talked to my mother since that last call, hadn't wanted to hear her voice. I followed the line of passengers flowing out the narrow doorway, and as the crowd of waiting people merged with the arrivals, I glanced again at all the faces around me. Compared to where I had just left, everyone looked so colorless, like the underbelly of a fish.

I stood there as the crowd dispersed, all the people and bags and sound moving away from me, none toward.

A man's voice spoke behind me. Paul the flight attendant had paid particularly close attention to me when I was on the plane, bringing me extra soda and one of those small blue blankets that barely cover your knees.

"Well, Isla." With his southern accent, he pronounced the name *ee-slaw*. "You waitin' on someone?" His blond hair looked painted on, like the molded hair on my old Ken doll, and his grin reminded me of a ventriloquist's dummy, to the point that I swore I could see hinges on either side of his wooden jaw.

I decided the less information, the better. "Yes."

He just smiled as the airport announcements blared overhead and I pretended to adjust the strap of my backpack.

The pilot walked by at that moment, flanked by three of the other flight attendants, all of them pulling their rolling suitcases behind them. Everything about them was crisp and navy blue like a fresh deck of cards. Just as I was about to turn away, I caught Paul exchanging a leering smile with the pilot that I knew was about me. For a moment, I considered kicking Paul in the crotch of his well-creased pants, giving up on my mother, and buying a ticket back to the island.

"Isla!" my mother called breathlessly, her high heels clicking across the vast expanse of floor. I saw her coming in a flurry of silk, her arm waving vigorously as if she were in the middle of a swarm of people. Purse over arm, my mother made a big show of hugging me, of kissing my cheek and wiping the lipstick stain she left there. She aimed a stream of words about working late and horrific traffic at me, but beneath the scent of mints, I caught the sharp edge of gin on her breath.

Then she noticed Paul.

My mother turned her body and all her attention in his direction. "Oh, and who is this handsome young man in uniform? I'm Isla's mother, Mr…"

"Paul, call me Paul, ma'am." He held out his slight and pale hand like a limp cod.

The two of them grinned at each other, holding the handshake longer than I cared to watch.

"I was just making sure Isla here met up with you all right."

Finally, my mother let go of Paul call-me-Paul's hand, and I made a point of sighing with extra emphasis.

"Paul, thank you *so* much for escorting my sweet girl," my mother cooed, and both sets of eyes fell on me. My skin suddenly felt oily.

"She's quite a charming young lady. Seems to take after her momma."

My mother giggled. Actually giggled. I was under the impression that giggling was illegal for anyone over the age of thirty. The flame behind my face flared. "Mom, can we go now?" I said behind clenched teeth.

"Of course, dear. It was lovely to meet you, Paul—"

I didn't wait for her to finish. I walked away, briskly following the signs toward the baggage claim, fantasizing about setting fire to my entire life. As I stepped off the escalator, my mother came up behind me and shoved her arm through mine as we walked toward the black revolving belts, asking questions about the trip in an excessively cheery voice that made my jaw tighten. I mumbled answers, hoping she would take the hint, but she kept asking, kept brushing the hair out of my eyes and talking about how much she missed me, about what was going on at her work.

I stared at the luggage going past on the carousel, around and back again like the electric train set my father used to set up around the tree at Christmas. Back when holidays still mattered. All the bags went by me twice before I recognized mine. I grabbed at it, dragging it over the metal lip of the bag belt, and hauled it through the doors behind my mother. As we walked through the parking garage, I was grateful for the sting of the bag banging against my sunburned thigh, the red of my skin the only memento of the island I'd left behind.

I didn't say a word on the drive home, but I was certain Mom didn't notice. She simply kept up her diatribe of inane one-sided chatter, while I thought back to that return trip from the airport years ago, the first time she'd left me there alone, and we'd stopped at the graveyard on the way. I thought about it every year as I transitioned from my summer life to life with her.

We pulled into the driveway and made our way up the walk. It all looked so different this year. I looked around while my mother unlocked the front door. The plots of daylilies beneath the windows were in full bloom, the riot of orange flowers rivaling the colors of Alma's gardens. I looked down the shady street and realized it was kind of lovely, noticed how much green there was. This was not a Puerto Rico versus New Jersey thing at all. They were both beautiful. I breathed deeply and told myself that perhaps it would be okay to be back. College was a new start after all. My mother opened the door and we stepped through.

I put my bag down and looked around. It wasn't just that everything *seemed* different; the entire living room was rearranged. My father's architecture books were missing from the Herman Miller bench that served as our coffee table, and his leather butterfly chair was gone. The familiar image of him in the chair reading the *New York Times*, a gin and tonic on the floor beside him, was pushed out by the trendy rust-colored armchair that replaced it. As I stood there, the ghost of my father evaporated. She'd made him disappear. Again.

I turned to my mother with my hands tightened in fury to find her smiling.

"Surprise! I thought a bit of redecorating would liven up the place!" My mother waved her arms around as if she were one of those vapid women on a game show, displaying the possible winnings to the contestants and studio audiences.

"Where are Dad's things?" My voice was cold and slow.

"Oh, honey, that old chair was beat-up and passé. And the books, I donated them to the library. At this point, they're so out of date that—"

"You had no right!" Rage filled my chest with fire so strong that I could feel the flames licking the bottoms of my eyes. It was as if my mother had created a black hole in the middle of the living room and had shoved whatever I had left of my father into its depths, along with what was left of our relationship.

But my mother showed no signs of remorse, only matching rage. "No *right*? This is my house too, missy! And if you think—"

"You had no right to bury him while I was away!" I shrieked, the accusation yanked up from some deep storage within, surprising even me.

My mother sputtered. "What? Isla, that was ten years ago! You were a child." Her lips quivered, but I knew no tears were coming. Instead, my mother lifted her chin and said, "I only did what I felt was best for you."

A flicker of empathy flashed through my heart, but rage was the overwhelming feeling, I guessed, for both of us. As I stared at the emotions playing across my mother's reddening face, I realized that the black hole was not new. Geography was not the problem; it was the woman standing in front of me.

I grabbed my suitcase and stomped up the stairs to my small, dark bedroom. The room always looked smaller, shabbier when I came home at the end of the summer.

I slammed the door, dropped my suitcase to the floor, and let it fall to its side as if injured. I looked around, and it was as if it wasn't my room. It had nothing to do with me. From the fake autographed eight-by-ten glossies of celebrities I no longer cared about, to the poster from the regional production of *Our Town* that Mom had dragged me to, to a pennant from my high school where no one really knew me.

Then my mother's falsely cheerful soprano hum wafted up from downstairs, footsteps across the hardwood floor of the dining room, the cracking of an ice tray.

The scalding heat flared again in my chest.

I looked around at the room and, with a lurch, started to tear things off the walls, pushpins flying like fireworks as tears burned in my eyes. Once the walls were bare, I continued to bang on them, wishing I could push my fists through and tear the drywall down piece by piece, until nothing remained but the wooden beams. Mom had to be wondering what was going on, had to be worried about it. Finally, when my legs could no longer hold me, I dropped to the bed and curled up in a ball. I cried quietly, afraid that my mother had heard and would come upstairs and try to comfort me. I stopped breathing for a moment and listened for footsteps. When I heard the stereo blare to life from the living room downstairs, I realized that I had been more afraid that she wouldn't come.

CHAPTER TWENTY-FOUR
a gift becomes a curse

I was beginning to nod off in Sociology 101, my first class after lunch, when my elbow slipped off the molded-plastic desktop and whacked against the metal arm attaching it to the chair. I shook my head and repositioned myself, trying to focus on what the professor was pontificating about—something about the theory of positivism—but gradually his voice became a monotonous drone in my skull.

Just as my arm began to slip once more, I jerked awake at a man's voice shouting in Spanish behind me. As I spun around in my seat toward the sound, my gaze swept over the students in the surrounding chairs. They were still absently taking notes despite the ruckus in the back of the classroom. I whipped around to look at the right-hand back corner.

A large, dark wooden desk had appeared and an aged, mustachioed man in a white suit was walking around it: the shouting was coming from him.

The whole room seemed to tip under me.

No. Not here. Not now.

A Black man stood in front of the desk. He was young, his curly hair cut short around his head, his eyes soft and dark. I would have thought he were another student if not for his clothing. He wore a white cotton guayabera, the traditional Latin shirt with pleats and pockets on the front, worn outside the pants. His pants were neatly pressed but stopped just short of his ankles. He wore no socks, only brown leather shoes that were carefully polished but clearly worn. I glanced to my right and saw the early autumn trees waving in the wind through the large window that looked out over the Columbia campus. Again, I surveyed my classmates. Yes, I was the only witness to the unfolding drama.

I turned back toward the front of the class, determinedly putting my back to the scene. The visions only happened on the island, I assured myself. Maybe if I ignored it, it would stop. *Please*, I silently begged whatever dead cuentista this story belonged to, *please, not now*. I felt a familiar pull from the island, like a ghostly umbilical cord had been reattached. No, that wasn't quite right. Umbilical cords feed you, support you. This was more like a leash, the other end firmly held by some dead Sanchez storyteller, pulling me southward, across the Caribbean.

The arguing voices grew louder, the Spanish blasting out like automatic-weapon fire, so I couldn't help but turn my attention back to the corner.

The man in the guayabera had his fingers wrapped around the brim of a pava, gripping the straw hat so hard I could hear the crunch of the weaving from where I sat. I had the fleeting thought that with the hat on, he must look just like the political flag I'd seen earlier that summer. The men stared into each other's eyes with only six feet of institutional flooring between them. Frozen where I was, I resigned myself to riding out the vision and tried to identify the players.

The younger man's eyes were large and rimmed with long, black velvet lashes. His lips were coral against the deep brown of his skin.

I wanted to stand up, to edge closer to the scene, but how could I explain my movements to the professor? Also, this vision was more intense than any I'd had before, even the hurricane. The edges were sharper, the colors florid. Shouldn't the signal, or whatever it was, be weaker this far away?

I looked at the old man, taking in the pale wrinkled skin of his face, how the dark, angry sparkle in his eyes reflected the light like the black volcanic sands of Punta Santiago. He had a full head of thick hair that was almost the same color as his white suit jacket and a black tie that matched his expensive-looking leather shoes. He stepped toward the other man, the volume of his voice rising as the Spanish words flew out closer and closer together, and I tried to catch their meaning as they were spat through the air. Something about disrespect and knowing your place, and then when responding, the young man addressed him as "Señor Sanchez."

I sat bolt upright. My thoughts were spiraling as the entire scene came into even higher relief. It was my great-grandfather! He looked exactly like his photographs, but he'd been dead forever. So who was the other man? Was he the one sending the vision? My hands gripped the back of the desk chair, and I rose onto my knees as though getting higher in my seat would relieve some of the anxiety tightening my limbs. The argument was heating up, but the yelling was one-sided; the other man had not lost his composure, and this seemed to infuriate my great-grandfather even further, the professor's unimportant words a continuous hum in the background. My grandfather poked the man in the chest with his fingers, the color of his face flushing with blood.

There was a change in the air, then, like the crackle that courses through the atmosphere just before a lightning storm hits, and fury rose off Great-Grandfather like heat. Suddenly he was punching at the man, who tried to ward off the blows. They struggled, becoming a mass of scrabbling limbs and shuffling feet.

"Ms. Larsen?"

I pulled my eyes away from the vision and stared at the professor, who was standing in the front of the class, chalk in hand, aggravation clouding his face. As I looked around, I noticed that all the other students' faces were turned to me as well.

"Is there a problem?" he asked in a condescending tone.

I mumbled a quick, "No," adding an awkward smile, anxious to turn my attention back to my great-grandfather.

"Good. As I was saying, metaphysical and theological claims cannot be verified…" I didn't hear the end of his sentence. As I looked back, the fluorescent lights gleamed off the shiny surface of an old-fashioned revolver and everything began to move in fast-forward.

The men were still bound together like two awkward dancers, their hands struggling for control of the gun. I felt tears threaten as I sat higher in my seat.

Then the sound of a gunshot boomed off the walls, and I jumped as I alone stared at the pair in the corner, their shuffling halted, all four arms tangled up between them. My great-grandfather's face grew pale, and he stumbled forward, his left hand groping for the desk to steady himself. The gun fell from between the men and clattered across the floor and under the desk. It was then I saw the dark-red stain growing on my ancestor's white shirtfront like a wilted hibiscus flower. His arm could no longer support him, and he slipped off the side of the desk and downward. The other man lurched forward. It was then that both he and I turned at the sound of a woman's panicked voice echoing outside the room.

"¿Papá? ¿Que pasó?"

For one frozen moment, the man seemed to look right into my eyes as we both realized to whom the voice belonged. My chest tightened as if in a vise.

And then he was moving, his long legs hurtling over the body on the floor, leaping headfirst out the open window behind the desk. The bottoms of his shoes flashed in the window's frame, the tough skin of his feet showing through the holes in the soles. They disappeared just as a door opened. A young version of Alma, my great-aunt, stood in the doorway, mouth agape, her hand quickly rising to cover it, eyes wide with horror.

Alma and I screamed at the same time. My great-aunt for her mortally wounded father, and me because there was only one thing her part in this vision could mean, since Great-Grandfather had died a very long time ago.

"Papá!" Alma cried, rushing to the unmoving man, his empty eyes staring up at the white plaster ceiling. I was vaguely aware of the entire class looking my way as Alma dropped to her knees by his side, palms hovering as if to touch him but too afraid. She choked out strangled sobs, her hands moving rhythmically as if they worked a rosary, eyes sweeping over the scene. Suddenly Alma stopped. She was staring at something a few feet away from the desk. I followed her gaze, and there, on the floor near the chair, sat the man's pava.

The next thing I was aware of was the professor's face over me as I looked up from the floor. "Are you all right, Ms. Larsen?"

I nodded though I wasn't really sure I was. What had just happened? As he helped me to my feet, I glanced around at the class. Everything seemed big, like I was looking through a magnifying glass. Then I remembered Alma's face, and the image was like a weight on my chest, as if the big ghost desk had fallen on top of me.

"Why don't you go to health services," the professor said as he escorted me to the door. A roomful of eyes tingled along my back.

I made it outside, somehow, and walked along the campus's cobblestoned paths, barely aware of my surroundings. People passed by, jostling me, and I envied their purposeful and normal movements. They hadn't just seen a ghost, probably the ghost of the only person who truly cared about them.

I needed to sit down. Making a quick U-turn, I irritated several people with my abrupt change of direction but didn't bother to mumble apologies. I made it to the steps of Low Library, my hand on the base of the *Alma Mater* statue as I sat, my textbook falling from my arms and tumbling open-faced onto the marble steps.

I felt as if I was no longer in my body, as if someone else were moving my arms and legs. The one thing I was certain of from the experience was that Alma was dead. My great-grandfather had been dead for years, and the other man was not familiar at all. Could Alma really be gone? But my great-aunt had seemed fine when I saw her just a few weeks before. Then I remembered how Alma had been going to bed earlier and earlier. My eyes filled and my hand rushed to my mouth to stifle a sob. But I didn't want to cry, not then and not there. There were so many questions ringing in my ears: What the hell had just happened? What did this vision mean? Alma never told stories, ever.

Diversions for a lazy mind.

I took a deep breath and shook my head as if I could loosen the images and clear them from behind my eyes like a Magic 8 Ball. I tried to reconstruct what I'd just witnessed: my great-grandfather, Alma, an unknown man, a gunshot. I covered my ears as I remembered the tinny pop of the bullet. I took another deep breath and concentrated on slowing my heartbeat.

View-Master slides of Alma ran through my mind. I flashed back to my last visit to Puerto Rico, the way she had been so very tired, how the piano had stayed shut more nights than not. My great-aunt had not been herself. She had been pale and muted like a surface that had been scrubbed too much. And I'd spent most of the summer brooding and angry, avoiding spending time with her. Just thinking about it made my breath shallower and shallower, until I was certain if I didn't stop, I would pass out again.

I made myself focus on the vision, what it meant, avoiding the immeasurable grief that knocked on my heart. What did I know about my great-grandfather? He had shot himself, that was what Mom had told me, because he was sick. I was no nurse, but that man did not look ill, and that certainly was no suicide. I thought back to the conversation I'd had with Tío Ramón outside the ice cream shop.

My eyes filled as I remembered the pain on Alma's face, the splatter of blood across the desk. Clearly the story that my great-grandfather killed himself due to illness was fiction, but what had I just witnessed? I considered the possibilities: a political disagreement? A labor dispute? Perhaps even a robbery? If I'd learned anything about my bisabuelo, it was that he'd had a dreadful temper. Or was the story the vision told not really true?

Then it hit me. I thought of my cut arm after the hurricane vision. Was there a bullet hole in the blackboard on the classroom wall? Was I in danger?

I grabbed my books and ran. Getting on an early bus and home to the book of stories was my only goal. Though I already missed Alma and really wanted to know what it all meant, that was not a vision I cared to see again.

CHAPTER TWENTY-FIVE
full disclosure

"¡Vámanos, Isla!" Mom called from downstairs. "If we don't get moving, we'll miss our flight!"

I snapped my suitcase shut, the impact shaking the bed, and glanced around the room for anything I might have forgotten. At the last second, I spotted the book of stories on the desk and tucked it into my carry-on bag. I had written out Alma's story the previous afternoon, just before the call came from Puerto Rico, but I felt better having the book with me. It was a piece of the storytellers to keep with me for strength.

We ended up rushing through the long, glass-lined corridors of Newark Airport only to find out our flight was delayed, and we had to wait at the gate in the cavernous terminal for over two hours. Luckily, Alma's funeral wasn't until the following morning, so we wouldn't miss it.

Mom fidgeted as if the molded plastic row of seats was electrified. Finally, she jumped to her feet, grasping her purse tight in her shaking hands. "I'm going to go get a coffee. I need to stretch my legs. You want something?"

I lowered my book and looked up. At least it was too early to hit the bar, even for my mother. "Yeah, can you get me a muffin?

Thanks, Mom." I returned to reading my book, trying unsuccess-
fully to lose myself in the world of *One Hundred Years of Solitude*. I
still could not wrap my head around Alma being gone. Solid ground
had been ripped away. My attention was pulled away again at the
sound of shouting nearby. *Can't a girl read a damn book?* I thought.
Glaring up off the page, I searched for the source of the racket. My
body froze when I saw Great-Grandfather coming around his desk
toward the anonymous man.

"What the hell?" I said out loud. The sounds of the airport
announcements drained away, the milling people becoming mere
apparitions in the background. My paperback dropped to the carpet
as I groped for the book of stories in my backpack, hands shaking
and fumbling. I pulled it out and brushed through the pages until
I arrived at the last cuento in the book: Alma's. Yes, it was there, I
hadn't dreamed it. I searched the handwritten entry, scanning for
something I could have missed, some crucial detail, but I hadn't
missed a thing. Everything I saw was there. I looked at my watch,
2:10, the same time as the day before. Why was this happening
again?

Raising my eyes just as the struggle ensued, I realized I was in
the line of fire. I threw my body to the floor, the sound of the
shot echoing over my head. Lying there, flat on my stomach on the
orange and red carpeting, I didn't even look up when Alma entered
the room…as she screamed…as she sobbed. I buried my face in my
arms and cried with her until all sounds of the vision were gone and
I was left alone, my whole body shaking.

Tears soaked my sleeves as I tried to catch my breath. It was like
the time when I was little, playing in the surf alone as the adults
chatted on their blankets on the sand, and a big wave hit me from
behind. For a long moment, I couldn't tell up from down as I

tumbled, my legs a flash of white amid the deep blue of the water, seawater choking my breath.

A flight was announced, the hum of voices returned, and I peered up in the direction of the vision to find my mother standing above me, eyes wide. "Isla! What happened? Are you okay?" She put the coffee and muffins down and dropped to her knees beside me, lips tight with concern.

"Yeah, Mom. I'm…I'm okay," I said, unsteadily pushing myself up on my arms, my right hand still clasping the book. Brushing off my pants, I slumped into my seat and tried to ignore the furtive glances from the other passengers.

Mom felt my forehead as she pulled me around to face her. "How did you end up on the floor, honey? Did you faint? I think I need to get you to a doctor. Maybe we shouldn't—"

"No, Mom, really, I'm fine. It's just…" I was too startled to come up with an excuse, too tired and scared to lie. I opened the book to Alma's story and handed it over.

As my mother read, her eyes opened wider, her free hand grasping and working at the fabric of her skirt. She occasionally glanced up at me as she leafed through the book, skimming back through each cuentista's story. Finally, she closed the cover and held it in her lap, her eyes glued to it as if she expected it to bite. The disbelief I had anticipated wasn't there. Or perhaps she simply thought me insane.

"Isla, how do you know these stories? I mean, some of them… Well, there's just no way you could have known."

I started at the beginning with Abuela and Teresa and told my mother all: each cuentista, each vision, what I'd learned about the gift. I talked for almost an hour, the hubbub of the terminal forgotten. Throughout, my mother seemed distracted, her eyes distant as if she wished she were somewhere else. When I finished, ending with the vision that had just passed and its unexplained recurrence, I held my breath, unsure of how she would react but relieved all the same to finally talk about it. We sat there silently for what seemed an eternity.

I watched my mother as she continued to stare at the book. I couldn't read her face, didn't know what to expect, and that frightened me more than the violent vision.

"I can't believe you've held this in, suffered on your own. I feel… responsible."

I saw Mom's eyes fill, and she fidgeted in her seat. My mother never cried. "Mom, how could you be responsible? I mean—"

"No, I should have seen this… I should have known. And Alma—"

"I tried to tell her, Mom, after I had the first one about Abuela, and she just got mad."

"You told her? And she didn't tell me?" Her voice was shrill, like the planes' engines as they squealed to life outside the wall of glass, the sound getting higher and higher until I thought I couldn't stand it any longer.

"Yes." I felt like a child who'd been caught telling tales out of school.

Suddenly, Mom leapt up. "They're calling our flight! We have to make this!" She grabbed our carry-on bags and ran to the counter just as they were closing the door to the walkway.

On the plane, my mother ordered a rum and Coke before we left the runway. I thought the news must have been too much for her after all. I decided not to bring it up again, instead looking out the window at the men waving their orange flags, giving the plane permission to pull ahead. To fly away.

CHAPTER TWENTY-SIX
diversions for a lazy mind

We shared yet another flight measured by the emptying of tiny airplane bottles of rum and arrived at la Iglesia de Santa Cruz for yet another funeral late the next morning. But this time when I walked through the rubber-strip-covered entrance, I felt a wave of grief hit, nearly knocking me to the stone floor. By the time the service started, the church was packed to the rafters, people standing along each side, peering down from the balconies above, children sitting on the floor in the aisles. I looked around at so many faces paying homage to my great-aunt and felt a swell of pride. She'd influenced so many lives, but none more than mine and my mother's.

We were there for an hour after the mass concluded. So many people wanted to express condolences to my family, to tell us how much Alma had meant to them. I barely held it together, damming the tears in my eyes until I felt them slide down the back of my throat. But that was what Alma would have wanted, for me to be strong…to be like her.

By the time we returned to Alma's house, the hour of the vision was drawing nearer. Would it be back? Would I have another one? I hated being in the house without Alma. Each room felt like my great-aunt had just left, her scent of soil and powder on the air, notes on the piano still ringing. Her absence was something I could feel in my body, a pain that did not cease.

As the minutes ticked by, my heartbeat grew stronger and stronger in my chest, and I couldn't sit still anywhere in the house. Finally, I sought out my mother in the kitchen where she was talking to Tío Ramón. The slur in her voice was already apparent, but I assured myself that she would remember our conversation in the airport even through the alcohol.

But my mother wouldn't acknowledge me. She continued to roll up pieces of ham and pierce them unevenly with toothpicks as she swayed slightly on her dress heels, a battered palm tree in the wind.

"Mom." I tugged on the sleeve of her blouse, feeling very much like I was five years old again. "Mom."

Tío Ramón pointed to me. "Sobrina, I think your daughter is trying to get your attention."

When my mother's eyes finally swung my way, just a glance into their glassy surfaces told me I wouldn't be finding help there. But I had to try; there was no one else to turn to. Not anymore.

"What is it, mi amor?"

I pointed to my watch. "It's just, that thing we talked about yesterday? What if it happens again?"

My mother glanced nervously at Ramón, who was listening with a concerned look on his face as he cut pale white cheese into cubes. Mom grabbed me, her slim fingers digging into the flesh of my upper arm as she started to drag me out into the dining room. I wondered if that painful grip was a genetic trait with all Sanchez women.

"Perdónanos, Tío. Girl talk, you know." Mom flashed that false smile, the one she only used when she was playing the sweet, innocent act. The look was gone by the time she wheeled me around to face her, Alma's curio cabinet blocking us from view.

"Isla, I've been meaning to talk to you about that." She ran her hand over her hair and then the front of her skirt as if she were able to return order to all. "I don't think you should mention your *visions* to anyone here… I'm just not sure they would understand."

"But you said you felt bad I'd gone through them alone—"

"Forget what I said!" The words were a slap, the smell of booze completing the one-two punch. A deep sigh burgeoned with faux patience. "It's just that, Isla, I've been thinking about it, and perhaps they were all dreams. You know, psychic abilities also run in the family. I had this cousin who—"

"No!" I put my hand up between our faces in an improvised wall. "I can't believe you're saying this! How could I know the story of the hurricane? I never even spoke to Rosa! She was in a coma, for God's sake!" I spat out at my mother. I asked myself if this could really be happening again, and in the same room where Alma berated me when I told her about the first vision.

"Shh! Isla, tranquilate!" My mother glanced back toward the kitchen and then locked gazes with me.

As I stared into my mother's age-lined eyes, I saw fear, but what did she have to be afraid of? Obviously, she wasn't worried about me. Then it hit me.

She knew.

My mother knew about the gift before I had told her. "Someone else has seen these visions." My voice was quiet but sharp.

My mother straightened up quickly and looked ready to leave in a huff as was her fashion. But then her shoulders dropped. She pulled out one of the dining room chairs and sank into it as if she were suddenly exhausted.

I could hear my pulse in my ears, thumping with anger and antic-ipation, but I pulled out the neighboring chair, perched quietly, and waited. For what, I didn't know.

My mother sat with her face in her hands, her manicured nails bloodred against her pale olive skin. I was beginning to wonder if that was it, if that was all I was going to learn, when I heard her voice come from between her fingers.

"Alma."

My gasp echoed in the empty dining room. "She...she told you that?"

"Yes, when I was little, eight or nine, I think. Right around the time my grandfather died. Alma and I were close then, even closer than you two were. I was staying overnight here, but I couldn't sleep. In the middle of the night, I wandered out onto the front porch just as Alma was coming through the gate with her gardening gloves on."

I gave a soft laugh. "Yeah, she loved gardening late at night."

"She took off her gloves, and we sat on the front porch in the dark, drinking mango juice, talking, and listening to the coquis. I don't know whether it was because the darkness made her feel safe or what, but she began to talk about things she never had before. She confided in me that since she turned eighteen, she saw visions from the storytellers in the family when they died. About how sometimes they were scary, and sometimes they were marvelous. She told me some of the tales, and it was if her words lifted me off the porch and dropped me into her stories.

"The next day, all Alma had told me was pushing on my skin from the inside, dying to come out. Mother and I were driving to the store, and finally I couldn't stand it anymore and I blurted out everything Alma had told me. You knew your grandmother; you can only imagine what her reaction was. That woman's mind was as closed as a vault."

The whole room was spinning. "Was that why Alma never told stories? Why she said they were diversions for a lazy mind?"

Instead of answering, my mother reached over for the crystal decanter that sat in the center of the table, the amber liquid sloshing behind sparkling glass as she pulled out the stopper and brought the entire bottle to her mouth, ignoring the matching gold-rimmed glasses that sat nearby. After a long swallow, she sighed and wiped her mouth with her ivory silk sleeve, all coquettish pretenses gone.

"Well, that bit of mother-daughter sharing earned Alma an extended stay in the hospital psych ward and me enough of a spanking that I couldn't sit down for a week. Things were never the same between Alma and me after that..." She looked off into the distance, her eyes focused on nothing.

Suddenly, she looked at her watch and jerked to her feet, still holding the bottle to her chest. "Enough of this reminiscing, Isla. I've got to lie down." Clutching the decanter as if it held her afloat, she staggered off to the bedroom, the door slamming with the finality of a period at the end of a sentence.

CHAPTER TWENTY-SEVEN
the scene of the crime

I sat in the dining room for some time, staring at the dust particles dancing in the beams of sun shining through the dining room skylight. The sounds of family busy in the kitchen seemed off-key without Alma's decisive voice among them. Why were we even *in* that house without Alma there? It was like a body without bones, amorphous and lacking purpose. I glanced at my watch... It was 1:59. I could almost feel it coming in the way the air hung about, the tension electrifying the humidity. Then I got an idea.

I walked to the dining room door and checked in either direction. No one was nearby. Tiptoeing toward the front of the house and the foyer, I heard the hum of conversation wafting in from the porch. Reaching the door of Alma's secret room, I stopped for a moment with my hand on the knob, the brass still warm as if Alma had just held it. There was no sound of movement from the gathering now except for the lethargic squeak of rocking chairs and the clink of glassware.

I turned the knob and stopped again. Even though Alma was gone, it still felt wrong, like my great-aunt would suddenly appear and scold me. Actually, given my experience, that wasn't out of the range of possibility. For just a moment, I considered going back to my room to hide under the covers. No, if Alma was going to send these visions, I wanted to see them in the room where the events allegedly took place, the past superimposed on the present. I needed to figure out why they weren't stopping. I was missing something.

Turning the handle all the way, I opened the door only enough to slip through as I'd seen Alma do countless times. I pressed the door closed behind me, keeping my hand on the knob to facilitate a quick escape. My heart was galloping as I looked around. I stood there for a few minutes, sweat pouring down my face, and my first reaction was disappointment. All those years of wondering about the room, imagining all sorts of mysterious and even horrific things the walls could contain, and I found an ordinary room. What had I expected? Bloodstains on the floor? Ghosts hanging about?

Ah, but the ghosts would arrive momentarily.

The scant pieces of furniture were shrouded with sheets, and boxes of books lay scattered around the gray tile floor. The windows, closed and unadorned, allowed the afternoon sun to blaze in unapologetically, making the room impossibly hot. There were no decorations on the walls, but there were white bleached rectangles where mirrors or paintings once hung, and the air lay completely still, dust particles glittering lazily in the sun like confetti.

Noticing the largest piece of furniture near the window, I walked over to it, sidestepping an overflowing box of books. Grabbing the corner of the sheet, I pulled. As the far corner of the piece became exposed, it was what I had expected: Bisabuelo's desk.

Yanking the sheet off the rest of the way, I then ran my hands over the scratched, varnished desktop. In that instant, I saw movement reflected in the wood's surface and looked up just in time to see my great-grandfather, with only the width of the desk between us. I gazed deeply into his dark-brown eyes and saw strength. I also saw fury, but beneath, somewhere in the swirl of dark brown around his pupils, I saw Alma. If they shared blood, could he be entirely bad?

Whipping around, I looked right into the face of the other man. His young eyes were tired, but he had a kind face. What happened between these men to bring them to such a desperate moment? I studied the man's calloused hands and noticed that in addition to the pava in his left hand, he held something in his right. The gun? No, whatever it was, it was small. My bisabuelo approached and their struggle ensued. I crouched down to watch, just a few feet from the men but out of the range of the bullet. I still couldn't make out much of what was being said, the Spanish was too fast, the words blending in the heat of the moment, but I picked up something of Bisabuelo's rant about the dirtying of his roots, reminding me of Ramón's Spanish blood speech from the summer.

The man struggled to ward off the blows and dropped his straw hat to the floor. I tried to see between them, to decipher exactly what was going on—Who pulled the gun? Was it under the man's hat? In Bisabuelo's jacket?—but there was just a tangle of limbs and struggle. Just before the shot rang out, I heard a clink and the metallic sound of something rolling across the floor. My view was blocked by the other man, but above his shoulder, I saw my great-grandfather's eyes widen in shock, his mouth a perfect O as he slid to the floor, directly in front of me. Alma's voice called from the other side of the door, and the man ran to the open window that was locked shut just moments earlier. I heard his body thud to the ground and the rustle of bushes beneath the window. Then Alma rushed in, throwing the door wide, so different from all those years she slipped through. My great-aunt dropped to the floor on the other side of her father, pain and shock clouding her face until she noticed the hat.

Then they were gone, and I was sitting by myself on the dusty floor, still clutching the white sheet. The window was closed again, but the air was stirring like in the wake of a boat.

I tried to think. Had I learned anything new from this one? Then I remembered the clinking sound. If I was in the actual room where it had happened, then…no, it was crazy. What were the chances that whatever was dropped was still there after all those years? Obviously, they had removed the gun, but they wouldn't have known about that other sound, and Alma kept the room exactly as it was that day, and for all the subsequent years, like a shrine.

"Oh, what the hell," I said, my voice sounding unnaturally loud in the abandoned room. I threw the sheet to the floor and began to crawl about on my hands and knees, peering beneath the desk, the surrounding chairs, and tables, behind the cardboard boxes. I scuttled around the desk, shoving the cracked leather chair aside, and ran my hand along the edge of the floor under the window. My fingers trailed in the grime, but I continued all along the edge of the wall until I reached a small end table.

"¿Isla? ¿Dónde estás?" my mother called frantically, her Spanish thick and panicked. Then I heard the rattle of the door. It burst open and Mom was swaying, her fingers wrapped around the door's edge.

Tío Ramón appeared directly behind her and tried to pull her away. "Calm down, Sobrina. What's going on? I think you've had too much to drink. Here, let me take you to your room—"

"No! She's in here, I know it! She could be hurt!"

My mother stumbled through the door as it gave way, and I scrambled to my feet.

My mother's eyes fell on me, and she put her hand to her chest. "Ay, Isla. You're okay. Gracias a Dios." She swayed on her feet again, and Ramón grabbed her by the elbow.

"Yes, yes, querida, Isla's fine. Now let's get you to bed. It's been a hard day…" Then he called to me. "M'ija, what are you doing in here anyway?"

I looked over at the end table. "Nothing, Tío. I was looking for something to read, that's all."

"Oh, you won't find anything in here but boring old textbooks. You know your great-aunt—God rest her soul. She wouldn't have known good reading material if it bit her." He smiled at me and then looked me up and down. "Child, what have you been doing? You're covered in dust! Come out of here and get yourself cleaned up before the guests arrive."

Reluctantly, I followed them out of the room, but before my tío pulled the door shut, I stole a last glimpse of my great-grandfather's office. It looked forlorn, like an empty stage after a performance.

I would get back in there, one way or another. I welcomed a mystery to unravel, like the puzzles Alma and I spent hours putting together. I loved the clean click of the right piece fitting among its neighbors. It was something small I actually had control over. Plus, seeing her every day, in any form, forestalled the need to fully let her go, which I was not sure I'd ever be ready to do.

CHAPTER TWENTY-EIGHT
buying time

I got up the next morning before my mother and tiptoed out of the bedroom. I pulled our door closed and looked around at the empty house, and for just a moment, I wondered if Alma had already gone out.

And then I remembered.

Alma was gone.

The silence seemed oppressive then, almost cruel. It was still so unreal that I'd never see her again. Other than in the vision, but there was little comfort in that. The recurring vision had me feeling anxious all the time, as if the soundtrack of my life was now in a dark, minor key, signaling that something bad was coming. The night before, sleep hadn't come easily. The house felt weirdly unsafe without Alma there. All the gates were locked as usual, the doors shut, but I'd still felt vulnerable. It was weird how a little old lady could make me feel so protected. It was as if she *were* the house.

I made my way to the front room, my bare feet slipping along the tiled floor. After all those years of not being allowed in there, it was almost too easy. As I pulled the door open, it felt a bit like the year my father was first sick and I found my Christmas presents a week early and not only discovered that I had been lied to for years about Santa Claus but also had to pretend to be surprised on Christmas morning so my parents wouldn't know.

I went straight for the corner and the end table. Pulling it from the wall, I dropped to my knees and brushed away a filmy spider-web that joined it to the wall. At first, I saw nothing, but then, in the shadow, I spied something covered in dust. Hoping it wasn't a desiccated spider, I touched my fingers to it, brushing the years of dust away. It was a small gold ring. Grasping it with my fingers, I took a closer look. It was a thin gold band with a tiny diamond chip set into it. So the man had been holding this.

If the woman in the vision were anyone else but Alma, I would have imagined he had romantic intentions, but no. I knew where Alma stood on such issues all too well. "And what do you have to do with this mess?" I asked the ring quietly. But talking to inanimate objects was not going to get answers. I had to talk to someone who could help me figure out the next step to ending the visions. Then I remembered Claridad. The old woman would know what to do.

A door opened in the next room, and I jumped to my feet, brushing off my pajamas. I quietly pushed the end table back against the wall, but as I turned toward the door, my foot kicked something that skittered under the desk. I didn't have much time, but I dropped to my hands and knees and peered beneath the furniture, spying something in the shadow of the desk's far leg. I flattened myself on the floor, my head bumping the underside of the desk, and reached out to the object. I had to stretch my fingers way out but was able to grasp it with the very tips. The sound of running water and the clatter of pots came from the kitchen, and I lurched out, knocking my head again and picking up a length of spiderwebs in my bangs. I brushed them away as I stood and examined the object.

It was a spent bullet.

"Bingo," I whispered.

"Isla?"

I shoved the bullet with the ring in my pajamas' pocket and rushed to the door. As I closed it behind me once again, I thought about how we had a day of family obligations ahead of us. There would be no time to sneak out and go to Claridad's. We were supposed to fly out the next day, so unless I came up with another plan, I was condemned to witness a daily shooting for…how long? The rest of my life? How long before that bullet came *my* way?

That night, Ramón took us to dinner in the Condado, and before the desserts arrived, I said in a voice loud enough for my relatives around the table to hear, "Mom, I think I'd like to stay for a week more."

There was a flurry of enthusiastic responses from our family, and my great-uncle Ramón put his hand on my mother's and said, "I think that's a fine idea, Sobrina. It must be hard for her with my sister gone; they were so close. What do you think?"

My mother stared at me, her eyes seeming to probe for possible motive, but she was unable to say much in front of our family. "What about school? You're only six weeks into the semester."

I was a good student, so this was easy to argue against. "I'm caught up with all my work. My professors won't miss me for one short week. They'll understand. Besides, I can make up what I need to when I get back, I promise." The ball was in my mother's court now.

Mom twisted her lips, eyes still narrowed. "You can't stay all by yourself at Alma's, and I have to go back to work. The job in the Bronx won't—"

"She can stay with me in Old San Juan, Titi Elena. It would give us a chance to hang out some more," my cousin Maria offered from the other end of the table, winking at me, and just like that, I had a partner in crime. I thought I could get used to having people on my side for a change.

"I just don't know..."

A chorus of encouragement piped in, and I looked around at our family gratefully. My mother finally gave in. As Ramón was paying the check, Mom pulled me aside.

"What are you up to?"

I pushed down a flare of anger. "Look, I know you don't want to believe me about the visions, but I have to find out what's going on." *And I certainly can't go through every afternoon of my life getting shot at*, I wanted to add, but I was not going to give her any excuse to drag me back to New Jersey. Or to stay. I needed her gone so I could do some real digging.

My mother stood with her arms crossed tight over her chest.

"Besides, I think Alma's trying to tell me something, and that's why the vision didn't go away after I wrote it down," I added, knowing the connection with Alma would be important to my mother, especially given what happened to her as a child. Solving the mystery could be her chance at redemption as well.

Mom really looked at me now, eyes focused. "But what is she trying to say?"

I shrugged. "Maybe that her father was murdered. I don't know, but I'm missing something, and I intend to find out what." The smiling faces of our family passed by as they filed out of the restaurant. "There's something here, something more than I can see in the vision."

My mother looked away quickly and fiddled with the fabric at the neck of her dress. What was that look in her eyes, I wondered. Guilt? Fear?

But just as suddenly, the look was gone, and Mom threw her head back. "I don't think you can handle this alone. I mean you're just a child, Isla. I'll stay—"

Anger rose in my chest, and I started to push it down as I always had but stopped myself. I was done protecting my mother. "What, you don't think I can handle it? I'm eighteen, for God's sake! And oh, by the way? I've been handling pretty much everything around our house since I was ten!"

Mom turned with a huff. "That's just ridiculous. And if you're going to be disrespectful—"

I forced myself to speak calmly. "I can handle this. I'll be fine. It's just I don't—"

"You don't need me. I get it, Isla."

For an instant, I saw pain in my mother's eyes, and truth. I wondered if I should have held my words back, pushed down my anger as usual. It had felt good in the moment, but...

A woman walked by, and my mother's face changed. "Mercedes? Is that you? Amiga, you look faaaabulous! And so thin!"

And just like that, Mom's switch was thrown to "on."

My mother and Mercedes squealed at each other, and I made my way toward the stairs, following Tío Ramón.

I fingered the small treasures from Alma's front room that nestled in my pocket, as if they were talismans that could bring me peace.

CHAPTER TWENTY-NINE
the airport...again

The next morning, one of my uncle's workmen, Joaquin, drove me and Mom to the airport. As my mother slipped into the back seat, she moved over, leaving room beside her. I hesitated, then opened the front passenger door and slid in. Mom also hesitated, then settled into the middle as if she never expected me to join her and began chatting with Joaquin. Mom and I hadn't said anything to each other since our conversation in the restaurant the night before, and with a stranger in the car, I didn't dare open my mouth for fear of what might escape and poison the air.

I sat and stared out the window. When had all the tin shacks by the highway been replaced by apartment buildings? Clothing hung in garlands across individual balconies, drying in the hot afternoon wind, the blue glow of television sets peeking out from inside. The airport itself had grown big and sprawling. It had happened slowly, year after year. I remembered chickens running through the open-air building in the late '60s when I was little.

Joaquin double-parked in front of the departures entrance and pulled my mother's suitcase from the trunk. "Ten un bien viaje,

Doña Elena," he said with a bow of his head, and he retreated back to the car to give us some privacy for the confrontation that was clearly imminent.

My mother and I stood avoiding each other's eyes and shifting on our feet like kindergartners on the first day. Feeling the tension crescendo, I went to grab the suitcase. "Let me bring this inside for you, Mom."

My mother yanked it back, slamming it against her leg in the process. "I can get it, Isla. I can't help anyone else, so I might as well help myself, right?" The suitcase's plastic feet scraped sideways across the concrete with a nails-on-a-chalkboard screech.

"You've always been good at taking care of *yourself*, Mom!" I shouted back as passersby began to stare. But that was fine with me: I was done with being the quiet, well-behaved girl, tired of the family tradition of pretending problems didn't exist, of keeping secrets. Look where that had gotten us.

We stood there on the airport's sidewalk, glaring at each other, each refusing to budge. Finally, I huffed and turned away, heading for the car.

"Isla?"

I stopped with my fingers wrapped around the front passenger door handle and looked back at my mother.

"About what you said last night at the restaurant… I–I know I haven't been much support to you with what you're going through, with anything really. It's just that…doing this all alone, and all this…death. I'm so tired."

I let go of the door handle and took one careful step back.

My mother said in a whisper, "The visions…the last time I talked about them… Well, it ended badly."

"With Alma."

She nodded. "I just worry about this being misunderstood, you know? People can be so cruel."

My voice was hard, harder than I intended. "Tell me something I don't know, Mom."

I thought my mother would get defensive, angry, but instead, her face collapsed and paled as her eyes filled. "Isla, I guess what I'm trying to say is that I'm sorr—"

I watched as my mother's lips froze, waiting for the rest of the word that I knew would never come. She wouldn't say it. Or perhaps she couldn't. A year, or even a month earlier, that would have infuriated me, and I would have buried it deep where it could fester. But as I looked at my mother, I decided that the almost-apology was the best she could offer. I walked back, and after a moment when we just stood there, my mother pulled me in, hugging me as the morning sun beat overhead.

"I'm sorry too, Mom," I whispered into her hair.

"Please be careful," she whispered back. I could feel her tears soaking through the fabric of my shirt. Though I felt bad for her, I wondered if I should be crying. I wondered if I *could* cry anymore. Eventually my mother broke the embrace, picked up her suitcase, and walked through the sliding glass doors of the terminal without looking back.

CHAPTER THIRTY

two halves of a whole

On the way back from the airport, I asked Joaquin to drop me off in Bayamón so I could help Maria sort through things at Alma's house. I also planned to sneak out to see Claridad, but I didn't divulge that part of the plan to him. When we pulled into the entrance, I was saddened by the stones missing from the wall, by the vines that were slowly encroaching on the driveway, and by the increased volume of the city that pressed down on Alma's small square of jungle. I found Maria in Alma's bedroom, the radio playing a rhythmic cumbia, surrounded by piles of newspapers and magazines, a respiratory mask secured around her face.

I noticed the sweat running into the white fabric covering my cousin's nose and mouth. I gestured to the face mask. "That bad, huh?"

"Oh, Isla, you don't know the half of it! She has papers here that are fifty years old and falling apart in my hands. The woman threw away nothing!"

I smiled at the thought of Alma, then felt an ache in my chest. I cleared my throat. "Can I help?" I indicated a pile of papers and photographs that was teetering forward from the back of the closet in an impressive imitation of the Tower of Pisa.

"Ay, por favor, go for it!"

I rolled up my sleeves and sat on a wooden chair in front of the closet. Reaching for the top packet of envelopes—a rubber-band-wrapped stack of paid bills—I almost knocked the entire pile to the floor. I managed to shove it back up against the rear wall and began to sort piece by piece, throwing 98 percent into the overflowing trash bag that sat between us.

As we worked, we talked. Really talked, and I found that unlike most adults I knew, my cousin really listened. After a lull in conversation, Maria asked, "Prima, how is college? Do you have many friends?"

I felt my throat close up, and I started to push the words back down as I always had. But Maria was looking at me so earnestly, like she really cared. I couldn't lie, but I didn't wish to disappoint my cousin with the truth. "Not really. I mean, I've only been there for a few weeks, and I have to concentrate on my studies, you know?"

"Yes, that's most important, but a girl has to have some fun, verdad?" It was said with a kind smile, but underneath I could see other questions, other concerns. And so for the first time, the words made their way back up, slowly.

"School has always been hard for me."

"I don't believe that! You're so smart."

"Not academically..."

She nodded. "Socially."

I looked at her and wondered what she could possibly understand about that. "I mean, after my father died, Mom...needed me more at home. So I didn't have time to make friends, go to parties, things like that."

She kept working but looked at me with soft eyes that didn't hold pity but rather sadness.

"I've never really felt comfortable in social situations. I always feel like I don't..."

"Fit in?" Maria finished for me.

I watched her for a second. Was she mocking me? No, Maria would never do that. "Do you understand that feeling?"

She gave a bitter laugh. "Yes, Prima, all too well."

She was beautiful and outgoing and smart. I just couldn't see it. "But...how—"

Maria cut me off. "There are other ways one can be an outsider, Isla."

I felt as though I'd overstepped, so I quickly changed the subject and asked about her job. As she talked about ad campaigns and corporate clients, I pictured her clicking along on her kitten-heeled mules through marble corridors, her long hair pulled back, a stylish outfit on her trim frame, a pile of files balanced in one arm.

The cleanup work was tedious, but the conversation made it enjoyable. At one point, I looked out the window at the greenery that was rapidly enveloping the house, untamed.

Untamed.

Since Alma was gone, there would be no more workers on the grounds. I cleared my throat. "So do you ever see José? I mean, around?"

Maria smiled. "Yes, sometimes in San Juan. He just started his first year at the university. And no, he doesn't have a girlfriend."

"Really? I mean, really. That's great. That he started at college, I mean." I kept my gaze focused on the pile I was sorting through, wondering if my face was as red as it felt or if I could say "I mean" one more time, just to properly seal my humiliation.

"I could arrange a get-together, you know, a group of people including José—"

"No!" I didn't let her finish the sentence. "No, really, not necessary. I was just asking." The last thing I needed was an audience of Maria's friends to bear witness to my social ineptitude. She was watching me; I could feel it.

"Hmm. Okay, Prima."

We continued with our work, and I was silent, trying to think of anything other than José, or my mother, or…Alma.

"Oh! Look, here's a picture of Titi Elena when she was young! Your mother was such a beauty."

Maria handed me a photograph, and my mother looked out at me from within the white trimmed edges, her face framed by a tumble of auburn hair, her lips and nails red and glamorous, and her eyes clear, bright, and full of possibility. "Yes, she was." But it was as if the photograph began to take on weight, my fingers bowing with it, and I put it down on the sewing table behind me, turning my back on my mother's sparkling eyes.

I could feel Maria watch me put it aside and bury my gaze in the work once again. "Isla, I've been wanting to ask you, is your mother okay? I mean, I knew she liked to drink, but I was surprised to see her so…"

"Tanked? Out of control? Totally humiliating?" I was shocked by the words that came from my own lips, but I'd been taken by surprise by the straightforward question. It was so un-Sanchez. I looked at Maria for a moment and realized that my cousin *was* different, that she'd always talked more openly with me than the rest of the family. Was it a generational thing? Whatever the reason, my chest ached with gratitude, and the next words tumbled out like water as I stared at the floor.

"She's not okay, Maria. Not at all. She drinks every night, and sometimes I have to hide the car keys so she won't kill herself or someone else. I have to do the grocery shopping, or we won't have anything to eat, and the laundry, or we'd have no clean clothes. I never know what she's going to say or do that would humiliate us both. Luckily, she manages to make it to work every day, but that's about it."

Maria was openly crying now. "Isla, why didn't you tell us? Did you talk to Alma about this?"

"No, God no. If I did, she would have insisted on moving me here."

"But you love it here! We would have taken care of you!"

I was crying now. "I know. That's why I love it here, why the Sanchezes mean so much to me. But if I did, who would have taken care of Mom? She would have killed herself by now, one way or another."

"Oh, honey, that is not your responsibility. She's a grown woman who is supposed to be taking care of *you*."

I nodded, my throat tight. "I know. But now that Alma is gone, there's no point."

"What are you talking about? You could come live with me!"

My head snapped over to look at her, and I dropped the papers to the floor and pulled her into a desperate hug. As we cried together, I wasn't sure I could handle the expanse of love and gratitude that built in my chest. Maria gently ran her hands over my hair like Alma used to, and my breathing slowed. Riding on the humid midday air, I could almost hear the strains of "Für Elise."

When we finally separated and emptied half a box of tissues, I let out a deep breath, exhaustion flooding my body, but also relief.

"Maria, I cannot tell you how much that offer means to me. But at this point, I think I'm in this for the duration. I can't give up on Mom now."

"We can get her help."

I shook my head; I knew my mother too well. "It has to be her idea."

After a cold drink and the other half box of tissues, we resumed our tasks. I finished up one stack and began to tackle another, farther back, the papers more yellowed and the dates on the correspondence older with each piece. About three-quarters of the way down, I encountered a parcel of old photographs tied together with faded ribbon around their yellowed edges. The top picture was of a construction site, a foundation amid a tropical clearing. It appeared to have been taken in early morning: moisture hung over the ground as if the house were being built on a cloud.

I pulled on the end of the bow and the ribbon fell apart in my hand, dust rising from the pile as mist from the photograph. In the next image, the walls began to grow from the ground. Sun-toasted men with their bare backs to the camera were bent in examination of their work. As the photos progressed, so did the house; its roof appeared, then the windows. Like a child's flip book, the building magically materialized with each turn of a photograph, until the last, a torn one, where the house was completely done, and I could see that it was Alma's house, the very house in which we sat. The walls were new and clean, the foliage controlled and groomed, the white paint gleaming in the midday sun.

There was a line of people standing across the front walkway, many holding shovels and tools. Next to last from the ripped end was my great-grandfather, a broad smile below his thick mustache, his arm around a young woman's shoulders. I looked closely and saw that it was the young Alma I knew from the visions. She wore a white dress, her dark curls cascading down the high, lace-trimmed neckline. Her eyes were vibrant, alive, and I could tell that this Alma was fun-loving and mischievous, a far cry from her pious and matronly future self. To Alma's right was the edge of a dark arm: the line of people must have continued beyond the tear. Who tore it, and why?

Something about the photo seemed important, so I placed it near my backpack and returned to my work. When I was done with the second pile, my hands black with dust, I asked Maria where I should turn next. Soon I would have to find an excuse to run over to Claridad's, but I found I was enjoying the work. It felt like Alma was there with us, and I wanted that feeling to continue for just a little while longer.

"How about up there," Maria said, pointing to the narrow shelf that ran the length of the closet near the top.

I stood in front of the open sliding door and stepped onto the raised floor of the closet to reach, holding on to the edge of the shelf for balance. The wooden plank upended with my weight, and everything fell to the floor. I carefully laid the shelf back on its brackets before stepping down to clean up the mess. As I bent down, I noticed a rectangle of silver satin among the pile of faded hatboxes spilling lace handkerchiefs and recycled cookie tins rattling with sewing supplies. I picked it up and recognized it as an evening handbag with a rhinestone butterfly clasp. "Boy, this must have been from Alma's *way* past! A bit festive for her, don't you think?" I held it up to show Maria.

"Ay, Isla, you just never know what kind of youths these old ladies had." She winked at me as I tried to picture our matronly great-aunt with the glamorous accessory in place of her omnipresent patent leather purse. "On second thought, maybe not Alma!" Maria added as if she had read my mind.

We broke out in giggles until I had to sit down on the floor and catch my breath. "Maybe the dust is getting to us."

I turned the purse over in my hands. I pried open the glittery latch, the butterfly twisting before setting the purse's flap free. I bent back the silky top and peered inside. Except for a lonely safety pin, it was empty. Then I noticed the pocket on the back side beneath the designer's label. I slipped my index finger in and felt a piece of paper or cardboard. Certain it must have been a missed price tag or movie ticket stub, I lifted it out. Holding it between my fingers, I noticed a familiar torn edge. I jumped to my feet, knocking over a pile of magazines that had been teetering on my right.

"Isla? Are you okay?" Maria pulled her dust mask away from her mouth.

I glanced up toward the sound of my cousin's voice. "Oh, yes, I'm fine. It's just…this handbag would go perfectly with that dress you talked me into buying."

"Then by all means, Prima, take it! It's yours. One less thing we have to riffle through." She smiled and returned to her sorting.

I looked at my watch; it was already 2:04. Only a few minutes remained before our great-grandfather's daily appearance.

"Why don't you take a break, Isla. You've been a great help already." Maria gestured around to the surrounding piles. "Besides, this is my hair shirt, not yours!"

"I think I will take a break, thanks. My back is killing me." Feigning nonchalance, I grabbed the purse and the first torn piece from the desk and shuffled off to the kitchen under the pretense of getting a glass of water.

On the patio off the kitchen, I stood and looked out the gates to the foliage behind the house as the vision played out in front of me. I didn't want to watch it again; it was too frustrating not knowing what was going on. And it was so violent that afterward I always felt as if I had been in the middle, struggling with the two men. I concentrated on how the sun illuminated the dark-green leaves still wet from the noon rain and stared at the web of black iron bars, anything but focus on the drama unfolding yet again. But just as the scene was coming to an end, just after the man jumped through the open window, I caught sight of someone in the bushes beyond.

A woman.

Was she in the vision or really outside?

It was all blending together. I rushed to where the man's feet had just been at the ghostly windowsill and caught a glimpse of a gray flowered dress among the shrubbery, stepping back to hide among the branches.

Then she was gone. I rushed to open the gate and ran out into the trees, certain I would find the woman there walking among the palm trunks. My steps pounded hollowly on the soft earth as I searched. There was no woman other than Alma in the vision, was there? I would have seen her before. But I hadn't been looking at the vision this time; my focus had been not on the players in the room but beyond. I ran among the trees like a drunken squirrel but found no one. I would have to wait another day to get a better look.

I walked back to the house to give Maria an excuse so I could go on my errand and grab the other half of the photograph. I ran inside and picked up the handbag from the kitchen counter, fumbled with the pocket again, and pulled out the first half. I stared at it, the light pouring in through the window and illuminating the ghosts of the past. It was as I suspected: the other portion of the photo from the pile in the bedroom. I placed the original piece next to it, the torn edges fitting together like puzzle pieces.

In the new and smaller piece, the line of people continued with three dark-skinned men, each sporting a belt of tools around his waist or a building implement in his hands. I zeroed in on the man to the far left, along the torn edge, who stood next to Alma until they were so abruptly torn apart. I pulled the photo closer until my nose almost touched the cracked and sepia surface and gasped. With his neat but threadbare clothes, the deep-set eyes, he was unmistakable.

It was the man from the vision.

CHAPTER THIRTY-ONE
learning her place

"Maria, I'm just going to take a quick walk around the block." I waved my hand like a fan in front of my face. "The dust and all. I need some fresh air." I braced myself for the inevitable argument.

"Of course. Just be careful, okay?" With that, she went back to disposing of the ancient pile of newspapers under the bed.

I smiled as I walked toward the back. It was so unusual to be trusted to be on my own. I had expected Maria to say something like, "No! You can't walk alone. I'll go with you. Let me just get my straw handbag and my Smith & Wesson .22."

I locked up the back-patio gate and shuffled along the walkway, glancing back at the spot where the mystery woman had appeared. What I didn't know about the vision seemed to be increasing, and the answers remained elusive. I jumped the wall easily and took off for Claridad's at a jog.

As I rounded the corner, I saw several people waving goodbye to the old woman, greasy-bottomed bags in their hands. I could smell the bacalaito from where I stood, and my mouth watered from the bready, salty smell of the codfish fritters. The last time I'd been there, there had been no food left in the case so I imagined it must be good. I checked my pocket and found the twenty-dollar bill Mom had forced on me for emergencies. Well, as far as I was concerned, this qualified as an emergency as I could bring some back to Maria as a cover for the trip and because the smell had brought on an overwhelming craving.

I walked up to the counter, and Claridad's eyes widened when she saw my smiling face.

"Ah, the cuentista blanca is back."

I bristled at the classification as a white storyteller, but I had to be polite if I was to get help. "Señora, I..." The woman crossed her arms over her chest tightly in impatience, and I felt my courage leave in a whoosh. "Umm...I wanted to get two bacalaitos...and"—I looked around the golden lit case—"two alcapurrias de carne."

I watched the woman shove the food into a paper bag, and she gave me my change. I took a deep breath and spoke. "And I was wondering if you might be able to help me. About what we talked about the last time?"

Claridad pushed the bag across the worn counter and simply stared at me. She was not going to make it easy.

I pushed on regardless. "You know, the visions?"

Nothing, not even a blink of her large brown eyes.

I blundered ahead. "Since my great-aunt died, I've been getting visions of something that happened when she was younger. But they're not going away when I write them down, like the other visions. Do you know why?"

The woman sighed but left her guard well in place. "Every cuentista has their own way of dealing with the visions."

I waited for more, but Claridad just started to wipe down the counter. "But...do you remember a shooting that happened at our family's house back when Alma...and you were young?"

"I don't pay attention to the lives of rich people. I have enough to worry about with my own family." She reached forward with her thin, birdlike arms and wiped the counter right in front of me, spraying the cleaner so closely I could taste lavender.

"Oh, we're not rich! I'm—"

Claridad slammed down the bottle of cleaner and the rag and looked at me with fiery eyes. "Those shoes, are they new?"

I looked down at my Reeboks, confused. "Yes, but—"

"Does your family live in a nice house? New car? Do you go out to dinner?"

"Well, yes, but I don't see—"

"Have you ever seen *anyone* in your family clean a toilet?"

I stuttered at this seemingly ridiculous question, but then I stopped and thought about it. Once a week, I'd come home and the house smelled like ammonia and the bathroom was sparkling, the toilet water turned a magical blue. Lily. I didn't even know her last name, where she lived, or if she had children of her own. I looked at the ground feeling chastised, my eyes filling.

The old woman must have felt pity for me because she put her papery hand on mine and leaned forward a bit. "M'ija, I can't help you. You need to talk to someone who was there."

I lifted my eyes to meet Claridad's. "But my family doesn't talk to me like you do! They won't!"

"Did I say talk to family?" The woman smiled, her pink tongue pressing against her teeth, and I couldn't help smiling back. "No, m'ija, find someone who was there who is not a Sanchez, who has no horse in the race."

I thought of the photograph with the line of people and nodded, tears spilled onto my hot cheeks. "Okay, gracias, Señora."

Claridad, still smiling, wrapped up a golden tostón and handed it to me. "Here, amor, eat this and by the time you finish it, you will feel better. I promise."

I took it and breathed in its deep-fried goodness. "Gracias, Señora." I picked up the bag of food and headed back the way I'd come, taking a bite of the piping-hot fritter and closing my eyes as the tastes of salt and garlic and starchy plantain hit my tongue. As I walked, I thought of how Claridad viewed the Sanchez family, my family. I'd never thought about where we fit within the island's societal structure. In Leonia, New Jersey, our house was like hundreds of others. There were poorer people, sure, but there were many families who were wealthier. Then José's words from the political rally and the reason he wouldn't eat the quenepas came back to me, and I felt like I was seeing things I hadn't before.

By the time I arrived at the property's wall, the tostón was eaten and I was feeling good. Did Claridad have her own set of powers, or was it just the starchy nurturing of fried plantain?

I had my hand on the door latch when an idea struck. I turned around and ran toward the front of the house, took a right, and jogged down to the strip of businesses Ramón and I had driven by earlier that summer. I saw the simple storefront up ahead, the profusion of iron bars and security systems the only hint as to what they sold inside. I pressed the buzzer to the right of the door of "Esteban's Guns." If you had told me a week earlier that I would be waiting for entry to a gun shop on an urban street in Puerto Rico instead of sitting in philosophy class, I would have laughed. But there I was.

The buzzer sounded and I jumped, just a little. I opened the door and let myself inside. The air-conditioning was on full blast, the floor clean and polished to a high gloss. The small store had glass cases that ran along both sides and across the back, with assorted gleaming weapons lovingly arranged on each shelf. The wall was covered with pegboard where all sorts of accoutrements of the trade hung: holsters, silencers, cleaning equipment, and a plethora of unidentifiable weapon-related items.

"Good afternoon, young lady! May I help you?" A gentleman was smiling at me from behind one of the counters. He was tall, broad, and handsome, I guessed about my mother's age, his salt-and-pepper hair neatly styled, his matching mustache perfectly trimmed. Esteban, I presumed. I wondered if I should be nervous given this man ran a shop that carried nothing but deadly weapons, but he had the deepest dimples and the kindest brown eyes I'd ever seen, so my nerves dissipated.

"Hi. I hope so." I reached into my pocket as I walked, and for a split second, I wondered if that wasn't the best move in a gun shop, but then I caught my image in some mirrors behind the counter and realized how ridiculous that thought was. I couldn't even kill spiders, for God's sake. "I have this bullet, and I'm trying to determine what kind of gun it came from." I placed it in Esteban's palm.

He took it but kept his eyes on my face. "You're a little young to be a detective, I think, yes?"

I laughed and thought of José. "You'd be surprised. No, it's a family item. An antique. I'm just wondering."

He pulled a pair of black-rimmed reading glasses down from his forehead and examined the bullet. "It's from a 30/30, probably from the 1920s or '30s. Very common in those days."

"Would you say it was something that a farmer or businessman might have had around back then?"

"Seguro, of course. In those days, the island was much like the Wild West. A man had to protect his family, his property."

Damn. So that wasn't going to be all that helpful. It pointed to it being Bisabuelo's gun that fired in the vision. "So it was from his handgun…" I said more to myself than to the shop proprietor.

"Handgun? No. This is from a rifle."

My head shot up. "What? A 30/30 was a rifle?"

"No, there were 30/30 handguns."

"Oh."

He peered at the bullet again. "But there were also 30/30 rifles, and that was what this came from." He pointed at the marks that twisted around the sides of the bullet like candy-cane markings. "See these striations? You can tell by the length of them that it had a longer shaft to travel through." He gestured with the bullet as if it were turning while moving forward. Then he carefully put it down on the black velvet tray in front of him. "Definitely a rifle."

The shot in the trees. Alma's voice echoed in my head. Maybe she wasn't talking about Abuela's monkeys.

My heart was racing as we both regarded the small metallic cylinder. Such a tiny thing holding such big information. Did this mean there was another shooter? Was that what she was trying to tell me? Was *this* the bullet that killed my great-grandfather? Or was it from target practice or hunting? I came to get one question answered but ended up with so many more.

Esteban coughed. "Can I help you with anything else, miss?"

I felt my face heat up. "Yes, sorry, thank you! I mean, no! This has been very helpful." I put the bullet in my pocket, picked up the bag of food from the counter, and backed up as I talked. "Thank you."

He smiled at me, as if every day gringa teenagers came in with antique bullets asking questions. "A su orden, señorita. I am at your service." He bowed at the waist. Actually bowed. It was as if he had been transported from another era, but luckily that was just what I had needed.

My head was spinning as I walked back, and when I opened the front gate of Alma's house, I realized I was whistling. This mystery was getting interesting, and I felt I was closer to understanding Alma's message.

CHAPTER THIRTY-TWO
puzzle pieces

Maria had to go in to work for a meeting late that afternoon, so I spent a couple of hours listening to music in her living room, staring at the photograph of Alma, and thumbing through fashion magazines. When she got home, she insisted I borrow one of Valentina's formfitting black dresses, and when we stepped out the front door to head to dinner, I felt grown-up for the first time. We went to a restaurant on Calle de San Francisco that played loud salsa music and was filled with young people drinking bright frozen cocktails who all seemed to know Maria. The owner greeted her by name, and she kissed both his cheeks before he led us to a table in the back.

The waiter came up to the table, his eyes darting to Maria as he asked us what we'd like to drink. Maria smiled at me. "Would you like to have your first real piña colada?"

My throat tightened. I was, in fact, legally allowed to drink on the island. But when I thought of my mother... "Just a Coca-Cola, please."

I was afraid Maria would be disappointed, that this was a test of how adult I was, and I had failed. But she just smiled and said, "Bueno! Make that two Coca-Colas, por favor."

She ordered food too, and after the waiter left, I said, "You didn't need to do that. You could have had a drink."

Maria did that dismissing thing with her hand again. "Forget it, Prima. I have a meeting first thing tomorrow anyway. So what did you do while I was at work this afternoon?"

That was my opening. Though Maria hadn't been alive when the photo was taken, she would certainly know more than me. "I listened to some of your new-wave albums, read for a while...and then I cleaned up that purse I got at Alma's." I reached into my backpack. "And I found something inside. A photo." I laid out the two halves side by side on the table.

Maria turned them around and smiled. "Wow, *that's* a piece of history. Look at how clean and new Alma's house was! And she was such a beauty."

"I was wondering who this man is—" I pointed to the man next to Alma. "Here."

Maria peered at the photo. "Hmm...I've never seen him before."

I slumped down in my chair, disappointed at yet another dead end.

"But him I remember." Maria pointed to another person in the photo. "That's definitely Chachu. He worked for our family for years."

I perked up at this.

"He was a charming rascal. I remember him flirting with my mother." Maria smiled at the memory. "Not in a creepy way, just... charming in that old-school caballero way."

"Is Chachu still around?"

"No."

I slumped again. Why couldn't I make some sort of headway? "So he died?"

"Oh no, he's still alive and kicking, just not around here. He retired to Vieques a few years back."

I perked up again. I felt a bit like a jack-in-the-box. "Where's Vieques?"

"It's a tiny island off the eastern coast of Fajardo."

"I'd like to go talk to him. Is Vieques far?"

Maria looked at me, her interest piqued. "Talk to Chachu? Why?"

I had to approach this carefully, come up with a mundane response so as not to arouse suspicion. "I want to get some stories for an anthropology course, about the history of agriculture on the island. And since he's been around so long…"

Maria nodded. She seemed to accept this, and I took a relieved breath. "The trip would involve an hour drive each way and a ferry ride. It would be an entire day. I'd be happy to take you, Prima, but I have a presentation to give this week. We can ask Tío if he has someone—"

"No!" I hadn't intended to shout. Maria was staring at me now. "I mean, I don't want Tío to think I'd rather talk to Chachu than him. It might…make him feel bad." I gathered up the photo halves and placed them within the pages of the novel in my bag.

Maria narrowed her eyes but didn't press.

"I could take a cab to the ferry terminal."

"No way, I won't let you do that. If the return ferry comes in too late, and it usually does, I don't want you waiting around Fajardo in the dark looking for a cab. We'll have to think of something else."

I was focusing on cutting up the crackling pork on my plate when I heard Maria say, "Well! Look who's here!"

I glanced up with the fork halfway to my mouth to see José standing next to the table smiling down at me. I couldn't believe he could have grown any more handsome over a few short weeks, but the proof was standing right in front of me. He was wearing a thin, cotton shirt that was open enough to expose his smooth, muscular chest, his brown skin warm against the bright white fabric. His jeans were well worn and soft, and the curls of his hair looked like they were still wet from the shower.

"Uh, José, hi."

"Isla, Maria, how nice to see you." Then he looked just at me. "I heard you were back on the island, Isla. I hoped I would run into you."

My heart revved as if my foot were stuck on the accelerator.

Maria was beaming, and her insistence on the dress suddenly seemed suspicious. "Would you like to join us?" Maria asked, kicking my chair with her high heel. "Pull up a chair next to Isla."

As José sat, I caught the spicy scent of his aftershave, and my head spun a bit.

After he was settled, he put his hand on mine. "Isla, I wanted to tell you how sorry I am for your loss. I know Doña Alma was very important to you."

I looked down at the pile of our hands. "Thanks," I whispered. I felt the muscles in my throat constrict and prayed that I wouldn't begin crying.

José watched me for a moment and then changed the subject, seeming to sense my grief. "So what were you two talking about before I interrupted?" he asked. He took his hand away and mine felt exposed, cold.

Maria jumped right in before I could say a word. "Isla needs to get to Vieques tomorrow for some family business, but I have other obligations, so we were trying to come up with an alternative means of transportation."

"I have to go to Fajardo tomorrow to get some supplies for my father, and I would be happy to take you," José offered.

"No...really, I can—"

"Oh, don't be silly, Prima. This works out perfectly..." Maria dragged out the *r* and I fantasized about strangling her right then and there with her stylish designer necklace. "It's settled then. Now, José, what would you like? Waiter?"

The next hour was a blur. I continually reminded myself that this was just José, my childhood partner in crime, but then I would catch him staring at me and I would get all flustered again. Maria kept the conversation going and José was his usual charming self, but then his jean-coated leg brushed mine, and it was as if he were electrically charged. I jumped and knocked my soda into my lap.

He rushed to procure a stack of napkins from the waiter as I grimaced at Maria.

"Well." Maria smiled at me. "I think *you're* cut off!"

With the sticky soda drying on Valentina's dress, we called it a night. I muttered a rushed goodbye to José, mortified.

When we got back to the apartment, I tore off the dress and threw myself on the bed. Only then did my heart begin to slow. I was lying there staring at the ceiling, thinking it was easier to endure violent phantoms than be subjected to another evening like that, when I heard Maria in the doorway.

"Wow, you have got it bad for that boy."

I sat straight up. "What are you talking about?"

She came in and sat on the edge of the bed. "You're a wreck around him."

I dropped back down. "My whole life is a wreck, Maria."

Maria reclined next to me, using her arm to prop up her head. "I know, Prima, but maybe this could be a good part of your life, you know?"

I threw my arm over my face.

"José is such a nice guy, and he really seems to be taken with you."

I pulled my arm away and gaped at my cousin. "What? Are you crazy? What would he see in me?"

"Isla, *you're* the crazy one! You're cute and charming, and you have this funny little New Jersey accent when you speak Spanish that—"

"What?"

"Never mind. What I mean is, what wouldn't he like about you? And you're going to have to learn to talk to him if you're going to ride in a car with him for two whole hours tomorrow!" She smiled gleefully.

I smacked her arm. "Yes, I have *you* to thank for that!"

"You can thank me later." Maria stood and started walking for the door, then stopped. "You're not nervous about your safety, are you? José's an honorable guy, or I wouldn't let you take off with him alone. You know that, right? His father, grandfather, and uncles worked for the Sanchez family… We know them well. I mean, I promised to keep you and your honor safe and secure." She did an overly dramatic curtsy, fanning out an imaginary skirt over her tight leather pants.

"What? Promised to whom?" Somehow, I knew it wasn't my mother.

"Tío Ramón. He gave me a fifteen-minute lecture about how he trusted me to watch out for you, how you were young and impressionable, and that it was my duty to keep you safe. I didn't tell him that I thought you could handle yourself. I just nodded and said 'Sí, Tío, of course, Tío, I will, Tío.'"

"He actually called you to talk about *me*?"

"Yes. Why?"

"Wow. It's just...that's so weird."

Maria cocked her head sideways. "Weird? How is that weird?"

"I'm kind of used to no one paying attention."

"Welcome to my world, chica."

"It must be nice."

"Nice? Nice? You can't cross the street without some family member nosing into what you're doing. Can't sleep with someone without the whole world knowing on this tiny island!"

"Sleep with someone? You're not"—I lowered my voice to a whisper—"sexually active, are you?" I opened my mouth in mock astonishment.

"Of course not!"

Maria picked up a small decorative pillow from the edge of the bed and hurled it at me while skittering through the doorway and toward her bedroom.

I lay there for a while staring at the ceiling and processing. It was so odd to think that my family had discussions about me when I wasn't there. Even weirder that they worried about me. On one hand, it was slightly infuriating and invasive: I was used to being left to my own devices. On the other, the idea that my family here cared enough about me that they discussed my safety was a warm blanket around my shoulders.

CHAPTER THIRTY-THREE
little girl island

When I heard the honk the next morning, I considered hiding in the bathroom until he went away. Truthfully, I'd never ridden in a car alone with a boy my age, but the clock running down to the next vision lacked patience. José was standing by the truck, holding the door open. He had his work clothes on, olive-green khakis with a matching fitted T-shirt emblazoned with the logo of his father's company. The color brought out the warmth in his skin and made me think of lush green forests, not to mention how the soft cotton stretched tight across his chest. I said good morning in a small voice and slid onto the seat, staying so close to the door that he had trouble closing it. We didn't say much as we headed out of San Juan and merged onto Route 3 heading east. Normally people felt compelled to fill silence with jabber, but José seemed totally comfortable with it. Ironically, I was the one who finally spoke.

"I...I've never been to Vieques. What's it like?"

"Ah, then you're in for a treat. It's almost untouched, much less developed than the main island. And it has some of the most beautiful beaches in the Caribbean."

"I don't think I'll have time to visit the beach this trip."

"Perhaps one day when you have more time, I can take you there."

I tried to smile, but with the ice-cold fear in my belly, I imagined it manifested as more of a grimace. I was grateful when he changed the subject.

"You know that there's a bioluminescent bay there?"

"What's that?"

"It's a bay surrounded by mangroves where there are microscopic creatures in the water that light up when you move them. It's magic, like swimming among the stars."

I looked out the window and tried to imagine what that must be like.

"Are you going to visit family there?" José asked.

"Not really family…someone who worked for my great-grandfather. His name is Chachu."

José smiled. "Ah yes, I remember him from when I was little. He is quite a character." He said this last word like it was in Spanish, and I thought it should never be said any other way.

"You were quite a character when you were little," I said, imitating his accent. "Do you remember when you ran around Alma's house, like, twenty times with a towel tied around your neck, pretending you were a superhero?"

He laughed. "Yes, I would have made it twenty-one times if you hadn't tripped me!"

"Tripped you? Oh no, that was totally your fault, not mine!"

"My fault?"

"Well, I suppose you think I put that root there? The one you tripped on?"

"Well, the Sanchez family has always had a way with plants. I wouldn't be surprised."

We beamed at each other, and I began to relax as I always had with José.

He asked about Columbia, about my mother. I gave short, upbeat answers. Why spoil such a pleasant drive with the truth about my life? Besides, I was still exhausted from baring all with Maria the day before. Then it was my turn to ask the questions.

"How are things going for you at UPR so far?"

"Incredible! There's so much to learn and so many classes I want to take. That first day when I walked on to the campus, I was so... nervous."

I couldn't picture José nervous. Compared to me, he was always so calm, like the surface of a pool next to the restless ocean. "Why were you nervous?"

His attention was on the traffic ahead, the dart and dodge game that was driving on the island, but I could tell he was thinking about my question, translating the Spanish of his thoughts and emotions to the English of the conversation. "It's that...I'm from a very different place than San Juan. It's hard to imagine how different when it isn't that far on a map."

I remembered Alma's comment from so long ago about his "backward town." I felt old anger stir my blood.

"I guess I thought all the other students would be from rich families and know so much more about the world. I've never been off the island. I was afraid I wouldn't—"

"Fit in?"

He looked at me, and in that instant, an understanding passed between us. It wasn't just Maria and me; it seemed he too knew what it was like to be on the outside looking in. When his eyes finally broke away and returned to the road ahead, there was a moment when the air felt thick and neither of us looked at each other or said anything. It was like sharing a secret with someone close to you, handing them a part of you from deep inside, which brought on a temporary shyness. It seemed right to me that we would share this. He had been the first person I'd talked to about my father, about how scared I was.

I saw the sign for the rain forest and knew we were not far. I had been dreading this trip earlier, yet it was flying by.

"I'm taking a class about the history of the island, studying the Taino Indians. Did you know, this part of the island was considered very sacred?"

I glanced up over the side of the highway, above the stores and the rows of houses, and up at the mist-framed peaks of the rain forest. "I haven't been to El Yunque since I was little. The last time I was there was with my mom and d—" The word stopped short on the percussive *d*, and I froze. I could tell José was sneaking looks at me, but my mind could form no words. I waited for him to attempt to pull feelings from me like so many people tried to, but instead, we drove in silence, and I was grateful.

His soft voice gently broke the surface. "I was very close to my abuela. She took care of me and my brothers when my parents worked, was always there when we came home with food for us, sewed our clothes, cut our hair. When she died, no one could console me. I spent a week lying in her vegetable garden, yowling up at the sky, at God, for taking her. But in time, I moved on, let the garden get overgrown. After a couple of years, I realized I could no longer picture her face or remember what her voice sounded like." He glanced over at me. "The thing is, I was angry at myself for that. How could I forget someone so important?"

I knew José was trying to help, but the thing was, I could still clearly see my father, all six foot two of him. Premature white hair, cherry-scented pipe smoke, a huge personality and a booming voice that filled any room. The problem was that whenever I saw him in my mind, he would start like that but would always deflate into the shrunken visage of his last days, like a forgotten balloon a week after a birthday party, the wrinkles in the lifeless rubber the only remnant of its former robustness.

"We're here, the ferry terminal."

How had we gotten there already? I chastised myself for spending too much time lost in my own dark thoughts.

"I'll be back before five thirty, which is when your ferry should arrive. If you have any problems, here's my father's office number." He handed me one of his father's business cards, the 787 number below a logo that matched his T-shirt.

I still felt a bit lost and very nervous, but I managed to say "Thank you" and give a little wave after I closed the truck door behind me. I expected him to drive away right after, and that scared me. This was all so new. But as I stood in line and bought my ticket, the truck was still in the same spot, his face shadowed by the vehicle's top in the late-morning sun.

It was only after I stepped onto the ferry's deck that the dented brown truck inched away from the curb, and my mood dampened. But I reminded myself that I would see him again in a few hours, after my visit with Chachu. After the next vision. My life was now being marked by the vision's occurrences.

One half of the passengers were casually dressed tourists, and the other half locals returning from the mainland with groceries and housewares. I helped one woman who was hauling a large, boxed baby crib, then went to sit on the ferry's top deck, the salty spray coating my face and hair, the conversations around me lost in the whipping wind. I was excited to visit the tiny island. José told me that the

U.S. Navy used parts of the island for maneuvers and the locals had become accustomed to the sound of shelling. I had an image in my head of crabs and seashells exploding on an otherwise pristine beach. There were other beaches that were open to the public. I hoped to see them someday, maybe even with José. My throat tightened and I swallowed that idea down. It was such a normal wish, so typically teenage. I wanted it so much it frightened me.

In my experience, caring about something meant I was going to lose it.

CHAPTER THIRTY-FOUR
esperanza means hope

The ferry docked just after noon and I easily found a taxi to take me to Esperanza, the little fishermen's village where Maria said Chachu lived. I asked to be dropped off a few blocks away so I could walk along the malecón, the sea wall that ran along the beach side of the main drag, Calle Flamboyán. I ran my fingertips over the elegant white stone balustrade as I walked, the classical white columns giving it the feel of a Roman ruin. At the center of town, the railing opened to a staircase that disappeared into the white sand of the narrow beach like a travel poster, the turquoise water lapping the shore. A line of restaurants faced the water on the other side of the road, where people sat in the open-air dining rooms sipping colorful frozen drinks or icy beers, the sound of salsa floating out over their heads and the heady scent of fried plantains beckoning.

I stopped to check out a street vendor's wares, eventually buying a blank book covered with banana leaves and shells for Mom. Maybe I could convince her to write down some of the family stories, especially those of family members who were getting older. After all, forewarned is forearmed.

I turned on Calle Tintillos right after a small guesthouse. Since it was midweek, there were no children playing, and the street was so quiet it seemed abandoned. I followed what numbers I could find on the houses until I stood in front of a tiny house painted the same blue as the ocean that matched the address that Maria had gotten for me. A hammock hung between the front supports; a salt-eaten 1950s Buick sat forlornly nearby. The building was simple but well maintained, the roof patched, the paint fresh. I started up the walk but stopped when I heard a voice coming from down the street.

"¡Buenas! Halo! Are you lost, young lady?" a deep voice called.

For a moment, all I could feel was annoyed at the English. Why did everyone immediately assume I was a gringa? Well, I *was* a gringa, but I was also Puerto Rican, and at that moment, I wished I looked it. I forced a smile and the feeling passed. I walked out toward the man who I assumed was Chachu, though it was hard to tell since all I had to go by was the ancient photograph tucked in my bag. He was more than eighty years old, according to Maria, but nothing about the man appeared elderly. He was tall, not as tall as my father but probably six feet, with wide, straight shoulders. There were lines etched deeply in his face, but his skin was warm and ruddy, not the ashen tone I associated with old age. He had a full head of hair, so white the midday sun made it glow, and his smile reached up to his eyes. But it was his walk that really surprised me. It was more of a stride, his hips shifting smoothly as he moved, one hand casually in his pocket, the other holding a fishing pole over his shoulder. This was a man who had to beat the ladies off with a stick in his day, probably still did.

"Buenos días, Señor. Me llamo—"

"My dear, these days I crave opportunities to practice my English. Indulge me."

And he was as smooth as sea glass. "My name is Isla Larsen Sanchez. I'm—"

"Ah! Elena's daughter! What a pleasure!"

I put my hand out to shake his. Standing with his heels together, he bent at the waist, brought my hand to his lips, and kissed it like a gentleman from an old movie. I felt a blush rise to my face.

"Ay, Señorita, you are as lovely as your mother. Your father—God rest his soul—would be so proud. But where are my manners? Let us sit down out back where it is cooler; you must be tired from your walk."

I followed Chachu to the rear of the bungalow where a rather elegant patio was laid out in octagonal stones framed by manicured bushes. In the center sat a white wire table and chairs with a view of a spectacular flamboyán tree that edged his property. He brought out two frosty cans of Coca-Cola, and after we settled at the table, he asked after my mother. I told him as little as I could without lying; I didn't want to get off track.

We caught up with news and he told me funny tales of my mother's childhood. Like the time when she was three and my great-grandmother was scolding her for some transgression, so Elena politely took her abuela by the hand, led her to a closet, and locked the old woman in. It was almost an hour before someone let the nagging abuela out. They found my mother outside, digging in the dirt with the good silver, singing a little song. I laughed heartily, but as I pictured Mom, I felt my throat catch a bit. It had been so long since my mother had looked happy. I took a sip of soda so Chachu wouldn't notice.

He started telling an anecdote about the first time Tío Ramón had Barrilito rum, and as he spoke, I studied his strong, calloused hands, thinking how incongruous they were with his educated English, his gentlemanly manners. But his laugh was raucous, and his eyes twinkled with a mischief that the years had not dimmed. I could see him at ease in the finest parties in San Juan or drinking cerveza with the maintenance crew that worked my family's land. I looked around at the simple life he had chosen and wondered how one with such a big personality ended up in such a small, rural place. So when he was done with his cuento, I asked Chachu about his life on the tiny island.

"I tell you, joven, I spent so many of my long years working hard in the hot sun or driving rain. I am not complaining, you understand. I was grateful for the work, but I just got…tired. Vieques is like Puerto Rico was in the '50s, quiet, peaceful, everyone knows everyone else. My life is simple, and I like it that way. I am happy here." As if in emphasis, he melted farther down into his chair, resting his soda can on his still-taut belly, a Cheshire cat grin spreading across his face.

Neither of us said anything for a time, and I realized I couldn't hear a car or a television, but the sounds of the ocean caressing the malecón reached us from a block away. The only sight in the back of the property was the thick, twisted trunk of the flamboyán topped with the last of the electric orange-red flowers that spilled onto the wiry grass. The air smelled green and salty, of land and ocean. I just nodded to him, and he nodded back. I understood.

We chatted for a while longer, no direction or rush to the conversation. I was comfortable with the man. I could see why my great-grandfather trusted him so much. When the hour of the vision arrived, I waited until I saw Bisabuelo, then asked Chachu if he might have a little something to eat, that I hadn't stopped for anything, and I was feeling a tiny bit dizzy. He went inside and I could hear his shuffling around the kitchen superimposed over the beginning of Alma's familiar drama.

I strode over behind the desk, occupying the space my

great-grandfather had vacated. I crossed my arms and glanced around. The room looked different from that vantage point, larger, the sitting room like a continuation with the open door. The desk was pin neat, piles held down with nautical paperweights, probably from his time in the U.S. Navy. He had upset a pile of papers on the table, legal documents, deeds, and what I recognized from my architect parents as a survey map entitled "El Tesoro." Wait, wasn't that the land Ramón had showed me? Then I remembered the new woman. I walked through the phantom window, my eyes trained on the back of the woman in the flowered dress who appeared to be pruning the greenery, a floppy hat guarding her head from the afternoon sun. Was she a neighbor? A gardener? The sounds of the struggle reached us, and in that moment, the woman turned her head to look toward the house, the brim of the hat shadowing her face.

She pulled the hat from her head, and I gasped.

"Abuela?" It was a whisper; very little sound could make it through my tightened throat.

Stunned, I stepped farther and farther back toward the house, staring at my grandmother's youthful face as the sound of the shot rang out from the trees and the bullet whizzed by my right ear just before going through my great-grandfather, my hair lifting up with the breeze of it. I felt it go by. Physically felt it.

And the shot had indeed come from the trees.

I stood, frozen in place as Alma's scene continued to play out as always, as if nothing had changed, as if my grandmother hadn't just materialized. As if I hadn't almost been shot in the head by an unseen assailant.

Shaken, I spun around and headed toward Alma, kneeling by the body of her father. And then even she was gone.

I stumbled back to the wire chair on shaking knees, my heart beating a merengue rhythm inside my chest, sweat beading on my forehead. I brushed my hand across the side of my head and brought it in front of my face and saw a very thin thread of blood across my palm. At the sight, I felt my stomach roil and ran over to some side bushes and vomited, my head reeling, blood running warm beneath my ear.

I heard Chachu gasp. He put the sodas on the table and rushed over, standing next to me with a look of concern. "M'ija, are you all right?"

I forced a smile, holding my stomach and hiding the bloody side of my head. "Yes, I'm sorry. My stomach is not good. Do you have some ginger ale?"

"Probably from the ferry ride; they are so hard on the stomach. Sit down, over here, querida, and I will get you some ginger ale and crackers." He led me over to the nearest chair and went back to the house.

I was reminded of Rosa's vision, of my bloody arm. I had had the sense it was a warning of sorts. Could it be that these visions would put my life in danger? I put my head between my knees and rocked back and forth, the wind ruffling my hair.

I missed Alma. I wanted her back. Why was she doing this to me?

I heard ice crack in the house and grabbed some napkins off the table to wipe the blood off my neck. I had to talk to Chachu and find out what I could; the stakes were getting too high.

I had to find a way to end this.

As I took deep breaths, I thought about what I'd learned. My abuela had played some part in the events, but in my heart, I knew the real key to the mystery lay with the two men. And I hadn't gotten to my great-grandfather yet when the bullet had whizzed by. So there had to have been another shooter. As I wiped the last of the blood off with the condensation-soaked napkin, I resolved to get some answers.

I heard Chachu's sandals scuffling across the patio, and he placed an icy glass of ginger ale in front of me and a small plate of soda crackers. He sat down but looked over at me with concern. "Are you sure you're okay, Isla?"

I nodded and smiled gratefully. "Yes, thank you." Though I wasn't entirely sure I was. But it was time. I pulled the photograph from my bag and placed it on the glass table. "This is why I've come, Señor. I was wondering if you could tell me who this man is." I pointed at the picture.

"Ah, okay." He took a pair of black wire reading glasses from his shirt pocket, unfolded them, and used them to peer at the photo. There was a reaction. I could see him control it, but I couldn't read it. Then he looked up at me. "May I ask why you want to know?"

The question took me by surprise. Until that point, he had been almost deferential, but with one sentence, it was as if I were a curious little gringa girl who was getting my nose into places it didn't belong. I had to admit I kind of was, but all I was looking for was the truth. "There is something involving this man that my aunt wants to be known, Señor. I really can't tell you how I know—that's between Alma and me—but I owe it to her to find out."

"Yes, I was sorry to hear about your tía's passing. She was a good Christian lady."

I waited to hear more, certain that was a segue to my answer, but Chachu just continued to study me, his eyes narrowed in query, saying nothing.

"All I'm asking is that you trust me with this information, Señor. I just want to understand who he was, and maybe a bit more about Alma, that's all."

At this, Chachu rubbed his hand over his chin, the stubble making a scraping noise against his palm while he continued to watch me. He seemed to reach a decision and sat up straighter in his chair. "Bueno. I like you, Isla, and your mother would not have raised you to start trouble. But the story is not a pleasant one. It caused your family much grief, so I don't enjoy dragging it up again. However, I'm sure you have your reasons. So I will tell you what I know, and we will see if you find the answers you seek.

"Your great-aunt was a lovely young woman, as you can see, her skin pale and flawless, her hair wavy and shining in variations of brown, like polished mahogany. She was a good girl, a well-behaved girl, always courteous to her elders, treated everyone with respect, from the governor to the woman who washed their floors. Her father worshipped her. He was so proud of her, cared for her like a jewel. He made sure she had all the necessities of life…and a few luxuries, though she seemed to have little interest in those. She was different from the other girls her age, even from her sister, your abuela.

"As Alma came of age, the sons of many of the good families hoped to win her hand. She was smart, as you know. She did well in school, particularly in math and science, and her father was torn: Should he send her off to college or select an upstanding young man to marry her? Then there was the issue of her being the younger daughter. Who would care for him and his wife when they grew old? After he got a troubling medical diagnosis, it was settled. He decided he wanted her to stay close to home, to be with her family, as a good daughter should. Besides, no man was good enough for his Alma. That was near the time we began building the new house, the one in the photograph.

"I hired Pedro—the man you are inquiring about—the day he showed up on the jobsite. I had worked with his father and had the honor of dining at their home in Cayey on several occasions. They were a God-fearing family, hard-working and kind. Pedro was no exception. He was a talented stone mason and an honest fellow. He kept to himself, mostly, not getting involved in the—what is a polite way to say it?—macho conversations among the other tradesmen. He came, did his work, and left.

"He was a quiet man, except for one day when he got into an argument with another worker on the job. The man, Beto, was an idiot. He had less sense than a stray dog, tu sabes? And tiny, beady eyes like a rodent. Anyway, that day, he had made a lewd comment about Alma after she passed by, and one of the men who was there said that even with Pedro's dark skin, he could see the blood rush to his face. Pedro stood toe-to-toe with Beto and insisted he apologize. Beto just grinned back at him—the man knew nothing of respect— and when he refused to apologize, Pedro jumped him and began punching. We pulled him off and sent them back to their work. The other men told me what had happened, and since I had already suspected that Beto was padding his time, I fired him that very afternoon. We finished the job with no further incidents, and I thought no more of it.

"The day that Pedro came back to the house was a dark day for the Sanchez family. The construction was done, and everyone was happy. When Pedro appeared at the house, I was speaking to the landscapers, and I assumed he had come to see me and would wait. What business could he have with anyone but me? I did not see him go inside.

"I heard the sound of a gunshot from where I was in the backyard and ran around to the side where Ramón's house is now. I saw a figure dashing across the nearby field—the land was open then— and I gave chase, but he had too much of a lead, and no matter how fast I ran, there was no way I could catch him or see who it was. I have seen that figure in my dreams many times and wondered if I should have kept running, kept trying to catch him.

"By the time I got back to the house, for I had run far trying to pursue the man, Alma met me at the door and was very composed, but I could see her eyes were red and no one could get a ratty old straw pava out of her hands. I called the authorities and told them about the man I had chased and where we had gone, but they could not find him. I did not mention that Pedro had been there, for he was not the type of man one suspected of such a thing.

"I know what you're thinking, Isla. I thought it myself at first and your abuela hinted at it, but it could not have been him. Pedro could not have killed your bisabuelo. He had not a violent bone in his body. That disagreement with the other worker was about honor, not vengeance, and it certainly was not on the scale of murder. I knew his family—a guava is only as good as the tree on which it ripens—and I knew that the police, they never would have understood. They would have assumed it was him, made assumptions based on the color of his skin, not on who he was as a man. But your great-grandfather? He had a fiery temper. Quick to anger, Señor Sanchez was. And he ruled with an iron fist. He was very proud of his Spanish roots and had very particular ideas about one's place in life, and when it came to Alma—well, I can only imagine what he would have done if... Bueno, enough of that.

"Your grandmother arrived and wanted to avoid an investigation, thought it would bring too much scandal to the family, so she told the police that your bisabuelo was ill and it was a suicide and that the man I had seen running away was an employee frightened off by the shot. I accepted this without question. It was a matter of honor and protecting the family that remained, particularly Alma. Your grandmother sent Alma away for a while after that.

"When she returned, I tried to talk to her about it, to tell her I saw Pedro that day, but she didn't want to hear it. I guess she wanted to put the nightmare behind her. I never spoke again of the events of that day. Only Alma knew what really happened. Oh, and your bisabuelo, but he was in no position to recount his particular version of events. Ironically Alma was left with no options other than to be the caretaker her father had envisioned for her, even though he was no longer around. She was left with the responsibility to look after her aging mother.

"Pedro's family would work for Alma on occasion, but he never came back to the house in Bayamón. He contacts me every so often. He ended up attending la universidad and becoming an engineer. It was as I had predicted: he had potential. Though we never spoke of the incident, to this day I am certain he was guilty of no wrongdoing.

"Pero todo eso es, como se dice, water under the bridge. Alma, as you know, has left us." Chachu looked at me and added, "So it would seem Pedro is the only one, m'ija, who knows the truth of what happened that day. Alma never talked about it to anyone. At least not that I am aware of."

"Does Pedro still live in Puerto Rico?"

"Seguro. In Loiza."

I was trying to process it all, then I remembered. "Señor, was my abuela there? When my great-grandfather was shot?"

"Marisol?" He scratched his stubbly chin in thought. "I don't believe so. Afterward, of course, but I don't remember if she was when the incident occurred."

I sat there as the sun faded below the trees, the sound of children returning from school echoing around the side of the house. I had more pieces, that much was certain. But I was no closer to a solution. Then there was the issue of the bullet. "Did my great-grandfather have a rifle?"

Chachu tilted his head in surprise. "¡Seguro! All landowners did in those days. They had land and people to protect."

"Do you know what caliber?" I was pushing my luck and I knew it.

He regarded me with narrow eyes. "That is a very odd question, young lady."

"Sorry, just wondering." I kept going before I talked myself into a corner. "Gracias, Señor, for telling me what you knew of that day. But did you have suspicions about what really happened and why?"

"Ay, m'ija. There was much talk about it in the parlors of Bayamón. About a murderer on the loose and other rumors… Your family worked hard to put it behind them." Chachu looked away, his eyes distant. "The Sanchez family employed me through diffi-cult times. The work I did for them paid for my children's dental work, the home they grew up in, their college educations, my wife's hospital bills—God rest her soul. Your bisabuelo, he was not an easy man to deal with, but I would never think of gossiping about him. And that's all it would be, gossip. There is no way for me to know what transpired." He leaned back with his hands together on the table.

I wanted to press him, to find out what he suspected, what people had been saying. There had to be more to why he didn't push to find the details of his boss's violent death. I thought he knew what happened, but I understood then that his silence was a matter of honor, of respect toward my family. I put my hands over his. "I respect that, Señor, and I am grateful for your taking the time to talk to me, to tell me of your experiences. Alma would have appreciated your showing such kindness to her crazy gringa grandniece."

At this, he smiled and affectionately squeezed my hands in his. "It was my pleasure, Señorita Sanchez. You are a lovely and kind young lady."

He escorted me around to the front, though we walked slowly, neither in any hurry. Just a few hours on the little island and I knew time moved differently on Vieques, even from the mainland, and I liked it.

"Señor, do you know anything about El Tesoro?"

He smiled at me. "You're not looking for buried treasure too, are you?"

"Why, do you know of any?" I grinned. "No, it's just some land my family owns in Bayamón."

He scratched his growing beard, the sounds surprisingly loud in the quiet afternoon. "The Sanchez family has owned much land over the years. The only land I know of from your great-grandfather's time was a piece he was going to donate to the Coalición."

"Coalition?"

"For statehood. I think it was called the Pure Republican Party before that. He was one of the founding members."

I refrained from rolling my eyes. I wasn't sure where I stood politically yet, but I did know that our family was way too conservative for me. When we arrived in the front, we argued about whether I was well enough to travel and about my wanting to walk to town by myself and grab a cab to catch the four-thirty ferry. When we stood in the road, he relented, exhaustion crowding around his eyes. The remembrance had taken a toll on him. "Please give my regards to your mother. She was always my favorite, a very mischievous young lady. Perhaps it runs in the family, yes?"

I smiled at Chachu, stood on my toes, and gave him a quick kiss on the cheek. His skin was warm and scratchy and smelled of sun and sea. As I was walking away, I turned back and asked, "What's Pedro's last name?"

"Alvarez," he called back. "The last I heard he bought a nice little house on Calle Heliconia. He never married."

I thanked him and took my leave. As I walked down the street, a big-headed Chihuahua yipped at me from inside a gated front yard, and a group of children, still in their plaid school uniforms, waved hello as I passed. Before I turned the corner, I looked back and could just make out Chachu, lowering his body slowly into the hammock. I could almost hear the groan of relief as the woven rope cradled his aging bones.

CHAPTER THIRTY-FIVE
embellishing the truth

I sat by the ferry's window and looked out at the water rushing by, the drops of spray snaking down the ferry's scratched windows. I was still lost in Alma's story, caught in another time. Claridad had been right about talking to someone outside the family: Chachu had helped, but I was still struggling to make sense of it all.

"Hi."

I jumped at the sound of a voice right next to me. I looked over and saw a girl about my age, with ice-blue eyes that glowed in her tanned face, her straight blond hair held back by a pair of designer sunglasses.

"Hi," I responded, then looked back at the deepening colors of the horizon, aware of the girl next to me, suddenly conscious of how I held my head, not sure what to do with my hands. Why didn't she leave?

"Are you on vacation too?"

I dragged my gaze from the window. "No. Well, yes. Kind of."

"My family and I come down here every year."

The girl pointed to a handsome couple sitting nearby, the mother's arm around a young boy with a sherbet-colored golf shirt and tousled hair. All three were blond and tanned and beautiful like the girl, and they were surrounded by piles of luggage as if entrenched in a brown leather fort. They looked happy and—though I had to guess at the definition—normal, like the families I saw on television.

"I'm Cara," she said, offering me her hand as if we were two grown-ups at tea.

I had to admit, I liked it. After a week of being treated as if I were a child, it was refreshing. I shook Cara's hand. "My name's Isla."

"What a cool name! How old are you?"

"Eighteen."

"I'm seventeen!" She said this with total glee as if it were such a coincidence that we were close in age. "I'm glad to finally meet someone my age. This year, all I've met are old people. If I have to sit around listening to another boring adult conversation, I think I'll totally scream!"

I liked to think of myself as an adult; I was eighteen after all. The difference between last year and this was immeasurable in so many ways. Then I remembered all the nights spent watching my family rock back and forth on the patio chairs as I sipped Coca-Cola and tried not to fall asleep. I smiled. "I know what you mean."

"And cute guys? There wasn't *one* on the beach this year. I bought a new bathing suit and everything! Maybe there'll be some at our hotel in San Juan."

It wasn't lost on me that Cara chose the word *our* to describe the hotel, as if everything was there for her family's taking. And I supposed it was. I had never considered what we had and didn't have as a family until that year. From Cara's perspective, however, I would guess the way my mother and I lived in New Jersey would fall on the side of "didn't have," though according to Claridad, we were well off. There were way more levels to all this than I had ever imagined. We both looked out the window now and watched the sun begin to melt into the horizon, orange light spreading across the sky like taffy.

"This is nice, isn't it, taking the ferry? We usually fly back to San Juan, but our flight was canceled, and we have dinner reservations for tonight."

I watched Cara out of the corner of my eye. I liked the way she gestured with her slender hands, nails painted a pale pink like the inside of a seashell, her gold bracelets making a clean tinkling sound as she moved.

"Is this your first time in Puerto Rico?" she asked.

"No, I come here every year too." I didn't tell Cara that my family was from the island. Or, for that matter, that they were secretive and bizarre and I was haunted by my dead great-aunt. For the moment, at least, I wanted something in common with this girl from the television family.

"That's great! Where are you staying?"

My mouth opened but nothing came out, my mind flipping through possible answers like clothes on a rack I could slip on, none of them the truth. Luckily Cara's mother called her before I could answer.

"I'll be back, Isla," she said cheerfully. But the boat began docking soon after, and Cara and her family scurried to manage their mound of luggage. I was forgotten in the melee, and as I stood to join the line of disembarking passengers, I tried to decide whether I was disappointed or relieved.

I walked down the shadowed dock toward José's truck parked at the end of the pier. I knew it would be there. There was so little in my life I could depend on, but even after so many years apart, I knew that José was one of them. I drew closer and my heart fluttered when he came into view, leaning against the vehicle's side, waving at me, the golden light of the setting sun painting him a rich, deep walnut.

"Isla!" I heard from behind, my name punctuated with the slap of sandals on the wooden planks of the pier.

Cara appeared next to me. "My parents want to know if you'd like a ride back to San Juan. We have cars picking us up. We can even have one to ourselves!" She was gleeful at the thought.

I looked at the girl's parents who waved and held on to their hats in the rising wind. Then I glanced back at José, his smile like the flicker of a candle flame in the growing dusk.

I couldn't help but smile back, but as I turned to Cara and pointed toward José, I wasn't sure how to refer to him. Friend? Family friend? Boyfriend? No, that would be pushing it.

Cara followed the line of my finger. She smiled with recognition. I stood a little straighter, proud I had such a handsome guy waiting for me.

"Oh! Your servant is picking you up."

I froze in place and stared at Cara, the word repeating itself in my head as if there were an echo.

Servant.

Servant.

Servant.

"You'd think they'd have him bring a better car. Are you really going to ride all the way to San Juan in that beat-up old truck?"

Just then, her family bustled by, and I noticed the two black, shiny sedans that were pushing into the space in front of José's front bumper.

My stomach turned over and over as if it were a clothes dryer.

"Wouldn't you rather ride in the Town Car? I mean, maybe you could even go to dinner with us. I could ask my mom—"

The incessant sound of Cara's voice was like tires squealing against a curb, and I thought I would haul out and punch her if she said one more word, just one more word…

"Cara, honey, we've got to go! We're going to be late!"

Cara was looking at me. She was waiting for a response, but all the answers were backing up in my head. *Say something, Isla, damn it! She insulted your friend! Didn't she? But it wasn't like she called him a name. If it wasn't an insult, why does it make you feel so bad? Don't let her leave without saying something!*

Finally, Cara shrugged and took off toward her waiting family as I stood there, my throat tight with unspoken words, wondering if I was going to throw up on the dock with all those people walking around me.

"Isla? Are you okay?"

I looked up and into José's warm brown eyes. I leaned forward on my toes, just slightly rocking, part of me wanting so badly to wrap my arms tightly around him. Thank God he hadn't heard what she'd called him. Then I thought of Cara and her family. I murmured a quick "I'm fine" and started walking briskly toward the truck.

During the drive home, I sat with my arms tight around my body, as if I had to hold my heart in place or it would fly out the window.

José glanced over at me. "Are you cold, Isla? I could close the windows." He reached over to close the fan vents in front of me, and when his arm brushed my leg, I closed my eyes to keep the tears from coming.

"No, thank you. I'm just a little tired." I looked out the open window and watched Fajardo pass by, the roadside stores buzzing with after-work customers. José didn't say anything else; he seemed respectful of my silence, which only deepened the crushing feeling in my chest.

The words wanted to flow over my tongue in a flood. They pushed against the back of my clenched teeth in their rush to get out. Words describing my visit with Chachu and what I learned about Alma and her father, about Pedro; words that formed questions about what really happened between them on that day that I revisited every afternoon. But the words exchanged in my conversation with Cara were what held the others back. Words that spoke of my desire to ride in the fancy car with her shiny blond family, and the most painful of all, the ones that admitted that when Cara mistook him for a servant, how for just one moment...I was ashamed of him.

I had no right to judge Alma or Bisabuelo; I was worse.

As we bumped over the cobblestone streets of Old San Juan, José told me he had to rush off to take the supplies neatly stacked in the truck bed to his father. I was relieved and sorry at the same time. As soon as the truck came to a stop in front of Maria's town house, I started to slide off the seat but turned to say thank you just as he bent toward me and pressed his lips to my cheek. Since we had both been moving at the same time, he caught the edge of my lips, and it felt as hot as midday in the truck's cab. He sat back and smiled at me in a way that made my skin feel as though it were on fire.

"You seem to have had a bad day, and I wanted to let you know I'm sorry."

I mumbled thanks and almost tumbled out of the truck as tears threatened again. He waited until I was safely inside, and I watched through the large louvered window until the small red dots of his rear lights turned around a corner several blocks up. I leaned my head against the black iron bars and breathed deeply.

I had so much to think about and no energy to do it.

When I had suitably recovered, I found I needed to talk to someone about all I'd learned, but even Maria didn't know about the visions, about Alma's story. I felt as though I were going to jump out of my skin from keeping it all inside. It got so bad, I resorted to calling my mother, but the phone just rang and rang. I wasn't really surprised or disappointed. It wasn't like she was ever there for me, and conversations about the vision had only ended badly. I sat staring at the phone as if I could find answers in its shiny surface.

In that moment, it rang, and I leapt up in the air, knocking the phone to the floor, scrambling for the receiver as it skated farther away on the tiles, straining on its curlicue leash. I struggled to grab it and get the right end to my ear.

"Sorry! Hello?" By now I was totally out of breath.

"Isla? What the hell is going on over there? Are you having a wild party without me?" It was Maria.

"Uh, not even close." I told her a bit about my day without getting into the why of my visit, and Maria invited me out to dinner.

"Come on, Prima! I just finished the presentation and am ready to have some fun. And then you can tell me all about your drive with José!"

I looked longingly at the bed in my borrowed room but accepted. I showered, changed my clothes, and headed out into the old city. When I had first arrived to stay at her house, Maria had given me the lowdown on what streets to avoid at night and told me to be cautious when coming in or out of the building. She was clearly fulfilling her promise to Tío Ramón, but the city seemed different since I was walking around on my own for the first time, and I was grateful for the advice. I had always loved Viejo San Juan, with its blue cobblestoned streets and castle bookends. When I was a child, we would only come to town to visit El Morro, one of the forts built by the Spanish, or have brunch at the Caribe Hilton with our cousin Carlos.

Now, as I browsed in and out of shops, admiring carved wooden magi and hammered tin-framed saints, and walked by the squares with street musicians playing traditional Puerto Rican songs under pools of the newly lit streetlamps, I was reminded how much more there was to the city. I couldn't believe Maria lived her everyday life there, away from her family. I wondered if I would ever be that independent. If I ever *could* be, given the state my mother was in.

I stopped to look into a tiny storefront shoehorned between two larger buildings. Its window was filled with clay renditions of the colorfully painted doorways that line each cobblestone street in Old San Juan like candy necklaces. Being the child of architects, I could appreciate the artist's careful rendering of the architectural details of the sixteenth-century structures. I was a few minutes early, so I went in and wandered among the aisles, admiring the tiny painted trellises trailing with brightly colored flowers. Some of them were personalized, and as my eyes swept over the offerings on a wide glass shelf, they rested on a small one that was painted leaf green, a trail of bright-pink bougainvillea spilling over the top, a black iron lamp to the left of the white door, and right beneath it, a plaque that said, "Casa Elena." My breath caught, and I picked it up. I thought of my mother and cradled it in my hand.

"Can I help you, miss?" a woman's voice said behind me.

I clutched the clay doorway to my chest and stammered. "I... I'm... I want to buy this one," I said, reluctantly handing it over.

The woman smiled and walked to the register with a curious backward glance in my direction.

THE STORYTELLER'S DEATH   259

"That's my mother's name," I told her, not caring that I must have seemed more than a bit strange.

The little clay doorway carefully stowed in my bag, I set off to meet my cousin.

Maria took me to a restaurant called Bigote de Abuelo, Grandfather's Mustache. We got a table on the balcony overlooking the Plaza de Armas, and while Maria ordered, I watched the sea of pigeons in the park below swell and fall as people walked through the square. I asked about Maria's day as we sipped passion-fruit shakes, the velvet night rising behind the old stone buildings. Before her presentation, my cousin had spent the morning at Alma's, and though it was going slowly, she said it was getting done. We chatted for a bit about Alma's eccentric archiving and what each of us would miss most about her. The pain in my chest was not going away— how could it when I still saw Alma every day?—but I was getting more accustomed to it.

Then Maria surprised me with a straightforward question. "So, Prima, I get the sense you're looking for something during your extended stay here. And I'm not just talking about José." She smiled playfully, but I could see the edge of seriousness in her question.

I started to stammer a bit, my shoulders rising and pulling back, ready to go on the defense.

The body language wasn't lost on Maria. "Okay, okay, I won't intrude on your secret mission, but you will let me know if I can help, yes?"

"Actually, I do have one question. Do you know how Great-Grandfather died?"

Maria laughed. "My, you are getting into the muck and mire of the Sanchez mythology!" But she put down her glass and crossed her arms, clearly enjoying the gossip. "Some people say he killed himself because he had tuberculosis and didn't want to burden the family."

"Some? What do other people say?"

Maria looked around a bit as if the tourists at the next table cared. "Some say he was murdered by a black laborer in a dispute."

I played along. "Dispute? Over what?"

Maria shrugged. "Who knows. It's usually money in such things."

"What do *you* think happened?"

My cousin shook her head. "I haven't a clue, but he was actually sick. I've seen his medical records. He wouldn't have lived long anyway."

I processed this for a moment and took a long sip of my drink. When I put it down, I looked up at my cousin. "Maria, on that note, maybe you can explain something to me. The cuentos in our family—in any family—what if a lot of them you hear aren't really true? Doesn't that mean we've been lied to all these years?"

Maria's melodic laugh floated off the balcony. "Oh, Cousin, that's a loaded one! Been finding out that the Sanchez cuentistas embroider the truth a bit, have you? Boy, some of them were pretty damn crazy, the stories *and* the storytellers. But I'm going to answer your question with another: Why should that bother you?"

I pondered her query. "I guess I always thought the family stories I heard were real. Now that I'm finding out some of them weren't, does that mean I don't really know who the Sanchezes are? Who that half of me is?"

Maria could see that I was serious, and the laugh left her voice. "Look at it this way: What difference does it make? No, really, hear me out. You thought those cuentos were what made up the fabric of the Sanchez family, right? Don't the stories that aren't true say as much about us as the ones that are?"

I considered this. All the cuentos I had heard and seen ran through my head.

"And we won't even get into the concept of what truth really is. It's like different cameras all photographing the same object. We all experience events differently and with our own particular angle."

Teresa's version of Ramón's election. Alma and her father. I smiled at Maria. "Okay, okay, I understand. Besides, I've done some embroidering of the truth myself at times."

"See? What's fabric without a bit of embellishment? Boring, that's what it is! And as for knowing what being a Sanchez is"—she raised her glass to me—"take a good look in the mirror."

CHAPTER THIRTY-SIX

at the heart of it

My next step was clear: I had to get to Loiza to talk to Pedro himself and finally get the answers I sought. If I had had any doubt as to the urgency of this quest, all I had to do was look in the mirror and see the thin red line across the top of my earlobe where the phantom shot had grazed me. I devised a tale about traveling to Loiza to do some research on the history of Bomba music (I had found reference to it in a book on Maria's glass spiral coffee table) and was asking about cab companies the next night at a family dinner when Tío Ramón overheard. All part of my plan. I could have scripted his response.

"Absolutamente no. Isla, it is not safe for a young lady to ride with strangers, particularly to a town like that. I will have Joaquin pick you up tomorrow at 11:00 a.m. outside your cousin's house."

Not letting on that this was my hope all along, I simply nodded like a good girl. His comment about a "town like that" clawed at me, but I decided not to say anything. Loiza was founded by freed enslaved people and had a largely Black population. If that was what he was referring to, I didn't want to know and then have to face my uncle Ramón day after day. I promised myself that I would address this with my family at a future date, but my priority had to be stopping the visions before a bullet found a more vital part of my body.

The next morning, I went to sit in the front passenger seat once more, and Joaquin smiled and moved his folders of papers to accommodate me. He might work for my great-uncle, but I had no desire to treat him, or anyone else for that matter, as a servant of mine. I was realizing this issue with my family was as much about social class as the color of skin, and I was no longer willing to play along.

We drove a bit in silence, until Joaquin asked, "Señorita—"

"Isla. Please call me Isla, Joaquin."

He nodded. "Isla, would you like for me to take Route 187? It will take a bit longer, but it's very pretty. It goes along the ocean."

I nodded like a little girl, excited. As we drove, I recognized the narrow highway that hugged the Atlantic shore. The foam-tipped blue of the ocean stayed on our left like a constant traveling companion. As we drove through Piñones Beach, the traffic thickened so I had time to take in the chorus line of straw-roofed huts hawking identical brightly colored souvenirs with "Puerto Rico" painted on them. Ropes were strung along the road, dangling rows of swimming tubes with palm trees dancing around the edges, the sun glinting off the clear plastic tops. It was all so familiar. Then a strong memory of driving through there as a child resurfaced.

I remembered my greedy eyes wanting every item on the vendors' shelves. I begged and pleaded to buy everything, then anything, and suddenly the pen holders topped with reclining, plastic coquí frogs with jeering faces and tiny straw hats seemed like treasure. My mother only approved the purchase of more traditional souvenirs, handcrafted and less commercial, like a pair of maracas or a güiro. I remembered how my fingers vibrated as I ran the fork scraper across the crudely carved lines on the side of the gourd instrument. Things hadn't changed at all. There was a blond girl in a pink shorts set pulling on her mother's pants leg, and I imagined that a descendant of the same pen-holding coqui was probably staring down at her from the shelves.

On the left was a row of kioskos, the smell of deep-fried delicacies suspended in the heat above the blacktop; large vinyl photos of frosty beer mugs festooned the wooden plank shacks. As we drove by, the beats of different salsa tunes blared from massive speakers, overlapping as if a giant radio dial were being turned. Once we left the tourist area behind, the vendors began to thin out, and I breathed deeply of the heavy salted air that blew in the window.

We crossed the Rio Grande, entered Loiza, and were greeted by a row of brilliantly hued one-story buildings with rows of children's shorts and T-shirts waving from clotheslines in mother-may-I lines. I told Joaquin that I was going to Calle Heliconia, and we cruised slowly through town, past more low-slung concrete buildings with dirt front yards and a small bodega with bright fruit and shanks of meat hanging in front like edible garlands. He turned left onto a dead-end street, and I glanced at my watch: 12:10, exactly two hours until the next vision.

"Which house are you going to, Señorit—Isla?"

I bit my lip and gazed out at the parallel rows of houses, each looking alarmingly similar to the others. What house *was* I going to? Why hadn't I thought of this? I couldn't go knocking on every door asking if Pedro lived there. Joaquin seemed to sense my indecision.

"My mother lives not far from here, and I am very familiar with the town. Perhaps if you told me the name, I could help you."

"Alvarez."

"You mean Pedro Alvarez? The engineer?"

"Yes, that's him. Do you know where he lives?"

"Seguro, but…"

"Is something wrong, Joaquin?"

I could tell he was torn. Exasperated, he turned toward me. "It's just…I don't think your tío Ramón would want you talking to Pedro."

"What? Why?"

Joaquin gnawed on the side of his fingernail. "There was some kind of family feud, something that happened long ago between his father and Pedro. Though his family continued to work for the Sanchezes, your grandmother forbade contact with Pedro himself."

I wasn't going to ask why. I knew. Just like my grandmother to stir the pot. "I'm not in any kind of danger, am I?"

He shook his head vigorously. "No, not at all, Señorita Sanchez—"

"Isla, please."

"Isla. Pedro is a gentle and thoughtful man. I wouldn't let you go talk to him if I thought you would be in danger."

Let you. I was just not accustomed to all these men telling me what to do, but Joaquin was only trying to protect me. I smiled at him. "Then Tío Ramón doesn't need to know, right? It could be our little secret."

"Yes, that would be best." Then he pointed to an immaculately cared-for house a few doors down from where we had stopped. "That's his." He inched the car in front of the concrete structure. "I will wait for you here, okay?" Joaquin smiled and I smiled back with relief.

But the relief was short-lived. I felt the weight of each of my steps as I approached the house. My hand hesitated over the cast-iron gate, and for a moment, I considered going back to the car and asking Joaquin to take me back, to drop me in San Juan where

I could hide in Maria's apartment. But it would be hard to go back to a "normal life" when you knew a ghost would be shooting a gun by your head every day for...what, ever? Sighing, I swung open the short metal gate and found myself standing amid a tiny but beautifully tended garden. Thanks to Alma, I could identify at least five varieties of orchids, a rainbow of waxy bromeliads, and a small, neatly trimmed African tulip tree that danced with the breeze within the gated yard. The scents of flowers and greens were intoxicating. Chachu implied that Pedro lived alone, so I assumed the garden was his. The gardening obsession was certainly something he and Alma had had in common.

I turned to go up the stone walkway, my thoughts racing. Just then, the front door opened, and an elderly man shuffled forward, swinging wide the gated door to the porch. Watching him through the curlicues of the black iron bars, I had no doubt it was Pedro. He was moving slowly, and his hair was almost completely white, but he stood tall and proud, his bright russet eyes just like those in the vision.

"Buenos días, Señor. Soy—"

"Sí, sí, m'ija, lo sé. I know who you are, Alma's grandniece, God rest her soul. Come in, come in," he said quickly, making sweeping gestures with his hands toward the inside as if he had been impatiently expecting me.

CHAPTER THIRTY-SEVEN
it was just a dream

Confused, I followed him in, pulling the doors closed behind us as we entered the house's cool interior. The living room smelled of lemon disinfectant and, underneath, the comforting smell of old books.

"I'm sorry, I... Did Chachu call you?" I asked.

"Sit, joven, sit. I will get us some hibiscus tea."

I stammered, intending to ask again how he knew I was coming, but I had the distinct feeling my line of questioning had just been dismissed. I could hear the refrigerator open, the sound of ice cubes clinking into glasses coming from the kitchen. The room was small but immaculate, with shelves of books lining one wall, a series of wood West-African fiddles along another. The furniture was rattan like so many living room sets in Puerto Rico, and the pillows were covered with what I recognized as woven Andean fabric. He was a man with cultured interests.

As I examined the books on the shelves, I came upon a series of framed photographs, generations of people I assumed were family. It wasn't until the last one that I stopped short. It was a five-by-seven of a smiling boy with a man and a younger version of Pedro.

The man's round face I thought might be familiar, but the young boy was unmistakable: it was José.

Pedro came in bearing a tray topped with a pair of frosty glasses and a plate of pastries, and at his entry, I jumped.

"I'm sorry to startle you."

I waved it away, embarrassed. "No, no. It's fine. I was just… looking at this photo." I indicated the last frame. "Is this José?"

"It is. He is my great-nephew. That's his father there." He pointed to the heavier man in the middle.

I recognized him now from our days playing in Alma's jungle. "I–I didn't know. José and I are…friends." I'd had no idea that he was connected somehow to this vision business, but in another way, it made total sense.

Pedro regarded me for a moment. "And how does your family feel about that?"

I shrugged. "My younger cousin likes him. The older generation… Well, they're more stuck in their ways."

"That's one way to put it," he mumbled.

He put the tray down on the glass-covered coffee table, and I was grateful for the diversion. "Oh! Guava cake, my favorite!" I delicately lifted a piece from the top of the pile, not hiding a child-like glee.

"Buen provecho, Isla."

Glancing up when he said my name, I again couldn't shake the feeling that he had been expecting me. But I was too busy glowing in the treasured warmth and excess calories of Caribbean hospitality. We talked politely for a few minutes about the town and how it had changed over the years, about my favorite beach in Luquillo, which was nearby, with its ground cinnamon-sugar sand and turquoise-blue water, about how he could see the mist-shrouded mountains

of the rain forest, El Yunque, from his roof. He took me up there
to show me the view. As we looked at the green velvet range that
seemed to breach the clouds, Pedro sighed. "Your great-aunt used
to love the rain forest."

I turned to him. "What? She refused to take me there when I was
a child, said it was a place for the young. I thought she hated it."

"How could someone who treasures plant life not appreciate the
miracle of the rain forest? No, no, she loved it there." He said nothing else, leading me back down and into the house. My heart was
racing. I felt like the answers were in reach. I could almost touch
them with my fingertips.

We returned to the living room, and as soon as we had sat down
once again, Pedro asked, "Well then, Isla, what is it you wish to
ask me?"

My eye caught the clock on the far wall: 1:15. Less than an
hour remained before the next vision. Just as well he was blunt.
Basta. Enough. "Señor, I have some questions about my great-
aunt Alma."

"Go on, child."

It started slowly, like water through a small crack. "I heard
this story from a cousin, and I want to understand what the truth
behind it is—" Gradually the dam broke, and the story came out
in a torrent, my hands gesturing wildly as I described the details of
the vision disguised as a family tale heard secondhand. His face was
impassive; nothing, not even my emotional description of the shooting, brought a change to his expression. When there was no more
to be said, I fell back against the cushion, my hands in my lap. We
sat in silence for a while, the ticking of the clock and an occasional
distant car rattle the only sounds. I wondered: Should I ask him
outright if he was involved in the murder of my great-grandfather?

Ask him what his connection was with my aunt? No. I couldn't. Then I remembered the bullet and ring in my pocket.

"I found this in the room where it supposedly happened." I placed the bullet on the table.

He regarded it coolly, then looked back at me. "I am not a fan of guns, so I'm not sure of its significance."

Then I dropped the ring onto the table beside the bullet, and we both stared as it danced on its edge on the glass, eventually settling on its side with a final clink.

His face dropped, the wrinkles next to his eyes and mouth lengthened with shock, and he appeared as he had when he was younger. He leaned forward, his eyes only on the thin, gold circle. "Madre de Dios," he whispered. "I never thought I would see it again." He picked it up gingerly, his eyes passing over it as if they saw something else entirely…or someone. Then he sighed and the years returned to his face as he slumped back into his chair.

"I just want to understand what happened, Señor. Alma was very important to me."

"She was very important to me too." Pedro sighed again, turning the gold band over and over between his fingers. "So much so that I had hoped to make her my wife."

Make her his wife? What? Did bigoted Alma love this man back? My pulse thundered in the silence in anticipation of answers. Staring at Pedro, my long-held images of Alma erased and redrew themselves like pictures on an Etch A Sketch. I didn't say anything, not sure I could have if I tried, just continued to watch him, his eyes still locked on the ring.

I could almost see his mind traveling back in time. His voice rose as if it were coming from a far distance.

"I hadn't gone there that day to make trouble, you understand.

And though he never seemed to care for those of us who had darker skin, your great-grandfather was an honest employer. Yes, I had heard rumors of his mistreatment of his Black work staff, was shown scars of injuries supposedly inflicted by him. But until that day, Señor Sanchez left me alone to do my work. I never wanted to hurt him. I know what people thought. I know what the police would have done. If it hadn't been for Alma, I would have died in prison; there is no doubt in my mind. But I get ahead of the story.

"I met Alma when I was brought on to the job of building her father's house. I was a stone mason then, and my father had worked with Chachu for many years, so I felt comfortable there, welcomed. I'll never forget the first time I saw her. It was through the trees in the back. I looked up from my work and saw Alma standing with her father, dark hair spilling over her shoulders like silk. And her laugh, it was like an embrace that reached across the yard. It took me weeks to finally embolden myself to speak with her. Men like me, poor laborers, do not often speak with women like your great-aunt, unless of course it's related to the work we are doing for them.

"I do not even remember what we discussed, the plants she was working on in the garden or something, but it was as if I had never felt full or happy before that moment. From then on, we sought each other out, talking whenever we could, exchanging plant cuttings from our gardens. In time, we shared a hidden kiss near the shed in the back. It was fleeting—she ran off back to the house, nervous about being discovered—but I could feel the feather touch of her lips on mine for hours, days. We fell in love. The love only the young can feel. It becomes everything—food, water, the air you breathe.

"We had one precious afternoon alone together. We met in San Juan—she had left on the pretense of a shopping excursion—and headed east in her father's car, searching for a place where no one would know us. We found ourselves traveling to El Yunque. We spent several hours walking along the trails, identifying plants, dangling our feet into the pools below the waterfalls, and holding hands. When we climbed to the top of the highest peak and looked around the island, the sides of our bodies touching, it was as if Bayamón didn't exist. As if it were our island, ours alone. I visited there many times after that day, and when I breathed in the fertile green scent, my skin moist with the humidity, I could almost feel the coolness of her hand in mine. But later that afternoon, we had to return to the fiction of our separate lives, to pretending.

"I worked hard and got myself into college to study engineering. I wanted to make sure I had a steady future to offer her. Finally, I convinced her that it was time for me to approach her father.

"I went there to ask for her hand. This was to be her engagement ring. It is nothing, I know, a trinket to someone from a family such as hers, but I was a poor student then, and she said she didn't care, she loved me anyway. I went to the back door—as your bisabuelo required all Black workers to do—and I was shaking like a ceiba leaf, my head sweating as I pulled off my pava and entered the dark, cool house. The maid showed me to Señor Sanchez's office. I stood there in front of his desk for some time, my hat in my hand, but he wouldn't acknowledge my existence. Eventually he barked—still without looking up: '¿Sí? What do you want?' I stammered a bit, I was so scared, but as soon as I mentioned Alma's name, his eyes shot up, glaring at me as if fire burned from them.

"'I was told about you! The other worker you fought with, Beto, he followed you and saw you together. Kissing!' His face became redder and redder. 'You've ruined her! Brought shame to my family!'

"'Señor, nothing happened! I would never damage her honor! It was nothing more than a kiss—'

"But at the word 'kiss,' he became completely enraged. He jumped from his chair, and I was certain he was going kill me. He continued to threaten me, accused me of insulting his family, of trying to sabotage the purity of his bloodline. Insane with fury, he jumped at me, and I just tried to hold him off. Then from within his jacket, he produced a gun. We continued to struggle, and somehow, the gun must have gone off. Honestly, I don't remember. There was a bang, then he was falling.

"At first, I thought it was me who had been shot, but then I saw the blood spreading on his shirt, tried to hold him up as he slipped to the floor. In that one moment, everything had gone wrong, and I knew that our dream of a future together died with the old man. What could I do? I had no choice but to run. No one except for Alma would have believed me, and Señor Sanchez was dead, the only other person who knew what happened.

"I do not blame him for his reaction, though. He had plans for Alma. He didn't want his daughter with a man such as me, and he was probably right…" Pedro's voice trailed off, and he gently placed the ring on the table as if the action ended his tale, his eyes clouded.

I was trying to imagine it, Alma's secret romance. I was boiling over with questions, thoughts, feelings. My mind turned to José and the beginning of our friendship years earlier. "I'm so sorry, Señor. For you and for Alma."

He looked up, startled, as if he had forgotten I was there. "Oh, child, with the wisdom of time, I now know that Señor Sanchez was only trying to protect his family. We were only children, and it was just a dream."

He slouched in his chair, the proud posture gone, his color ashen. "Your abuela Marisol was there that day."

"Yes, I know."

"Alma told her everything. Marisol was furious, spouting the same things about bloodlines to Alma. She told Alma she would turn me in to the police if we ever saw each other again. She made Alma go to that hospital so that there would be no talk, so that the family's reputation would stay secure. Alma went to protect me."

Tears filled my eyes, blurring the image of Pedro's sunken form in the rattan chair. Fury built in my chest on my mother's behalf. All those years, Abuela made her feel it was her fault Alma was hospitalized. Made her think it was because she told about Alma's visions.

"It was an accident, you understand. I never wished any harm on Señor Sanchez. I offered to give myself up, to tell the truth, but Alma begged me not to. After that, I stayed away." His eyes were glassy as he stared at the ring on the table.

"The thing is, Señor, the bullet here? I found it in the room where it happened."

He nodded absently.

"But the bullet is not from a handgun."

His eyes rose to meet mine. "What? Was it the one that killed your great-grandfather?"

"I don't know. But I want to find out."

He deflated again. "Oh, what does it matter anyway? Now everyone else who knows the truth is dead. There is just me, and who listens to an old Black man?"

"I do, Señor." My voice sounded strong and sure despite the choked-back anger.

He offered me a tired smile. "I know, child. And I thank you for that. I know that your abuela and many in your family thought I had shot him, but they graciously didn't turn me over, and I was not going to make things more difficult for Alma. But I always wished... Our feelings for each other were so important, so strong as to come but once in a lifetime. I hated that we had to keep our love a secret. Who knows, perhaps someone would have wished us well." His eyes were unfocused, like they were still seeing the past, and I let the silence be as my mind swirled.

I jumped when a horn blew somewhere outside, and my gaze flicked to the clock. 1:58! Did hearing Pedro's story, the real story, mean the visions would stop? I couldn't take that chance. I turned to Pedro.

"Señor, you have been so kind to share your story with me. I now know there was so much more to Alma, and I wish you could have lived out your lives together as you both had hoped."

"Gracias, joven, but it is the way God willed it." He took my hand in his, his grip surprisingly strong, and he looked right into my eyes. "She was a good woman, your aunt. She deserved so much more than a tired old man like me."

I squeezed his hand in return and let the tears trail down my cheeks. "With all due respect, I don't think she would have agreed with you on that one, Señor." In fact, after the last week of seeing her vision over and over again, her untold story, I was *certain* she would not have agreed. "And neither do I."

He escorted me to the door. When I was halfway down the walk, I stopped to wave, and as I turned back to continue on, I saw my great-grandfather in the bright sunlight coming toward me, the desk blocking the garden gate.

"Oh no. No."

I thought finally learning the truth would stop the vision. It hadn't. As I stared at my great-grandfather, I felt hope seep out of every pore, my shoulders weighed down with the lack of it. Would the visions ever stop? I stretched to try to get a better look at the papers on the desk, but Pedro was still watching, so I changed directions and went to step toward the gate but twisted my ankle on the edge of the path. Everything seemed to move slowly as I lost my balance, my arms pinwheeling as I fell directly into the tangle of bodies that was the younger Pedro and my great-grandfather, just as the argument was reaching its peak.

It was in that split second that I looked right into my great-grandfather's eyes and fell through him, right into the bullet's path.

My only thought was: *This is it.*

Just as the shot's blast echoed in my ears, I was pulled up by the arm. In that instant, the bullet whizzed by my shoulder, right where I had been a moment before, and my feet were placed on the concrete path.

I looked up and saw Pedro's warm, concerned eyes, his hand still holding my arm firmly as I caught my balance. I started to cry hard then, sobs breaking free from my chest.

"Are you all right, child? You must be careful. Are you hurt?"

I tried to breathe; out of the corner of my eye, I saw Joaquin rush from the car with concern. "No…no, Señor. I'm not hurt. Thank you for saving me."

"Saving you? Oh, I don't think my plants would have killed you, m'ija." He let go of my arm and smiled.

I laughed and cried and hugged him as Alma kneeled next to us, clutching Pedro's straw hat.

I nodded to Joaquin and opened the front gate. Pedro turned

and started walking back to the house as we started toward the car. When he got to the last step, Pedro turned around and looked back down the walk.

"Pity," he said, and I turned.

"About what, Señor?" I asked.

"That was my favorite pava." He shrugged and shuffled back inside. I was still gaping as the door shut.

CHAPTER THIRTY-EIGHT
untold stories and other regrets

On the return trip from Loiza, I sat in the back of the car. I was too flustered to sit next to anyone, and after my crying session on the sidewalk, Joaquin looked relieved at the choice. As he drove, I concentrated on breathing normally while a thousand emotions cycloned through my body. I only spoke to ask if we could take the more populated Route 3 for the return trip. I wanted more people around, even anonymous people standing at bus stops, workmen gathered around food trucks. Just...people. As we drove by a gas station in Canóvanas, I spied a pay phone. I asked Joaquin to stop, fished out all the change from my pocket, and made a beeline for it. I needed to speak to someone who understood. I had to.

The bouncy voice of the receptionist at my mother's architectural firm answered on the first ring.

"Hi, Cindy! It's Isla. Can I talk to my mom?"

"Isla? Honey, aren't you down in PR with your mother?"

My hand tightened on the receiver. "What? What do you mean?"

"In Puerto Rico? Aren't you down there with her now?"

"N-no. She flew back a few days ago."

Silence on the other end. Something was wrong. "Isla, honey, your mother never flew back."

"What?" My voice was shrill.

"She called to say she was going into the hospital down there earlier this week."

"Hospital?" My throat squeezed on the word.

"Let me just—"

I didn't let her finish. I slammed the receiver back on the cradle and ran to the car, legs shaking. I yanked open the car door and fumbled for my purse.

"Isla, is everything all right?" Joaquin leaned over the seat.

"I have to get more change. I have to call Tío. Do you have his number?"

"Yes, of course, but why?"

My change purse flew open, and coins rained down on the car's carpeting. My head hurt so badly, and I couldn't hold the tears back any longer. "My mother…she's in the hospital. I don't even know why or which one—"

Joaquin nodded. "Santa Cecilia Hospital de Psiquiatria in Santurce."

I froze, half in the car door, half out. "A psychiatric hospital?"

"Yes, but she's not there anymore."

"What?" The pain in my skull was bordering on unbearable.

He stared at me for a moment, and the soft look in his eyes was so much like pity I thought I'd sob again. "Get in, Isla. I'll take you to see her." He turned around, twisted the key in the ignition, and the car rattled to life.

I climbed in and closed the door, feeling as if I was no longer in control of my body. I stared at the back of his head as he negotiated the car onto the busy road. This man knew more about what was happening in my own family than I did. The Sanchez family secrets were going to kill me. They'd already come close in

Pedro's front yard. At the next light, I asked in a quiet voice, "Is my mother dead?"

Joaquin jumped at that. "What? No! No, m'ija. Your mother is…all right."

I nodded and took a deep breath. Of course, there would be no stories to alert me if she were. My mother was not a cuentista. She listened to stories but never told them. "But why was she in that hospital?"

"I'm not sure that I should tell you, m'ija. I think this should come from your family—"

I leaned forward, reached over the seat, and put my hand on his shoulder. "Please, Joaquin. My family never tells me anything, and I need to know now."

He sighed. Then nodded. "Yes, I would want to know too. She never got on the plane. After we dropped her off, she called your great-uncle and asked to be taken to the hospital. He made the arrangements, and I went back to pick her up and take her there from the airport." Joaquin stopped at a red light and looked back at me. "Your mother wanted to go to the hospital to get help to stop drinking."

I fell back in the seat, the leather letting out an exasperated breath as I sank down. My mother was detoxing? I'd read about detox in a novel earlier that year but never imagined my mother…

"But this is good news, no?" Joaquin asked.

I nodded, not certain if he even saw me, but not caring either. I was silent for the rest of the drive. What prompted my mother to go to detox then and not six months earlier? Was it what I'd said to her at the airport about only taking care of herself? What did it matter why? She was trying to stop drinking. I was both happy and totally raw at the same time, as if I were whistling while walking naked through the center of town.

The scenery began to look more and more familiar. When Joaquin pulled onto Calle Santa Cruz, I leaned forward. "She's at Alma's? But…there's no one there. It's half packed up."

Joaquin said nothing as he pulled into the carport, the gravel crunching beneath the tires like cracking teeth.

I sat in the car and stared at the house, the white paint peeling off like layers of sunburned skin. Joaquin came around and opened the door, putting his arm out for me, seeming to understand how shaken I was. I let him lead me to the front door, and he only let go of my arm to open the gate with a key from a large ring in his pocket. At the swung-open door, he gestured in. "I'll wait for you out here, Isla."

I looked into his kind eyes, the beginning of wrinkles spreading out from either side as if in a permanent smile. I gave him a quick hug and stepped into the dark, cool interior.

CHAPTER THIRTY-NINE
the truth hits everybody

I had been going in and out of Alma's house my entire life. For ten years, I'd spent every summer there, alone with my great-aunt. I'd been there just a few days ago with Maria. But on that afternoon, it felt different, like someone else's house. A stranger's house. Had it always smelled so musty? As I walked through the sitting room, my gaze rested on the piano, its cover down like a closed eye, waiting for Alma to awaken it. I walked over and ran my fingers through the dust along the cover, missing my great-aunt like a limb that was no longer there.

There was a sound in Alma's secret room or, as I now knew it, my great-grandfather's office. I knew Joaquin was just outside, that it was the middle of the day and the room was unlikely to be filled with snarling demons, but still my heartbeat took off at a run. I walked over to the door silently, my sandals padding along the waxed floors. A thump. I put my hand on the doorknob and remembered my earlier image of the room, before the vision, my grandfather's blood spattered over the desk surface, the tile floor, over the bookshelves that had been empty my entire life. I swallowed as I slowly turned the brass knob.

As I swung the door open, I drew in a sharp breath. The room had been transformed to the one of my vision. The furniture was uncovered and polished; a thin-as-paper Oriental rug lay in the center of the floor, the ornate design faded but elegant. The shelves were filled with leather-bound books, and there were oil paintings on the left-hand wall, one a richly colored portrait of my mother as a child, her smiling head supported on her hands with black-and-white tiles beneath her and a receding grove of trees in the distance. And sitting right in the middle of the desk, Pedro's pava. But more than just the accoutrements that filled it, the room seemed alive, moving, as it did in the vision.

I took another step into the room and noticed my mother's silhouette sitting behind the desk, her body impossibly small in the worn leather chair. She was looking out the window that was now framed with cobalt-blue raw silk curtains.

"Mom?" My whispered voice sounded young to my own ears, like I was eight again.

She turned and smiled. "Hi, honey. I suspected Joaquin might bring you here." Her voice was worn thin like the rug beneath us.

I stepped closer, but not too close. I was still so unsure of everything. "Mom, what's going on? Did you do all this?" I gestured around the room carefully, as if afraid to disturb the time-traveling magic.

"Yes. With all this talk about the past and Alma being gone…I just wanted to spend a little more time here, remembering."

I pointed to the straw hat on the desk. "Where did you find that?"

"On the top of the cabinet in the back storeroom. I always wondered why she kept that beat-up old thing. Now we know."

We both looked at the hat, and I felt gratitude for my mother remembering all I had told her in such detail. "Why didn't you go home?"

She chuckled, a sound bitter like citrus rinds. "Home. You know, I'm not even sure where that is anymore." Mom swung around and put her hands flat on the desk in surrender.

I felt as though I was looking at a different person. This was not the mother I'd hated and loved in equal measure these past few years. All her carefully constructed pretenses were gone, the sharp edges worn down. "What do you mean?"

My mother let out a long breath and put her head in her hands. "I'm just not sure where I belong." She spoke in a faraway voice, like she was no longer talking to me but to herself.

It felt like my insides were swelling, that I was going to burst. I couldn't stand hearing that Mom felt that way too, that we were both so…lost. My voice caught as I said, "I don't belong anywhere."

Her head shot up at this, and she stood to walk over to me but stopped a foot away, as if concerned she wouldn't be welcome. "Honey, that's just not true! You're loved! In New Jersey and here."

I snorted. "Yeah, right. My life is full and enriching, Madre."

Her eyes got glassy. "That's mostly my fault, Isla. That's why I checked myself into the hospital."

There was a space then, a silence that felt cavernous. I wondered if I was supposed to argue, but I couldn't. It was the truth: it *was* mostly her fault. It was just surreal to hear her say it out loud.

My mother walked over and gently put her hand on my cheek. "I'm taking the last flight out tonight. The doctor down here arranged for me to go to a rehabilitation center not far from our house at…home. It's going to be a long fight, but it's time I faced my demons. For both of us."

So many years, I had wished for this, but now that it was here, I wasn't sure what to feel. I hadn't anticipated the overwhelming sadness. "For how long?"

"A month. But I called Columbia and they said you can talk to your professors and get work to do remotely and stay down here until I get out. This way, I'll know you're being taken care of while I'm away."

"I can take care of myself, Mom."

She sighed. "Yes, I know, but with all that's going on, I think it's better for you to be here with the Sanchezes." At that moment, a car backfired in the street and we both jumped. My mother put her hand to her chest. "That scared me! Sounded too much like the shot."

"*The* shot?" I searched my mother's eyes and saw something flittering at the edges, just out of sight. There was something else going on. Something more than her drinking. "Why are you *really* in here?"

She looked around absently. "Because this is where it happened. The…incident."

I brightened, remembering. "Mom! I just came from visiting Pedro! The man in my vision!"

My mother brightened too. "What did he say?"

"He didn't murder your grandfather. It was an argument."

She paced around the room. "That's no surprise. If Abuelo was anything, he was surly. And a bigot to boot. And I didn't know Pedro well, but he just did not seem the violent type. But what was the fight about?"

"He had gone to ask for Alma's hand."

Mom froze. "When you told me about the ring, I wondered, of course, but that makes no sense with the Alma I knew… I–I can't believe this."

"Me neither. Especially after the hard time she gave me about José!"

"Wait, who's José?"

"Oh, that's a long story. But there's more. The bullet I found? It wasn't from your grandfather's gun."

Her eyes narrowed. "Whose was it then?"

"There was another shooter."

Her mouth hung open, her eyes wide. "This is starting to sound like a telenovela."

"It gets worse. Abuela was there that day. She knew what happened."

Mom shook her head. "No, that's not possible. I would have known."

"She was! And she sent Alma to the psychiatric ward because of her relationship with Pedro, not because of the visions."

"What?" The word was long, disbelief spreading it out over a full breath. And then she just stood there, motionless.

"Mom? You okay?"

"That bitch!" The words spat across the room. "All those years, she made me think that she had sent Alma away because of what I told her about the visions."

"I know. But, Mom, it wasn't your fault! That has to be a relief."

"It is, honey. You're right. Of course." She started pacing again, and I could tell something was still wrong. If the room had felt alive before, now it was electrified, the curtains billowing, the overripe smell of neglected flowers riding the breeze.

I had to tell her that finding out the truth hadn't helped. It would be hard for her to hear with all she was going through, but she had to know. "And, Mom, the visions didn't stop after I talked to Pedro."

She was about to say something when a man's voice burst behind us. We both stumbled a bit and whirled around.

My great-grandfather was coming around the desk, gun in hand, and Pedro was standing next to us.

"What the hell?"

My mother stared at them, mouth open. "But today's vision already happened. This is impossible…"

I gaped at her. "You see it?" I gestured wildly. "You can see them?"

My mother rushed around the desk. "No, no, this doesn't make sense!"

I was about to corner her and make her tell me what was going on when I looked out the window and saw the edges of my grandmother's hat in the bushes.

The shot in the trees.

I would deal with my mother later. There were other answers I had to get first.

As Pedro and Bisabuelo began to argue, I leapt out the open window just as I'd watched Pedro do over and over. I bashed my knee on the edge of the concrete windowsill but landed on my feet and took off at a run. It was surreal to see wide-open lawn next door instead of Ramón's squat concrete house, a space that was overgrown with trees, bushes, and fruit in my time. I skidded to a stop right near my grandmother's peering figure and glanced around to get my bearings as sounds of the argument carried on inside. I heard my mother calling my name from the open window and was turning around to respond when I caught sight of movement just ahead in the greenery. I crept closer, and though I knew I was not visible to anyone in the vision, it still felt dangerous.

I stopped short at the sight of a man pointing a long, thin rifle barrel toward the house. So here was Alma's other shot in the trees. I rushed around him and was looking into his beady eyes when he pulled the trigger. The shot exploded right next to my head, and I clasped my hands over my ears, an unbearable ringing buzzing through my brain like electricity. If I had thought the sound loud in the visions before, it was ten times worse from this perspective. My brain was still vibrating as Abuela appeared and yanked the man around by his arm, her mouth twisted. That was how I most remembered my grandmother, lips tight, derision coming off her in waves. The soft-filter version of her with the monkeys had almost made me forget. I took my hands off my ears, and though they were still ringing, I heard my grandmother whisper to the man with the rifle, gesturing threateningly at him with her garden shears.

"What is wrong with you, Beto? You only got the old man! I'm paying you to get them both!"

The *old man*? Wait... Abuela had *wanted* to kill her father?

The man gaped back in response. "Doña, they were struggling. I couldn't get a good shot!"

"You imbecile! What am I going to do now? My idiot sister is throwing it all away, all for one piss-poor moreno!"

I stood and stared at the pair, angry tears clouding my vision, wishing I could yell, scream, even strike them, anything to affect some change, any change, in the way things had played out.

"Don't you think I wanted to get Pedro too? Bastard made me lose my job! But, Doña...your own father?"

We both looked to her, waiting for an explanation, though nothing could justify this turn of events.

As she spoke, my grandmother's hands flailed as if trying to stoke a fire. "You know nothing! That man treated me like a second-class citizen my entire life, and then he has the gall to try and give away *my* land to his meaningless cause?" She shoved the man away, her gardening shears cutting the fabric of his shirt. "Never mind. I'll find a way to deal with this myself!"

My grandmother and I watched as the figure of Pedro sped across the yard and Beto used the distraction to escape, the true murder weapon tucked under his arm. I caught the achingly familiar sound of Alma's cries coming from the house, and then my grandmother and the open field vanished, not as the visions usually did but with an audible pop like a soap bubble that had stretched to its end. And there was my mother, standing in Ramón's front yard, staring at the exact spot where Abuela had stood, her mouth open, fists clenched at her sides.

"You weren't content to ruin my life! You had to ruin Alma's, Pedro's, my daughter's, *and* kill your own fucking father?" Mom shrieked at the empty space. "I hope you're rotting in hell!" Spit flew from her lips as she yelled at the air, arms flailing, tears streaming down her reddening cheeks. Then it was as if her bones simply dissolved. She dropped to the ground in a defeated pile like a rag doll and began to sob in earnest.

Joaquin came running from next door, and Ramón rushed out the front door of his house and stopped at the sight of the two of us. "Que pasó, Isla? What's all the screaming about?"

I moved over to Ramón, my hands out. I couldn't blame him. The woman had just come from a mental hospital, so he probably thought she had totally broken down. "Tío, we're okay." I looked over at Joaquin, who had just joined us. "Can you guys just give us some time? Mom and I need to talk."

Ramón looked uncertain, glancing at Mom over my shoulder, but finally he gave me a brisk nod and turned to the other man. "Come, Joaquin. Let's have a café while they talk." The two men disappeared into the house, and I walked back to my mother.

I sat on the ground next to her and rested my hand on her shoulder. "Mom." My voice sounded calm after such chaos. There were so many questions pushing to be asked but one that couldn't wait. "How come you could see the vision?"

She looked up at me with red-rimmed eyes. "Because I have the gift of the cuentista too."

"The *gift?*"

She nodded and sniffed. "I see the visions too, when the storytellers die."

At any other time, I would have been furious at this, the worst of all secrets she'd kept from me, but in that moment, I felt only pity. "But why didn't you tell me? Why did you let me think I was alone in all this?"

"Oh, Isla, I thought you had found your own way to deal with them. That it was manageable for you. Until Alma."

I stared at her. "What do you mean? How do *you* stop them?"

She just shook her head and squeezed her eyes shut.

"Wait, you don't?" My voice was a whisper, but the thought was screaming in my head.

My mother opened her eyes, new tears spilling into her lap. "Why do you think I drink? My mother had us believe the gift was something to be ashamed of, to hide. But all those stories, all the voices." She put her hands over her ears as if the rifle shot had sounded again.

Realization flooded through me in a wave. "All the storytellers' visions…they go on around you every day? Every storyteller who has died since you were…eighteen?"

She nodded. "It's not all the time, but on and off during the day and night. Except when I'm drunk. It mutes them, like voices in another room. It's the only time I can stand it. But then I wake up in the morning, and they begin again, like a series of movies that run over and over."

I tried to imagine the daily parade of ghosts around my mother—at the supermarket, at work, in the shower. "Couldn't you write them down? Like I do?"

"No. I tried that, years ago. I think that solution is yours and yours alone. I think we all have our own way of dealing with it, and I haven't handled mine well. I always wondered why Alma spent all her free time with her plants. Maybe that was her way of dealing with them."

Oh my God. "Wait. I found Alma gardening in the middle of the night many times. When I asked her about it, she got all defensive. Do you think that was what she was doing? Planting the stories in the soil?"

"Maybe."

I thought of Claridad's words, that it is different for every cuentista. "Is it just Sanchez women who get the visions? And why only some of us?"

She shook her head. "I don't know. My mother scared me out of talking about it, so I never asked anyone else. I think it's only those who are storytellers themselves."

"But you never tell stories. And Alma hated them."

"Yes, *after* she was put in the hospital. Before that, she told the most glorious tales about the island, the townspeople, nature, the family…everything. I could have listened to her for hours. I was so sad when she stopped. At least now I know why. And me? I think my mother scared the ability out of me."

"Did Alma know? I mean, that you had it too?"

"No. I couldn't tell her after all she'd gone through. I told no one. Except your father."

The air stilled. "Dad?" My voice was small. "Dad knew about the…gift?"

"Yes."

I was afraid to ask the next question. Afraid the answer would mean my father would be disappointed in me and I in him. "Did he believe you?"

"Oh yes! At first, he was concerned that I was sick, brain tumor, something. But in time, he helped me figure out what it was, tried to help me find a cure. But nothing worked. He kept telling me I should confront the family, bring it all out in the open, and make them explain it to me. He'd almost convinced me, but then he got sick, and I was just too…tired. When he was dying, he was worried about leaving me to deal with it on my own, to raise you with the visions going on around me. But what could he do?"

At the sleepover from long ago, she raved about how he'd left her alone…with all those stories. I had thought she was raving; I was angry she embarrassed me in front of the girls from school. A band of guilt tightened around my chest.

Mom was looking at the dirt in front of her, her shoulders slumped. "When he died, the last person who believed me was gone."

I took my mother's hand. "Not the last."

She patted mine and smiled sadly. "No, not the last. And I'm sorry you have to go through all this too, Isla."

"I'm not." I was surprised to find I meant that. "It's not that bad, Mom. I kind of like having insights into their lives. The only thing is, the one departed family member whose stories I want to experience more than anyone else's is the only one *not* sending me visions."

"Your father." Not a question but an answer.

"Yes."

I heard Tío Ramón's voice coming through the open windows, moving through his house, and I knew our time was short. "And Abuela hired that guy Beto to kill her father to keep him from giving away the land and to kill Pedro to keep Alma from marrying him?"

A tiny flame flared in each of my mother's eyes. "So it would seem."

It all became clear to me in that moment, what Alma was trying to tell us with her story, what all this was leading to. "Mom, the Sanchez secrets have hurt enough people. It's time for the truth to come out. It's time for you to confront them all as Dad suggested. But I'll be there with you."

Ramón and Joaquin walked out of the house and toward us.

My mother took my hand and we got to our feet. I watched her stand military straight like Alma and address her uncle Ramón, but not in the passive way she normally talked to him, rather like a peer. "Tío. We need to call a Sanchez family meeting."

"Elena, what is going on? I must insist—"

"Tío, tonight, at Alma's house." She looked into his eyes. "It's urgent."

Ramón was someone who gave orders; he didn't take them. But after a momentary pause and an assessing glance at Mom, he nodded, said "Bueno," and returned to his house. We could hear the whir of the rotary phone almost immediately.

Mom looked at me, and we fell into a deep hug, the buzz of insects and whisper of rustling leaves surrounding us. We stood like that for some time, and I imagined the warmth and camaraderie we shared was not like mother-daughter but rather like that of war buddies who shared experiences and battles no one else could understand.

Now I had someone I could talk with about the gift.

And maybe it really was a gift after all.

We walked arm in arm toward Alma's house. While Mom told Joaquin of the change of plans, I thought of something. I ran back into the office and grabbed the straw hat, returning to Mom's side. "I want to get this back to its original owner."

She smiled. "Let's go together."

CHAPTER FORTY
the whistleblowers

In Pedro's small, neat living room, my mother filled in the details of all we had learned. Pedro didn't seem surprised, though his tear-filled eyes betrayed the importance of it all to him. As we talked, I glanced at the photo of José smiling from among the shelves of books and instruments, his eyes beautiful and warm, and wondered how I could ever have been ashamed of him. It felt as if that ferry ride had been years earlier rather than just a few days.

That night, dozens of members of the Sanchez family gathered in Alma's sitting room, chairs moved from everywhere in the house, the fans spinning lazily overhead. The night was cooling as everyone settled down, and Ramón stood in front of them, hat in hand.

He cleared his throat and addressed the group. "Thank you all for coming on such short notice. We asked you here tonight because Elena and Isla have something important they want to talk to us about." He stepped aside and gestured to us with his hat, taking a seat on Alma's piano bench.

Holding hands to give each other strength, Mom and I stood at the front of the room, our backs to the open door leading to Bisabuelo's office. Just as Mom began to speak, I saw Maria run up the front stairs, Valentina behind her. But why had she brought her roommate to a family meeting? Maybe she just drove her here. Maria caught my eye and smiled, moving to the back of the room. I felt better knowing she was there.

My mother's voice started out small, then got stronger with each word. "Isla and I need to talk to you about a Sanchez family legacy. I should have talked to you all about this many years ago, before Alma got hurt." She looked over at me. "Before we got hurt. Something of which we Sanchezes should have been proud, not ashamed. Something we should have celebrated. My daughter, Isla, is the latest recipient of this gift, so it is only fitting for her to begin." She bowed to me.

And so I spoke of the gift of the storyteller, of my experience, my mother's, and Alma's. Of the visions and the cover-ups, the stories told and the stories buried. There were scoffs and small protests, but from the silence of the key players, it was clear this was not news to some.

Then we told the rest of our family the truth of the patriarch's fate all those years before. Of Abuela's guilt and Pedro's innocence. And of Alma's love for him. At least Ramón had the decency to look ashamed.

We told them we hoped that going forward, the Sanchezes could be a family built on truths, not secrets. The last words said, the truth laid bare, we thanked them for coming and for listening.

The meeting broke up, and there were expressions of incredulity, but there were also tears of gratitude from a cousin from Ponce, a male cousin, so the gift wasn't only for the women in the family. And two sisters who grasped each other's hands as I spoke and thanked me later for bringing their gift to light. I'm sure there were others who shared the gift but didn't come forward, but I hoped that one day they would feel safe enough to talk about it.

The dazed family members began to scatter toward their respective cars after some rather strained goodbyes. I watched them rush out of Alma's house, eager to put the whole thing behind them, as seemed to be the Sanchez way.

I turned to Mom. "How do you think it went?"

"Better than I expected. At least no one excommunicated us from the family. Yet." We chuckled.

Maria made her way to me, Valentina right beside her. "Well, Prima, so that was what you were investigating." A huge smile spread across her face.

"Yep. Sorry I didn't tell you earlier."

"Isla, you made them face the truth, something that should have happened long ago." Her eyes softened. "I'm proud of you."

I hugged her tight, then pointed to my mother. "It wasn't just me. My mom is the brave one."

Mom protested but smiled and gave Maria a hug as well.

When she pulled away, Maria gestured to Valentina.

"Isla, Elena, I'd like to formally introduce you to Valentina, my—"

I was about to argue we'd already met when she continued.

"My girlfriend."

Mom gasped, my smile was huge, and in turn, Mom and I gathered Valentina into a big Sanchez hug. "Ahh! I'm so excited!" I looked over at my cousin. "But why didn't you tell me earlier?"

"I haven't told anyone in the family. As you've seen, the Sanchezes are not exactly open-minded people."

"So no one knows?"

She put her arm in Valentina's and they smiled at each other. "Just some close friends. It's not a safe environment for people like us yet. I've had to hide this part of my life for so long, but tonight you showed me I could share the truth about who I am with you."

Her ability to relate to my feelings of not fitting in made sense then. All I could do was nod without crying again.

"Bueno, we're heading back to the house. Are you coming?"

"Soon. Joaquin is bringing Mom to the airport, and I want to go along. I'll have him drop me at your house afterward."

Mom hugged Maria goodbye, and I smiled at them as they walked down the front path, their heads together.

Ramón was the last to come up to us after the glasses were cleared and the chairs returned to their proper places. He stood before my mother, hands in the pockets of his farm-dusted pants. "Well, Sobrina. That was…enlightening." His eyes looked tired but clear. He turned to me. "And you, young lady. You must have gotten that truth-seeking gene from your father, no?"

I smiled at him. "Nah, that was all Alma. We had so much more in common than I ever knew."

Mom kissed Ramón's clean-shaven cheek. "Tío, thank you for all your help with my mother's estate. But I wanted to let you know that I'm not going to contest her will. I don't approve of how she came by that land."

His eyes opened wide. "What? But, m'ija, it doesn't matter where it came from! You could use that money. A widow with a child to support—" He pointed at me as if I were a toddler pulling on her skirts.

But my mother gave a small laugh. "Isla is no child, Tío. She could take care of both of us. I have a good job, and besides, I think we do pretty well on our own… Right, Isla?"

She put her hand on my cheek, and I felt warmth radiate from the touch, down into my chest, and wrap around my beating heart. "I think we will now, Mom."

Ramón sighed. "Bueno."

That word again. That complicated and intricate word.

He kissed Mom's cheek. "And now, I am going to go home, put my feet up, and smoke a cigar. That is quite enough talk of ghosts for me."

I squinted at him. "You don't believe in the gift?"

"I did not say that, m'ija, but if you had been paying attention to our discussions about your Spanish heritage…and there she goes rolling her eyes again." He turned to Mom, gesturing in exasperation. "Elena, did you teach her to be so disrespectful to her elders?"

My mother laughed and I rolled my eyes again, just for emphasis.

"As I was saying, if you had listened, you would have learned that we are descended from the family of St. Teresa of Ávila, and do you know what she was famous for, young lady?"

I crossed my arms, enjoying the petulant teen act but truly shocked that he would bring up saints at this juncture. "What?"

My great-uncle moved in to kiss my forehead and whispered, "Visions." He smiled beneath his thick, silver mustache, chuckled under his breath, and walked into the trees and out of sight.

Mom and I were both laughing as we turned off the lights in the kitchen and started to pass the breakfast table when she stopped short, looked up at the ceiling, and her eyes went wide. "Isla… they're gone!"

Confused, I looked back into the empty house. "Well, yes, but I think Joaquin is still—"

Mom grabbed my upper arms and looked at me with glassy eyes. "No! Isla!" She looked at her watch, then up at the ceiling. "The monkeys should be coming right now, but they're gone!"

Understanding began to spread. "What?" I looked back at the patio, even though I had ended that particular vision months earlier. I looked back at my mother. "Really?" I pointed to where the potted plant had stood. "Abuela's not hiding here?"

My mother shook her head, eyes brimming with tears.

"Do you think it was because you confronted them like Dad suggested?"

"I don't know, but I think it might be. All those years of pretending they weren't happening, of being afraid to talk to anyone about them, petrified someone would find out and I'd end up in an institution like Alma. Little did I know that all that fear and hiding would land me there anyway."

Oh God. I hadn't thought about it that way. I looked at my mother and realized I'd never felt closer to her, never felt more like her daughter. I pulled her into a tight hug, and we stood crying on each other's sleeves in the golden evening light.

A thought occurred to me, and I pulled back. "Wait! Mom, does this mean they're all gone? All the visions that you've been holding on to for all these years?"

"I don't know, honey." She wiped the tears from under her eyes. "I guess I'll find out at 2:00 a.m. when my cousin Nacho should be running by wearing only his fedora."

I put my arm around her as we walked from the kitchen. "Oh, you're going to have to tell me all about that one."

———

Later, as Joaquin drove us to the airport yet again for my mother's late-night flight, I wondered if that meant that Alma's vision was gone for me too. There was no way to know until the next day. I was glad I would still be on the island when I found out. I also wondered how our truth-telling would affect the family from then on. The Sanchezes had been burying the truth with their dead for so long, they no longer knew what they were fighting against.

I was no fool; I knew I hadn't "fixed" anything. Everyone was probably happier *before* they knew. But I had saved my mother... and myself, and we'd told Alma's truth, and that was what mattered most. As I rode next to my mother in silence, Joaquin humming along with the soft danza playing on the car radio, I knew that this was our fate, Mom's and mine. We were cuentistas, and I had learned that storytellers could not stay silent. What needed to be said would come out one way or another. Before or after death.

CHAPTER FORTY-ONE

kissing the horizon at the top of the world

The next morning, nestled in Maria's guest room, I slept late. It was that dead-to-the-world kind of sleep since it seemed like weeks since I had last truly rested my body and mind.

I dreamed of Alma.

My great-aunt was pushing off in a rowboat from the shore of a black volcanic-sand beach, the ocean glistening like mica where the sun touched it. I was running toward the water, calling to her, but Alma appeared unable to hear me over the roar of the waves, and I couldn't seem to close the distance between us. When I looked down at the sand retreating beneath my feet, I saw I was running in place, the same pile of seaweed marking my lack of progress. When my eyes swept up again, Alma was farther out, the small boat rocking with the chain of waves. She was rowing away from shore, her strokes relaxed but determined.

I finally reached the wet sand, the water lapping up over my bare feet. When I was in up to my knees, I stopped and yelled again, putting my hands on either side of my mouth for amplification. I wasn't even sure what I was yelling; I just wanted to get Alma's attention. When my great-aunt was so far out that her form was barely discernible, I saw her arm go up in a wave.

Standing there, silent, I watched the boat merge with the line of the horizon.

I realized, within the dream, that it was not a "Help me!" type of wave or even a "Hello, Isla" gesture but rather a leave-taking.

I heard a male voice as I slowly rose to consciousness.

"¡Buenos días!"

Huh? I lifted my head and remembered where I was: Maria's guest room. I laid my head back down on the pillow.

"¡Buenos días!"

I sat up and almost fell out of bed. Who was yelling? I slipped on my flip-flops and stumbled toward the kitchen, trying to pull myself from sleep.

The kitchen windows. Someone was calling through the bars over the open kitchen windows.

"¡Ya voy!" I called. "I'm coming!" The classic Sanchez bilingual bellow for these kinds of circumstances.

As I neared the kitchen, I saw the silhouette of someone standing at the louvered windows, the unrelenting morning sun forcing the face into shadow. Then the visitor seemed to hear footsteps and glanced in again, his hand shading his eyes as he peered in.

"Maria?"

I jolted, fully awake now. José! It was José? I hadn't seen or spoken to him since that trip back from Fajardo, when I'd been cold after that ferry trip with Cara. My mind sputtered. Why was he here visiting my cousin on a Sunday morning? My hands rushed to my sleep-disheveled hair. *I must look a mess! Do I have time to go and change even though he already saw me? No. What does it matter anyway?*

I stepped around the kitchen table and closer to the front windows.

"Isla? Is that you?"

I tried to clear my throat. "Yes."

"Ah! I didn't recognize your voice before. You sounded like a Sanchez." I could see him smiling.

Heat rose to my face. "I *am* a Sanchez."

"Oh, no, I know that. It's just… Well, never mind."

"Maria's not here, José. She left early. I could call her at her mother's—" I reached for the phone.

"Isla, wait. I'm not here to see Maria."

My hand froze midway.

"I'm here to see you."

I stood there in my rumpled T-shirt and boxer shorts. "Do… do you want to come in?" Then I looked down at my pajamas and resisted the urge to cover myself with my hands. That would be like closing the barn door *after* the horse has run away. "I could get dressed."

He smiled through the bars, the curlicued black iron framing his face. "No, I wish I could. I have to take my mother to church this morning and I'm late. I just wondered when you were heading back to the States."

I shuffled my feet on Maria's Spanish-tiled floor and crossed my arms over my chest. Why didn't I sleep in a bra? "Not for a while." The extra few weeks on the island suddenly held even more appeal. "Why?"

"I was wondering…if you weren't already busy… My family is having a party tonight in Adjuntas. I know it's a long drive and up in the mountains, but I was hoping you might…"

As he stammered, he became that little boy I knew again. But when I took in his angled mahogany face, his deep, dark eyes, it was abundantly clear he was no longer a boy and the feelings stirring under my skin were not those of a girl. I wondered once again how I could ever have been ashamed of him. I let him flounder for just a minute more as I admired him, until I couldn't listen to the insecurity in his voice for a moment more. "I'd love to come."

He let out a big breath. "Yes? Yes! Good! I'm glad. That's great. I can come back and pick you up here this afternoon, around five o'clock?"

My grin spread up into my eyes. "See you then." I was about to turn around and head back to the bedroom when I thought of something. "José?"

He was still at the gate. "Yes?"

"What are you doing after church today? I mean, between then and the party?"

He looked at the ground and thought for a moment, then back at me. "Nothing, why?"

"I was wondering… I was thinking of going to El Yunque this afternoon and wondered if you might like to come."

He smiled that smile again, the one that made my legs wobble. "I'd like that, Isla. I love the rain forest. I'll come back for you at eleven then?"

I calculated the timing of the trip in regard to the vision. "Perfect."

"Hasta luego," he called as his fingers slid across the bars.

As I walked backward through the kitchen, I watched him appear in each window as he walked up the block, our eyes not easily letting go of each other, until we waved and finally broke free.

I showered and dressed slowly, as if moving underwater. José was right outside at eleven, and I climbed into the truck. It was so right to be with him that day that I felt it in my bones. We headed east and I admired the way the bright tropical sun made everything clean, climbing in between houses and on the roofs of car dealerships, creeping into the open-air fronts of the bars along the highway, the pool tables waiting patiently for post-church patrons.

José turned the truck south onto Route 191, following the signs to the Caribbean National Forest. I was glad to have him with me, but I came up with a plan so that I could be alone when the vision was due to hit, when I would learn if Alma's nightmare was truly gone, Pedro never having to climb through that window again, the deadly bullet evaporating into the tropical afternoon.

We parked the truck, and as I waited for José to lock up, I stopped and took a deep breath, the verdant air filling my lungs, lifting the edges of my mouth.

"Which way would you like to go?" he asked.

I pointed up to the cloud-shrouded peak. "To the top."

We began to hike side by side, smiling at the people we passed along the way—red-faced tourists wearing cotton clothing, their children with sneakers caked in chocolate mud, skidding down the slippery passageways that hugged the footpath. Birdsong came from everywhere, overhead, beside us in the trees, an avian symphony.

"You know, the Taino Indians believed that a powerful spirit reigned from his throne on the top of this mountain," José said as I paused to catch my breath.

The carpet of waving palm fronds spread out all around us and I grinned. "Makes sense to me. If I were a god, this is where I'd want to rule from."

We hiked a bit in companionable silence. Then I said, "José, I met your great-uncle Pedro."

He looked over at me, head tilted. "Yes? Where did you meet him?"

I laughed. "It's a long story, but I liked him very much."

He nodded. "Tío is a good man. An honest man. He's the one helping support me while I study at college, you know."

I smiled. "I didn't." I hadn't known Pedro long, but that made so much sense. "Seems he and my aunt knew each other." I risked a glance at him. Did he suspect anything?

He was silent for a beat, then, "Yes, many generations of my family have worked for the Sanchezes. For your family." He kept his gaze on the path with a strained look around his eyes as if that was a source of shame for him.

"Did you know he and my great-aunt had wanted to marry?"

He stopped short and stared at me. "What?"

I nodded, smiling. "Yes. They were in love."

He shook his head as if clearing it. "Wait, you're talking about Alma?"

I took his hand and we started walking again, slowly. "Yes, Alma. I didn't believe it either, but let's just say I accidentally uncovered a Sanchez family secret."

He was walking as if in a trance, and I could almost see his mind struggling to make sense of this new information.

"It made me love her all the more."

He smiled at me, and we walked in silence for a bit, both lost in our thoughts of Pedro and Alma.

We stopped every so often, though I didn't think José needed to. He never even seemed out of breath as I sat breathless under the wooden shelters that marked the passage of miles on the trail. José sat beside me, and once again I was amazed at how easy it was to be silent with him, to not fill the quiet. Creatures scuttled under the bed of fallen leaves. A never-ending palette of greens surrounded us. José's palm rested on his leg, and I imagined running my hand over his thigh, feeling the smooth warmth of his skin. Heat rushed to my face, and I jumped up. "I'm ready!" After he rose, I discreetly placed my water canteen back on the bench and rushed to continue up the trail.

As we hiked upward, the muscles in my calves and thighs tightened and released, the heat spreading to them like logs catching in an autumn campfire. I listened to José's sure footfalls behind me. Everything seemed brighter, more intense.

We arrived at the summit in the early afternoon when the sun was still high and hot overhead, the light blinding after the trail's canopied darkness. I turned around slowly, breathing in the view of the entire island. La isla looked like a sleeping creature covered with a thick green blanket, the ocean spreading out beyond until it kissed the horizon.

I checked my watch: five minutes. Though I was grateful to have José with me, I wanted to make sure he wasn't there if the vision was not gone. I couldn't risk the kind of humiliation I'd experienced in class, or worse. Not with him. Besides, if anyone was going to get shot, it should be me. I sat down hard on the packed dirt.

"Isla, are you okay?"

I made sure to breathe even heavier. "No, I'm okay. It must be the heat. I just need my water—" I groped around in the dirt, though I knew where it was. "Oh no! I must have left it on that bench, about five minutes back." I started to get to my feet. "I'll just go and get it. You wait here—"

But José was already turning back down the trail. "No hay problema, Isla. You sit right there, and I'll go back and get it."

As I watched him pick his way down the path, I felt bad about the ruse, but I just wasn't sure it was over, and whether I was the one going back to get the water or waiting here, I knew I had to be alone.

I stood and took the book of stories from my backpack, clutching it to my chest. There was nothing it could do if the vision returned, but it was comforting to have all those Sanchez stories so close, the voices hushed beneath its cover as if they too waited to see if Alma's tale was complete.

Alma politely knocked on my thoughts, and as I let her in, I wondered what my great-aunt would look like. Would it be the armored Alma, wide-hipped and in a huff but still loving and warm? I should have been angry at her, for making me feel I had done something wrong in befriending José, for denying the existence of the gift of the cuentista...for not telling me the truth. If I stored this anger in my heart, she would forever be the old and pinched Alma who, in trying to protect me from the pain she herself had experienced, yanked the bad without noticing the good that was dragged along behind, battered and broken. But no, it was the younger Alma who entered my thoughts, with vivid eyes full of hope, a smile of a secret love teasing her lips. When I looked into her face, I saw my mother...and myself.

Two minutes.

Was this the exact spot where Pedro and Alma had stood so many years ago? It was easy to imagine that the island was theirs from that vantage point, to imagine there was no one else.

The alarm on my watch went off and my breath caught. I stepped farther back toward the center of the mountaintop. If I had to dodge a bullet yet again, I didn't want to end up misstepping and taking a tumble down 3,500 feet.

Nothing.

I spun around, the view blurring past as my eyes scanned for Bisabuelo, for Alma, and Pedro, even for my grandmother and Beto.

No one.

My mind was reeling in concert with my feet as I checked again and again. I let loose a moan as joy and grief vied for my attention as if I were at a wedding and a funeral at the same time. I frantically made one more spin to ensure there would be no gunshot, no dying old man. I was the only one there.

It was over. It was really over.

It was time to let Alma go.

I dropped to the ground, kneeling with my hands on either side of me in the packed dirt as I tried to catch my breath. As I crouched there at the top of my mother's island, I looked in the direction of Bayamón and imagined my family processing the tale my mother and I had told them the night before. Were they furious? Disbelieving? Moved? It didn't really matter. The truth was out, and that was all I cared about. All Alma cared about. And the end of Alma's vision for me only proved that it had been the right thing to do. No more secrets.

And what of the gift? How many Sanchez family members had it? When did it start? Was Mom's slate clean, or did she have to watch Nacho walk naked across the 747's aisle last night? And what would happen the next time a Sanchez cuentista died? These were all questions I looked forward to sharing and exploring with my mother. The only thing I was certain of was that I was a Sanchez, and I had the gift of the cuentista. I would continue to tell our stories on paper, from New Jersey, or Bayamón, or wherever my life took me. I hugged the book. Since I could bring the cuentistas' stories with me, home was wherever I chose.

José reappeared on the path.

Rising to my feet, I dusted myself off and reached for the canteen as José gave it to me, his hand holding on a second longer than necessary.

"Thank you."

"It was my pleasure."

I took a long drink, the cool water gliding down my throat, the warm sun on my face as I held my head back. I felt José take my hand, his skin cool against mine.

I opened my eyes, and he was standing right in front of me, so close the heat of his body reached me.

"Isla, are you sure you're okay?" His eyes squinted with concern.

I smiled. "I am now, José… I am now." If only he knew how much. "Thank you for coming with me."

He shrugged. "I like spending time with you. I always have."

My skin tingled. "Should we head to the party?"

"Yes, Isla, about the party…"

Oh God, he was changing his mind. I was too happy, things were going too well, I should have known—

"It's just that my family's house…it's not like what you're used to down here, you know?"

"What do you mean?"

"I mean you Sanchezes have very nice… I mean, we lead a simple life… Other than Pedro, well, some would say we're poor—"

In that moment, I pictured young Pedro in his worn shoes and hand-me-down pants and Alma in her custom-made San Juan dresses. José was still talking as I stepped forward, pulled his face to mine, and pressed my lips to his. After the surprise wore off, his soft mouth gave in to me, and it was as if the sun were warming me from the inside. I leaned in closer, his chest against mine, his arms wrapping around my waist as if they belonged there.

When our lips finally separated, it was like the sea pulling away from the shore. I whispered, "I'm sure it's perfect, José."

Voices carried up the path to the summit, voices speaking

English. I smiled at José shyly, and without a word, we pulled apart and started toward the trail. This was not a place or a moment I wanted to share.

Hand in hand, we stepped out of the sunshine and under the cover of the green canopy as a pale young man and woman appeared on the path, their toned legs pumping beneath khaki shorts, their eyes shaded by straw hats. José's hand dropped from mine as we approached them. Did he think I would be ashamed?

As we came closer, the couple greeted us with matching waves and smiles, and I took José's hand back firmly in mine, nodded hello, and continued on my way, side by side with José. A wide smile spread across his beautiful face.

I swung his hand back and forth in rhythm with our steps and asked, "Hey, would you like to hear a story? It's about a gift…"

Reading Group Guide

1. Family secrets play a huge role in *The Storyteller's Death*. How do family secrets start and take on a life of their own? Have you ever discovered something shocking about a relative's past that changed your understanding of them? Who are the storytellers in your family?

2. Describe Isla as a character. What circumstances make her an outsider both in Puerto Rico and New Jersey? What is her biggest obstacle?

3. What makes someone a cuentista throughout the story? How do stories gain power even when they aren't strictly true?

4. Alma quickly separates Isla and José when they first meet as children. When you first read that scene, why did you think she stopped their budding friendship? Does knowing more about Alma's own past change your understanding?

5. How do Isla's visions change her view of her family's place in

their community? What does she learn about their wealth, politics, and personal pride?

6. The Sanchezes are very proud of their Spanish heritage. Why do Alma and Tío Ramón emphasize this aspect of their lineage? How does that focus on the past contrast with the environment around them?

7. José dismisses Isla at the Partido Popular Democrático rally because he believes her family is pro-statehood. Why does he think that? Why does the PPD oppose the possibility of Puerto Rico becoming a U.S. state?

8. What do quenepas represent for José? How does sharing the fruit with Isla mark a change in their relationship?

9. What motivated Marisol, Alma's sister, to arrange for both Pedro's and her own father's deaths?

10. What's next for the Sanchez family? Do you think they'll be able to follow Isla and Elena's example and move toward greater openness?

A Conversation with the Author

What inspired *The Storyteller's Death*? How do you begin a new story?

Years ago, I had a conversation with two writer friends where we were discussing how different cultures treat their old people. I told them about how in Puerto Rico, the elderly family members are often right in the house. I said, "There was always some old woman dying in the back room when I was a kid." One of my companions yelled, "That's it! That's the beginning of a story!" I'm grateful for her insight as otherwise the whole story might have passed me by. I started it as a short story for my first MFA workshop, and it grew over the two years in the program. I worked on it for seventeen years, all told, but that was where it began. My stories tend to start in very similar ways, sparks that flare and either catch or fizzle out. Little did I know, this story was a looong burning candle.

Like Isla, you spent your childhood summers in Puerto Rico. How do your experiences compare with hers?

Though they differ in specifics, my experiences are at the heart of Isla's. My father died when I was eight, and my mother started shipping me off to her family in Puerto Rico for the summers while her drinking worsened. It was a very painful time but also beautiful, as it allowed me to dig some roots in that fertile soil. I credit my Puerto Rican family for saving my life. They taught me that adults could take care of things. At home, I did the laundry, the shopping, hid the car keys. When I was in Puerto Rico, I could be a child, though in many ways, that ship had sailed. As a result of my circumstances (and genes, let's be honest), I was a strange and somewhat feral kid, a sinvergüenza, as my great-aunt used to call me, or one without shame. It was those summers that bonded me so strongly with that side, with that part of my blood. In Puerto Rico, those who are born there are said to have "la mancha," the mark of the island, on them. Though it might not be visible, I like to think that I have something of la mancha on the inside, riding through my veins on tiny rafts alongside the platelets and anti-anxiety meds.

Who were your favorite storytellers growing up, either in your family or in print? How did they shape your own storytelling?

So many members of my family can tell a story. In fact, all of the cuentistas' stories in the book are based on Dávila family tales, but I grew up hearing mostly my mother's. They were rich and dramatic, filled with slashing storms and vengeful shootings. Later, I found out that many of those she told weren't exactly *true*. My mother had already passed on, and I was hurt and angry, feeling as though I'd been lied to. But then my cousin José Luis said, "Why does that bother you, Prima? Isn't our family as defined by the stories that aren't true as by the ones that are?" He changed my thinking about the role of storytelling in a family, that memory is a movable feast and there is more meaning in the telling of the stories themselves than the "truth" behind them.

As for in print, I was always an avid reader and was particularly drawn to magical realism and horror. Magical realism because so much of Latin culture seems infused with magic. No one questions the existence of ghosts, for instance. And I think I've always been drawn to horror because it made me feel better about my own difficult life, because though it might have sucked, at least there weren't zombies.

Puerto Rico comes alive throughout the story, and there are subtle signs that the times are changing. What do you feel the biggest changes have been in Puerto Rico in your lifetime?

First, I'm so glad I was able to bring some aspect of the island of my heart alive, thank you. But since I don't live on the island year-round, I hesitate to speak as an expert of any kind. That's why I set the book in the era when I spent the most time there: the 1970s. In part because I knew it best but also because it was a fascinating time in Bayamón and on the island. My older siblings had grown up with the family property surrounded by mostly farmland. They talked about chickens and pigs running around the property, miles of farmland, our tíos riding around on horseback. But in the seventies, all that started to change. It was interesting to see how much from summer to summer, interesting and difficult since not all changes were good. But one thing remains a constant: family is always first, and Puerto Rico survives hurricanes, earthquakes, political unrest, and a pandemic, sometimes all in a row! I am proud of that heritage of resilience.

How does Isla's lack of physical wealth prevent her from seeing the privileges her family holds? Do you see a difference between privilege and personal circumstances?

This is something I've been examining my entire adult life. Like

Isla's mother, mine made the choice to support herself, my brother, and me—the only ones still living at home after our father died—with no help from her family. It made for lean times, but we always had a roof over our heads, food in the cupboard, and clothes on our back. But this was because generations of her family had worked hard and built resources, putting the strongest emphasis on education, and had sent my mother to Columbia, where she studied architecture. So even though we lived simply, we benefited from the privilege of her family through the foundation of her education. During the summers I spent on the island, however, there were servants and swimming pools and dinners out, and as a kid, I felt as though we were the poor relations. With adulthood, I realized that wealth was entirely subjective, and though we lived differently, I grew up with a tremendous amount of privilege. It was such a revelation that it pretty much had to be a theme in the novel.

Maria is an important ally for Isla in the Sanchez family. How does each generation change the course of a family's history?

We're in such a time of change these days, and I'm grateful to be around to see it. I was raised differently in New York and New Jersey, and when I was on the island, I encountered shock about everything from wearing flip-flops off the beach to tattoos to living with a boyfriend before marriage. But that was from the older generations. With my cousins? I could talk about anything. As our generations and the ones after us have come into power, some of the old ways of thinking are falling away, like scales from the societal eye. I have tremendous hope for Gen Z. They are not as constrained by binaries and outdated traditions as we were, as my mother was. Each generation finds a way to honor those who have come before but also allow the family to evolve.

In many different ways throughout the book, love paves the way for learning and greater understanding. How do you view the relationship between love and curiosity?

Love has always inspired me to look closer, deeper, to explore. And it keeps things new and interesting. The only way to learn is to ask questions and listen more. This book was inspired by my love and gratitude to the Puerto Rican side of my family, and sometimes you must look into the dark corners to bring out the textures and patterns that make life interesting and bring greater understanding. The friendship with José was based on a real incident with a boy when I was a child. The realization that a family member who was so very dear to me was a racist was almost unbearable for years. But love sometimes requires discord to reach understanding. I think this book is, in many ways, the way I came to terms with that.

What books are on your bedside table right now?

What, you mean the teetering stack that's so big it might fall over and kill me in my sleep? Right now, I'm savoring Zoraida Córdova's novel *The Inheritance of Orquídea Divina*. I love her work, and this book feels like...family. I don't want it to end. I just finished *Tender Is the Flesh* by Agustina Bazterrica (translated from the Spanish edition). This dystopian/horror novel is very dark and not for the faint of heart, but it was one of the most thought-provoking books I've read in a long time. And finally, I'm relishing the essays in Kei Miller's *Things I Have Withheld*. His stunning "The Old Black Woman Who Sat in the Corner" captures the heart of what I hope *The Storyteller's Death* brings forth—the stories we dare not tell and the beauty of the women at the heart of them.

Acknowledgments

Since I have been writing this novel for seventeen years, the amount of people who have supported its creation is so very long. I hope against hope that I remember them all, but since I can't even remember why I went into a certain room these days, I fear I will miss someone. If I did, it is not out of a lack of gratitude but rather a breach in memory.

As always, I am so grateful for my friend and agent, Linda Camacho. She unfailingly believes in me and my work, and I appreciate her so very much. To my editor, Christa Désir, who loved this book and these characters almost as much as I do and saw the beauty in Isla's story from day one. Christa and the brilliant Findlay McCarthy showed me what was missing and supported me through the hard task of mining those difficult memories to bring authenticity to the story. They are the BEST. The incredible team at Sourcebooks who have helped make this dream a reality, particularly thanks to artist Sara Wood and art director Heather VenHuizen for giving *The Storyteller's Death* a beautiful cover that captures the spirit of the novel (and…quenepas!).

This book was born at Vermont College of Fine Arts (VCFA), and so many of my VCFA family supported me. First, I give particular thanks to my advisers, Ellen Lesser and David Jauss, for believing I could do this and helping me become a stronger writer so I could. My poet friend and former academic dean, Gary Moore, for his amazing feedback and emotional support from when this was just a kernel of an idea. To Amabel Siorghlas and Anne Connor for identifying the first line as a start of a novel and for years of writing encouragement. My friend Sharon Darrow, who supports me in all my projects and who, over martinis late one night, talked me out of quitting writing. And to all my VCFA workshop leaders and attendees for their early feedback, you are my community, and I am grateful for you every single day.

All the love and gratitude to my dear friend and hermano, the brilliant Rigoberto González for his guidance, feedback, and friendship in this wild writing world. Gracias to Lisa Alvarado, who predicted this novel many years ago in a living room in Chicago. Miciah Bay Gault, who has walked next to me as we navigate this writing life and given me thoughtful support, feedback, and occasional spa trips. Dawn Kurtagich, my literary sister in Wales, our biweekly video meetings keep me sane. And gratitude to Rachel Chelius for being my friend for more than fifty years. She lived some of the events in this book and stayed by my side through it all.

To my mentors, Cory and August Rose, who have taught me more about writing and navigating this career than I can possibly recount or thank them for. You are my family. To friends Renee Lauzon, Sabrina Fadial, Gary Miller, and Tom Greene for their support and encouragement early on.

A lifetime of gratitude to Andre Dubus III, who gave me the most challenging workshop experience of my life and helped me to step back from this story so I could step closer. He is one of the reasons this is out in the world, and I will always be grateful to him.

To my siblings, Ellen, George, and John Hagman, for unfailing belief in my work and helping me mine our history so I could give Isla's tale depth. My cousin Tere Dávila, a brilliant writer, friend, and creative comrade. Our cousin Carlos Dávila, who spent an hour talking about the different plants on the family property in the '60s, helping me bring color and scent to Isla's world. My tío Esteban Dávila, who answered questions about antique weapons without even asking why; he just understands me (and any errors are my fault, not his). Thanks to my husband, Doug Cardinal, who keeps me grounded but shares my dreams: I love you. And finally, to our son, Carlos Victor Cardinal, who is the reason I started writing in the first place and I'm proud to say is now my writing partner on numerous projects. You are the next generation of family cuentistas. Gather all the stories, then pass them on so that our ancestors, so that I, will always be with you.